HOMEWARD DOVE

ALSO BY JANICE LAW

HOMEWARD DOVE

JANICE LAW

WILDSIDE PRESS

Published by Wildside Press LLC.
www.wildsidebooks.com

CHAPTER 1

When my grandmother got real old she began to go strange. She bought stuff she didn't need, picked fights she couldn't win, and told the damnedest stories she could make up. She about drove my mom and dad nuts with crazy ideas and late night phone calls and monster bills from the shopping catalogues. The funny thing was that she could seem fine, normal, sane. She put on sanity the way you or me put on a shirt—a sleeve at a time and buttons up to the neck. And she'd get it almost right; then, just when you'd be thinking you were talking to a normal person, she'd tell you how Uncle Joe died of polio, even though he's running the lunch wagon in Plainfield this minute, or how Cousin Dorine hasn't talked to her in years, when you know Dorine, who's too dumb to recognize a hopeless case, calls her every Sunday four o'clock sharp.

I didn't appreciate Gram's efforts. I thought you're crazy or you're not, an open and shut case and not a damn thing you can do about it. Now I'm not so sure. Some days you can feel yourself getting crazy and you think why not? Shit, the whole world's crazy why not me? Other days, you decide to resist, you try to hold it together. You opt for sanity and hope it'll treat you better than the alternative.

I know; I've tried both, and between one and the other, or maybe with trying to decide between one and the other, I've gotten myself into some pretty strange places. Days like this when I'm not feeling so good and my legs, specially the right one, are acting up, I ask myself how I ever wound up where I am, because unlike Gram, I'm a sharp guy. Ask anybody; they'll tell you, Jeff's a sharp guy. I was even pretty good at the books, but I could see where that was leading. My cousin Vincent—two years at the university and an Associate Degree and where is he? Sub-sub manager at the Burger King just below the by-pass. Aggravation I don't need. Me, I went right from school to the auto body. I stayed there until Electric Boat got hit with cutbacks and Jimmy said they had to lay me off.

So I come back here and bum around some. I help Frenchie and his dad with their roofing business for a while, but I hate heights. Start the morning up forty—fifty feet and I feel like puking. Roofing about ruined my gut, and I got so I just had to look at a ladder to feel I needed a sixpack. Then I did some painting, and I worked one summer for a cut rate blacktop outfit until consumer protection got onto them. I was flat broke and ready to sell my truck when Bargain Barn opened its warehouse five miles down the road. I got a job in their shipping department—two dollars above minimum wage plus benefits, workman's comp included. If I'd been lucky, I'd of strained my back and gotten disability.

That's the racket I should of tried, but, instead, one night I'm in Dougie Donelley's, an Irish pub up near the Mass line and Frenchie introduces me to a cousin of a friend's cousin who's over from Rhode Island. You don't want to know the details, but what happens is that the Barn's overpriced Jap and Taiwan VCR's and TV's and stereos start finding their way into the back of a Delivery Dispatch truck that the C of FC, Arnie, runs for some electronics shops with good connections. Me and Cousin Arnie split the profits; I adjust my inventory sheets and figure I'm about earning what I'm worth for shifting imported crap for the guys in the fancy suits.

It's a no sweat operation. I'm good with math and I'm neat. Some of the guys in the warehouse can barely add 3+2 and their sheets look like cat barf. You ask Pat how many Toshiba 400's are on the shelf; he'll give you a different count every time. Me, I got all my inventory down cold and my sheets are so neat who'd believe they're off? And they're not—by much. The cousin had a bit of a greed problem, but I knew my limits: a TV here, a stereo there, a little "damage" to a VCR, a scratch on a console. I was never even questioned, and some weeks I was all square. You want to be careful, see, and not press your luck. And I didn't. I can say I was as careful as it made any sense to be, and though the cousin was always pushing me for "special orders" and big screen TV's, I knew where to draw the line. That's sanity, I think you'll agree. I pay off my truck and I'm making my rent on time and things are going about as well as they ever are around here, when the craziness arrives.

Her name's Michelle. She has connections, though I don't know it at the time and wish now I had, because I'm smart enough to spot trouble if I have even a hint. But all I know is she's the new inventory control checker, and she's got the official red and white Bargain Barn name badge pinned to a sizeable right tit. Michelle has a lot of brown hair permed to look like a grown up brillo pad, and she's basically the same as the last one except maybe more surly. Michelle chews gum and sucks on a diet coke all night instead of running out the back for a smoke every half hour which is what got the last one fired.

I keep an eye on her anyway for a couple of weeks. Then I start again with a few modest donations to Delivery Dispatch, but Michelle doesn't break a sweat. She double checks my inventory sheets and says I've got great handwriting and how she wishes all the guys were as neat. She's making so nice I'm sorry that she isn't my type. Then she goes back to her paperback and pretty soon I'm shipping out more than ever to the C of FC. I'll tell you how things got: things got to the point where I stopped wanting to blow off the damn job and started to worry about holding onto it. Talk about turning into your old man! That kind of anxiety should of warned me, but I'm making some real coin and I'm getting used to the little extras. I've got my eye on a Harley 883 and I'm even thinking about a little boat to use bass fishing up the lake, when outa the blue, Michelle stops me one night I'm signing out.

"You gotta problem," she says. Michelle wears contacts that are tinted different colors. Tonight's are kinda maroon which gives her werewolf eyes.

"Oh yeah?" I says. I'm still thinking about boats and Harley 883's and sanity.

"You gotta discrepancy."

I furrow my brow and look all worried and concerned. "I don't see where my count's off," I says.

"Oh, tonight's fine," she says, working over her gum. "Tonight's fine." Then she pulls out a sheet with my tallies going back for three weeks. She's got them cross referenced against the incoming shipments and the legitimate delivery invoices. Three weeks she's been watching me! She musta been hiding invoices behind all those Stephen King's and Danielle Steele's she reads, 'cause she's got me cold. I feel just the way I used to feel up on Frenchie's high ladder—bouncing around in the wind with a square of shingles on my back and my gut having contractions.

"It's these nights," she says.

She's holding out the figures, but all I see is the Correctional Institute: leaf raking and raising marigolds behind the razor wire—or maybe even Somers: Latin Kings and gang rape and home made knives—when Morrissey, the shift warehouse boss comes over. He's stout and suspicious with little piggy eyes and a mustache thick as a siding brush. He looks at me like I'm a pile of dog shit and says, "You gotta problem? What's the problem here?"

Morrissey is always nervous about the stock. He's over-paid to be, but now I remember he's been on the last month or so about inventory losses. I should of taken the hint and layed off Delivery Dispatch for a while, but instead I was a damn fool, and now I hear the cell door closing, clang, just like in the movies, when Michelle turns around and smiles. She shoots Morrissey a pink tinged death ray and says, "I spilled some coffee on my form and I wanted to double check some figures with Jeff."

I'd just about wet myself, and there she is smooth as Pennzoil. If you'd asked me at that moment, I didn't know whether I wanted to kiss her or strangle her.

Morrissey hikes his pants another few inches toward his armpits and says, "Drinks confined to breaks, Michelle. You know the regulations."

She parks her gum in one cheek and calls him "Mr. Morrissey" and tells him it'll never happen again. He gives her a look like a rat after cheese and jaws a minute about company policy and company morale, and she sits there looking fascinated. I'm recovering fast and thinking flat out, wondering what she's up to. She's got enough to bust my ass and get promoted right into decent money and decent hours. I can see she's watching me all the time out of the corners of her werewolf eyes, and I think, "Love Slave to a Female Werewolf," and curse my good looks and the C of FC and all Irish pubs everywhere. Then Morrissey is gone and I'm saying good-night and feeling cold now and wondering how to get my hands on that inventory check sheet she's holding, when Michelle says, "Walk me to my car. We've gotta talk."

It turns out, <u>she</u> has to talk. She's honest as the next person, she says—there's a laugh—but I'm screwing with her job. I'm thinking maybe I can pull out the charm and promise to be a good boy, when she says, "One third should do it." Just like that. "Retroactive," she says, 'cause she's taking a risk, blah, blah, blah.

"And if I don't?" I says.

She shrugs. "Morrissey'll have an orgasm," she says. She don't need to say what'll happen to me.

"I want that sheet," I says.

"When I get what you owe me," she says. "I'm figuring $1300 would keep us square."

She wasn't a werewolf; she was a bloodsucker, a leech, a goddamn lamprey eel. With red tinged eyes.

"Don't get me mad," I says.

"I got friends," she says. "Friends you want to stay friends with." Just tone of voice I'm inclined to believe her. Later the C of FC confirms she's got connections in Providence. "Low level", he tells me. "Nothing we can't handle. Her half sister married a soldier in one of the families. That's all I know."

"Christ, I don't want that kind of trouble," I tell him.

"Who's got trouble?" he says. "She's a businesswoman."

He wasn't so cheerful when I told him how she shot the shit out of his profit margin.

"Far as I'm concerned, we can forget all about the business," I says.

But he doesn't want to do that. Family trees should be rewritten to eliminate cousins of all kinds. He wants to expand now that we've got

Michelle "working for us". He doesn't know the bitch. She has me by the balls and before he knows it, she'll have him, too, and we'll both be working for her. I could see it coming and it came.

First it was suggestions and then it was orders and pretty soon I'm getting a hernia just from looking at all the crap I'm humping. Worse yet, she's craziness, and she and the C of FC together are greedy craziness. I'm working twice as hard for a pay cut and I'm starting to get nervous. I flash all the time on the Correctional Institute, and I feel like puking every time I pull into the Bargain Barn lot. About the best thing I could of done was left town and not come back, but with Dad feeling cruddy, and Mom getting old at the Discount I hated to do that. And then there was the usual shit, the slumlord tangle of rental deposit and yearly lease and money tied up. Besides, trout season was coming. One of the sweetest streams in the east is just miles away and, south of town, where the river runs wide and shallow, ain't so bad, neither.

Finally I figure wait til trout season's over, take the loss on the last two months of my lease, and call the folks collect from Denver or Spokane. I sweet talk Michelle, stall the C of FC, and start handing in clean sheets. I'm living smooth and easy and broke, an employee theft dropout, when Michelle says one night, "I need money." Just like that.

"Talk to the boss," I says, and I get myself out the door. She catches me half way across the parking lot. Seven-fifteen, white arc lights, smell of rain, a few early peepers calling. I'm already seeing the stream with a big rainbow lying in the pool below the bridge, when she pulls up in her Datsun. Piece of junk.

The lot's almost empty. She rolls down the window. "We had a deal," she says.

"Listen", I says, "we had a deal. Now I'm sick of the deal, all right?"

She shakes her head. Tonight she's got her blue contacts in, making ultraviolet eyes that remind me of bug snappers and cheap grocery stores. "I'da gotten a raise for busting you," she says.

"Yeah and you wouldn't have been spending my cash for the last six months." I didn't even want to think how much I'd paid her. Every time I looked at her, I saw my Harley 883.

She makes a sour face. "That was short term gain," she says, and I see that the C of FC was right, this is a business woman. "Long term, I'm better with the raise."

"Christ!" I says, "They coulda closed the fucking Barn by the time you made it back. You coulda been fired, taken a hemorrhage, won the Lotto. You got yours up front and no problem."

"None whatsoever," she says. "So call Arnie. Cash by the end of next week." She puts the Datsun into gear and burns out the yard. I'm running through my vocabulary, but I'm not feeling so good. Ms. Vampire knows the C of FC's name, which means she knows even more of my business than I thought she did. If she's onto Arnie, too, it means she's got a way to back up what she says; it's not just her word against mine any more.

I'm in a helluva fix. My first impulse is to call that troublesome little bastard, the C of FC, and lay out the situation. My next is to say the hell with them both. Anything can happen in a week, and tomorrow's the opening of the fishing season. After sticking around and ruining my digestion this long, I'm going to be out tomorrow morning sure. I jump in my truck and head for The Kitchen, where I figure to drink a couple beers and have a pizza with everything. I've gotten through the first part of the program, when in walks one of my old high school buddies, third base on the softball team and the foulest mouth on the school bus, Lynn Santori.

"Hey, Red Gal!" She stops just inside the doorway. Lynn's maybe 5'9 or 5'10, blonde, wide face, kinda Scandinavian looking despite the Greek name. She carries some weight but it's artistically arranged, with the better parts hidden at the moment under a baggy red and gray sweat suit.

"Hey, hey, hey, Red Man!" She comes in and gives with the high fives over the bar, the traditional Red greeting. I've had just enough Rolling Rock to miss the old school with the Redmen out on the football field and the Red Gals warming up next door in their soccer shorts and hockey kilts. I have fond memories of Lynn's strong thighs, red and cold to the touch under her hockey kilt after a windy November game. I put my arm around her shoulders and give her a kiss.

"What you drinking?"

"I came in to use the phone. Sorry, Joe," she says to the barman.

"You gotta have a margarita," he says. "You never come in without buying a margarita." Joe was a few years ahead of us at the regional. He's a nice guy, but the glummest looking bartender you've ever seen. He's tall and thin, and he looks as if they assembled him out of skin and a skeleton without remembering to put any meat between.

"I gotta call Gina," Lynn says without saying "yes" and without saying "no".

"Yeah?"

"Yeah. Mom's keeping the kids and we're going to play the slots at the Pequots."

"I like that theater they've got there," Joe says.

"Yeah? Me and Gina are going to the slots," Lynn says. "If I can get hold of her. I thought Mom couldn't keep the kids, see, since her back's been bad. But she saw the chiro today and she's moving pretty good."

"Yeah?" I says but I've still got my arm around her, and I'm going on autopilot. I don't know how it is, but I take spells of being wild about Lynn and sometimes these coincide with spells of her being wild about me, too. It just takes a certain atmosphere. The smoky bar at the Kitchen, a few Rolling Rocks, maybe the old red and gray Red Men colors—who the hell knows? "So your mom's keeping the kids tonight?"

"Yeah. She and Dad are crazy about them."

Crazy, they'd have to be. Lynn has seven-year-old twins, a boy and a girl. They look completely different but they're both wild and bratty and too much like their dad, Buddy, who ran off soon as he saw what family life was like. They're even too much for Lynn sometimes, so that once and a while she drops them off for the grandparents to spoil. She gets her friend Gina and runs down and plays the slots at the Pequot casino. Then she stays overnight at Gina's, where she wins her losses back playing poker with Gina and her old man and her Uncle Tony.

That's sometimes. Other times, she tells her Mom she's going to the casino and comes over and plays games with me, instead.

"So how's life treating you?" she asks me.

"Not too bad," I says. Actually, as you already know, it's pure shit, but I hate to grouse to Lynn. She was dealt a crap hand with Buddy, who had more muscle than brain and more prick than muscle. All in all as lousy a card as she could of found in the deck, but she keeps cheerful, and I admire that. So I says, "Not too bad. Considering."

"Yeah," she says, "considering the general fuck-up of the universe. Right, Joe?"

"How you want that margarita?" he asks.

"Cold," she says. "I guess I want that margarita cold and strong."

"Now you're talking," he says. Joe likes to fix fussy mixed drinks and things with frosted rims and fruit floating on top. I tell him he's wasted at the Kitchen, and he and Lynn both laugh and she says, "You look like you're getting wasted, too."

"Naw," I says. "Warehouse is thirsty work. You need a couple beers just to settle the dust."

"Yeah?"

"Yeah. You want some pizza?"

"Naw. I'm going to call Gina and go to the casino."

"Don't try to delay a woman in the gambling mood," says Joe, setting her drink on the counter.

"With everything," I says. "Pepperoni, spinach—look at that—the salad comes right on the damn pizza."

She laughs again. "I gotta call Gina," she says, but I can feel her hip against mine and she's not moving it away.

"You got time for a slice of pizza," I says.

"You want nachos with a margarita. Am I right, Joe?"

He nods his cadaverous head. "A margarita takes nachos."

"So get some nachos," I says, slipping my arm around her waist. "They make nachos here, don't they?"

"Can't sell margaritas without nachos," Joe says. "State regulation," and he winks just in case we can't recognize the joke.

"I maybe got time for some nachos," she says.

Up on Joe's big screen tv, the Knicks have just gone ahead of the Rockets. "You want to see the Knicks win," I says. "Save your money and root for New York."

"I like Ewing," she says as if she's thinking things over.

"He's terrific when his knee's okay."

"You like nachos?" She asks.

"Sure I like nachos. But I'm eating pizza."

She holds one out anyway, dripping with cheese, and pretty soon my crotch's running a fever, and I'm beginning to forget about the Bargain Barn and Michelle and the C of FC. I have another beer. "Don't call Gina," I says.

She raises her eyebrows and doesn't say anything. Lynn likes to be persuaded even if she's already made up her mind. "I got a tape of the last Red Men football game," I says.

"I like that theater the Pequots got now," Joe says. Is he thick or not?

"You hear that," Lynn says. "What do I want to watch the Red Men for?"

I wonder if I've made a tactical error: Buddy was a Red Man. Captain, quarterback, All-Conference. "This was the Turkey Day game," I says. "A vintage game."

"A vintage game is one we won," Lynn says to Joe.

"My cousin plays," Joe says. "Travis. He's a pulling guard."

There must be weight somewhere in Joe's family. But probably no more brain.

Lynn looks at her watch. "I gotta call Gina," she says. "You've kept me here half an hour and I haven't phoned yet." When she pushes back from the bar, her sweatshirt rides up and I feel the satiny flesh at the top of her hip. Have I said she's covered in one hundred percent pure silk? The underlying upholstery ain't bad, either.

"Don't call yet," I says. I've figured out that all she's wearing is the sweat suit. I flash on my apartment with the lights low, Garth Brooks on the stereo, a mess of sheets and pillows on the floor, and my head starts reeling. Sometimes she affects me that way. "You can call from the bank," I says. "Where's your car? They got one of those outside phones by the bank."

"Mighty cold out there," says Joe.

Maybe you see why I sometimes wonder if Joe is dumb or if he's got a lot of hidden agendas.

"My car's other side," Lynn says but she's kinda leaning against me in a way I find hopeful.

"I'll drive you over," I says. "My truck's right in front. I'll drive you over. With the heater on."

"I can imagine," she says. But she looks at me as if she's seeing nights watching "Star Trek" with the twins, and Sunday dinners at her folks, and the day shift at the Donut Shack.

"You gotta coat?"

"Do I need a coat?" She asks.

"Not in my truck. You don't need a coat in my truck."

She laughs then. She's got a big laugh. Maybe that's what gets to me cause I'm beginning to see everything with a red tinge around it.

"Come on," I says. "Night, Joe."

"You don't need to drive me," she says as we go out the door.

"Come on," I says. "It's one of those drive up phones. You've got to drive up." I open the door and she climbs in. I go round the other side and get in and lean over and kiss her. I feel the universe contracting—no Bargain Barn, no Michelle, no C of FC, no Kitchen, no bar, no parking lot. I get my hands under her sweat suit and my guess was right and I'm trying to pull up her top when The Kitchen door opens and there are voices and she stops trying to swallow my tongue and gives me a look.

"I don't think you want me to call Gina," she says.

"Come home with me."

"I can't leave my car," she says. But she's running her hand up the inside of my leg.

"I'll bring you back," I says. "Christ, we can take your car if you want."

She gives me a squeeze. "I'll follow you," she says, hopping out. "You got room in your garage?"

"Yeah," I says, though George, the landlord's brother's got his Toyota all in pieces on one side and with the recycling cans and the garbage, there's barely room for my truck. "Yeah," I says again, cause I know she won't leave her car out on the street where some busybody will see it and tell her Mom and cause problems about leaving the twins next time.

"Hey, hey, hey," she says, and I understand the deep meaning of lust, at least. Then I put the truck in gear and go lurching out of The Kitchen's lot with my whole life focused south of my navel.

Down the highway, I keep watching her lights in my mirror. Times like the one I'm telling you about I used to wonder why I didn't marry Lynn. Or at least raise the subject with her. Back then I'd have said I'd checked out the gene pool: those twins were enough to scare Attila the Hun. But now, I think it was other things. She liked me sure, but I also knew she'd loved Buddy, the loathsome. And me, I liked her, I liked her a whole lot, but I didn't love her or anyone else, really, though I'd gotten a glimpse of the possibilities one night at a high school dance. That was the night Jess Portinari sat crying in my truck trying to decide if she should marry Andre Simeone.

If she hadn't, a whole lot might have been different, but she got married, and Andre became an almost war hero, and I learned that love's not rational. Not even close. It comes up and hits you like water out of a pothole. There you are soaked, and there's not a damn thing you can do if it happens to be muddy. Or dangerous. Or stupid. Or impossible. I learned about impossible long ago, and I know about stupid now. But driving out of The Kitchen lot after Lynn, I'm thinking mostly immediate gratification with the fewest complications, which means it wasn't love—which has some of the same details, you bet, but a whole different floor plan.

I reach my street and park and throw up the garage door for Lynn and wave her in. I run the truck into the drive, squeezing its nose against the garage until the back end is off the side walk, step inside and pull down the door. It's dark and cold and I can smell the grease and oil from George's gutted Toyota and Lynn's saying, "What the hell you doing?" when I find her and pull her against me. There we are, heading for the point of no return against the trunk of her Ford, when the side door opens. Lotsa light, Lynn untangling, me working on various buttons and zippers, and George's standing there, shit-faced, saying, "Sorry, I couldn't get around your truck" and Lynn says, "I shoulda gone to the slots."

As soon as we're outside, I start telling her about the sexual merits of Red Gals in general and of herself, in particular; all of which she says she already knows. But she's willing to listen, and I've had enough brew to be persuasive. Upstairs in my apartment, I haul out the margarita mix I laid in last time Lynn stayed over, and she puts Mary Chapin Carpenter on my stereo. When I come out of the kitchen with a brew and a margarita, everything is dark, Carpenter's singing about passionate kisses, and Lynn calls, "Hey, hey, hey, Red Man," from the bedroom. I set down the drinks, hop out of my boots, and shuck my troubles with my Bargain Barn uniform.

CHAPTER 2

I wake up around five as it's coming light. My head feels like my brain's gone solid, and I lie there thinking about density for a minute. Cement, lead, squares of shingles, bags of sand. Combined, in the case in point between my ears, with feathers, big, blood stained, sharp pointed turkey feathers like the ones that used to be left after Dad cleaned the Thanksgiving bird bought from the turkey farm. That's how my brain feels at the moment, heavy, but with lots of sharp points floating through it. Then I hear Lynn breathing slow and steady, and I remember drinking a beer and a margarita at some point in the proceedings, or maybe it was beer and a tequila straight up. That was some time after the Mary Chapin Carpenter disk finished and before we got doing complicated, exciting stuff on the living room couch. As I stretch my legs, the creaking bed springs remind me of various night noises and pleasures, and I'm about to slide over and wake Lynn up, when one of those sharp points lands. There's Michelle and the C of FC and the Bargain Barn all after my ass.

So instead of starting in on a pleasant half hour, I study the ceiling for a bit and wonder if I'm going to like Seattle or Yuma or wherever I'm going. Then I know why I'm awake three hours before I need to get up. I slid out of the warm, rumpled blankets and head for the john: it's opening day.

My dad never had to set a clock in fishing season. Not once, though the alarm rang regular at 6 a.m. the rest of the year. He used to say the fish just called him. I understand that. The river's been calling me for several weeks now, not just the water alone or the fish, but the whole thing: early morning mist with the sunrise breaking through, a cold smell of water and earth, the whirl of a line running out, and a spinner winking in a pool where trout are rising. I'm thinking that I should of called Dad last night and asked did he want to go up the river. Probably he would of said "no", which is why I didn't—that and running into the Numero Uno Red Gal—but maybe he'd have liked to sit in the car. He does that sometimes now that his emphysema's gotten bad. He goes down to the shore and sits in the car with the windows open a crack and thinks about surf casting and tells anyone who is willing to listen how many flounders he used to catch and how good the blues were before they made a toilet out of the Sound and poisoned all the creeks with runoff.

He and Mom used to like surf casting a lot. I have some pictures of them, both young and good looking, standing in baggy, old fashioned swimsuits beside big surf poles. "That's real fishing," Dad says, and he gets this wistful look as if the young fellow with the black hair and the faded t-shirt is still behind his eyes, trapped forever now by lungs getting brittle and by arteries clogging up like old pipes. It's an odd feeling to think that Dad and Mom, who I've known all my life, really live elsewhere, back in that unreachable foreign country, their youth.

I've got a lot of odd feelings this morning, which is what you get with tequila and all those crazy mixed drinks that alter the composition of your brain, solidifying some bits and putting others in flotation. But though I feel sand, lead, and feathers settling every time I move my head, I put on my thermals and my overalls. Then I shut the bedroom door and get on into the kitchen to make a pot of coffee for my thermos. While I'm waiting, I'm so thirsty I drink another Rolling Rock, and it's five-thirty by the time I write Lynn a note and carry my rod, waders, and tackle box down to the truck. Maybe it's the beer, but my stomach isn't feeling too good. I stand beside the garage, thinking it over, and then I stash my thermos in the truck and say the hell with it; I'll walk to the river and save the trout stream for tomorrow.

That's how come opening day I'm down on the river no more than six blocks from my apartment. The rain hasn't come; it's all hanging around in mist, and when couple of pickups pass me with guys heading further out, I regret my decision but don't feel like walking back. I cross the big intersection, empty except for a couple of heavy tractor-trailer trucks barreling through on their way to Providence, and reach the new park that's supposed to bring folks out to enjoy the river. What it'll mean will be more crap in the water and kids tearing up the benches at public expense, but at least the politicos left some gaps in the railing. I scramble on down the slope, holding my rod out to one side so I don't break the tip and using my tacklebox for balance.

This part of the river bank's rocky, with big ledges that start far back on the land and jut into the water, breaking up the flow and creating pools and shallows. I walk south with only the sound of the river running noisy over its stony bed. The old factory buildings on the west side are empty and quiet; the highway is muffled by the slope. A few mallards drift on the swift current, and big, silent gulls float in and out of the mist. I feel the cold of the river through my waders before the sweet sound of the reel letting out line.

I take a few minutes to get the rhythm again, then suddenly there's just the river and calm and the spinner flashing below the surface, gliding carefree and deadly. After I've been there an hour maybe, I catch a brown trout—the state stocks them by the thousands. The brownie's a bit small, and since I don't feel like cleaning it, I take the hook out. The fish struggles slimy in my hand but goes still when it feels the river again. I hold it for a minute, watching the gills soaking in the oxygen laden water, then it dips to one side before regaining balance and slipping effortlessly into the stream. While I'm tying on another spinner, I think I could of brought the trout back for Lynn. I decide to keep the next one, but my hand is off or the fish are spooked or there's too much food cause that little brownie's the only one I catch.

By eight o'clock, the sun's behind the mist, and, though my feet and hands are frozen, I'm sweating in my thermals. My gut's about settled, too, and I'm beginning to think breakfast and coffee. I pack up my stuff, put on a pair of gloves to thaw my fingers, and climb up to the park. I'm standing by the fence, putting away some spinners I'd stuck on my vest, when I hear a rattle. First I think something on the highway, which is out of sight behind the new trees and shrubbery, but no. Here comes a woman rushing along with her head down, pushing a little fat faced kid in a baby stroller. She looks up and puts on the brakes just as she's about to run me over. Michelle's got plain brown eyes this morning, and she's as surprised as I am and no happier.

"Your box there's on the walk," she says like she can't get by and this is holding up her life.

"You going to a fire?" I says.

"I got things to do," she says, and she heels the stroller over at a 45 degree angle and starts by. I put out my hand to stop her.

"This is a good a time to talk," I says. I'm wondering who the kid is and is it hers and whether this is something I can use to get out from under.

"What's to talk about? We've got an agreement."

She starts working on her gum, and for the first time it strikes me that she's stupid. Shrewd but stupid which is the worst combination cause it doesn't give you flexibility. "What's the matter with you," I says. "You don't like where you're living? You want to wind up in Niantic?"

"I've got proof," she says. "What have you got?"

Like I should have written her checks and kept the stubs. "We couldn't have moved that much stuff without your knowing," I says. "Anyone with half a brain will see that."

"I wanted to be sure," she says. "That's what I'll say. And what'll you say? You say anything, you're all finished. Arnie, too."

"So why should I take the risk?" I says. "That's all I'm telling you: no more."

"I need the money," she says. "I turn you in, I get a raise."

"Maybe you get a raise, maybe you get fired. Morrissey will want a clean sweep."

She gives a little smirk and that puts another idea in my head: Michelle plus Morrissey. This is worse and worse, cause if he's having it off with her, she'll turn me in sure.

"I got proof," she says again.

The little kid's restless. He's got blond hair and brown eyes and he's drooled a bit on his blue sweater. He pulls at one sleeve and then he starts chewing on a leather strap. The strap ends at the black purse as big as a back pack that's stashed behind him. Michelle's never without it; she won't even walk across the warehouse without that damn bag.

"Yeah?" I says, and I reach over and whip it outa the kid's grasp before either one can stop me. "Names and dates and invoice copies, maybe?"

"Give me that!" The kid's cheeks get all red; he wrinkles up his face and starts high decibel yelling. Michelle starts, too. She's got less imagination than my favorite Red Gal but a whole lot more venom. I open the flap and see a shit pile of stuff, wallet, makeup, little plastic boxes for this and that. Probably has her werewolf eyes in one of them. She's grabbing for it, but I'm taller, and I keep pushing stuff around, which is hard with gloves on, and then I hear something crackle, and I turn away from her. While she's pounding on my back, I unzip a compartment and see papers—pink and yellow invoices, photocopies, a little notebook. I scoop them all out and start stuffing them into the pockets of my fishing vest. She's trying to get at my face and I'm keeping one elbow up, when she takes the stroller and runs it into my shins. The kid's hollering and wrestling around and my leg hurts like hell and I ask her what the fuck she thinks she's doing? She's screaming about her purse and her papers. I pat the purse—no more crackling and rustling—and hand it over.

Instead of saying "thanks", she gets behind the stroller again and starts using it as a battering ram, screaming kid and all, which is crazy. Pure, pointless craziness. And I'm no better, because I'm caught against the rail and I stick out my fist to stop her and catch her off balance. When she falls, she tips over the stroller, the kid, the purse, the baby junk, and I see everything without any emotion but satisfaction until there's this bad thud. Which is her head hitting a bolt that's holding down one of the new benches. It hear it even with the kid wailing and the stroller wheels rotating and a truck shifting gear just over behind the knoll.

I go cold and hot at the same time and grab for the stroller. The kid, I guess it's a boy, is okay, though he's had all the noise scared out of him, and he's scraped his cheek. I can see the lymph oozing off the raw patch and, just for an instant, his big eyes are very close to mine. He doesn't say a word, just looks at me like he's some sort of automatic camera. Beyond the stroller, Michelle's lying with her eyes open and a funny expression on her face. She looks surprised, really, really surprised. She puts her hand on her chest and gasps, and I'm puzzled and relieved and figuring how we'll settle things, when she gives this funny noise like she's had the wind knocked out of her, only she hasn't, she's hit her head. There's some blood now and a shit smell and fluid darkening her legs. She's not moving at all, not even breathing, and I just go crazy. I grab my pole and I'm through the opening and halfway down the slope before I remember my tackle box. I scramble back up, half blind with sweat. By this time, the kid's started in crying and chewing on the leather strap again, but Michelle's still lying there surprised and motionless. I cut back down to the river, where I puke up that unwise a.m. Rolling Rock before I start running. I stumble over the ledges and splash through the shallows until my gut hurts so much that I have to stop.

I'm expecting witnesses and disaster. What I hear is the river rushing and gurgling. No one's following me. There are no shouts, no sirens, no eager, pursuing footsteps. The sun hasn't burned through down by the water yet, and with the trees starting to leaf out, I'm pretty well hidden. I tell myself to get a grip. To wash off my face. To walk down under the bridge and come up over the chain link fence on Water Street and go home like any other morning. I haven't seen a soul and who's to say I was ever near the park?

So I start along, telling myself at every step what I'm wishing was true: that I've been fishing along the river, that I caught a small brownie and let it go, that I've seen nothing unusual, that whatever happened up on the sidewalk—if anything happened up on the sidewalk—has nothing to do with me. And at every step, the papers in my pocket are shifting and rustling and telling me that I was up on the walk and that Michelle's dead—or maybe that she's not dead but even now is putting the finger on me—or that she's dying and I should of gone back, flagged a truck, gotten an ambulance. The kid'll be screaming his head off and maybe he'll get out of the stroller and fall in the river and I should go back. I actually stop and stand still, the shallow water running cold and fast around my waders, and it comes to me that I was happy an hour before. I thought I was hung over and bummed out. Now I realize I was happy. I realize I could have fished another hour, maybe caught another trout and taken it back. Lynn might still have been there, and I'd of fried the trout up for breakfast and we might of gone back in the sack for an hour before she left for the Donut Shack. That would of been happiness. Now I see that everything else, even the Bargain Barn and the Correctional Institute, even telling Mom and Dad, were just difficulties. This is different, and, standing in the shadow of the bridge with the morning traffic starting to get heavy and the smell of diesel, I realize my life has changed beyond control.

So I go crazy again, which maybe is nature's own protection, cause I pick up my tackle box and my pole and I tell myself again I've been fishing right near the bridge. And when I see there's no sign of life above the bridge, either, I tell myself I was there the whole time.

I'm not sure I believe that, but I walk upstream anyway til I'm near my street and come out at the parking lot by the feed store. Since there's a truck out front, I walk around back. I'm expecting to see someone unloading big dusty bags of oats or chicken feed or shiny sacks of dog chow, but, though the door's wide open, nobody's on the loading dock. My heart is pounding away, my waders are beginning to rub my banged up knees, and I have to tell myself twice that I've just been fishing, just fishing, before I can walk around the loading dock and cross the road and the old rail line. When I get to Water Street, I loiter behind the electrical repair shop until a car pulls away from the curb, then I walk, as casually as I can, toward my house.

I'm coming back from the river where the fish weren't biting worth a damn and what does the State know about trout, anyway, because that brownie was hardly bigger than a minnow. I keep that in my mind along with the bridge and the idea of a spinner bright for a moment in its shadow and of the mist filling up the spaces between the railroad girders. I've got to think of that and not the sidewalk, cold and bare in the wind, or the odd noise Michelle made or the child, speechless and watchful, or the sound of rocks and dirt scattered by panic flight. I've got nothing to do with them. Nothing.

If I can only get back inside my apartment, it will be all right. I've just got to walk down the sidewalk with my tackle box and rod the way I walk dozens of days every year. And if old Claire Wilkins looks out and asks how did I do, I'll say "nothing worth keeping, but if I get lucky I'll bring you back a mess of trout." I say this over to myself, although I've barely enough breath to get the words out, and then I repeat them, because they sound so strange. They're like words out of a different life and not the one I'm in now, the one that started as soon as I heard the bad thud, the bad thud which was the door between one life and another closing.

My truck's in the drive, and I'm behind it when Danny next door comes out and waves to his little girl. He doesn't see me and neither does his wife, Carmelita. That's all to the good, let me tell you. Danny's Chevy pulls out and bumps down over the sidewalk cause he's got it riding low, which he claims is style but which is really stupid when you get as much snow as we do. Bump, I hear him, then the screen door shutting. I slide around my truck, ease the side door of the garage. I put down my tackle box and pole and take off my waders. I leave everything there, though normally I take my stuff upstairs, since the garage isn't always locked. I cross to the house and use the back stairs. It's so quiet in my apartment, I wonder if Lynn's up and gone, and I kinda hope she has, because I don't know what to say to anyone and Lynn's known me long enough to notice how all my words are strange. But when I look through the bedroom door, she's lying in a big lump of covers with a pillow half over her face and seeing her gives me a shock. I got to stifle this urge to check her breathing and make sure she's all right. I stand there listening for bad noises, for gasps and thuds and queer little rasping sounds. Then I tell myself to use my brains: Lynn's asleep and nobody's seen me.

I stand there shaking—like the chance of escape is scarier than being caught for sure. Then I go into the bathroom ultra quiet and take off my overalls and hang them up behind the door. Everything else is soaked in sweat. I smell like the old Red Men's locker room with thirty guys whooping and dancing and snapping towels after a win over the Whips. I jam everything into the laundry bag, turn the hot on all the way, and step into the shower.

I don't know how long I'm in there. I stand with the water beating on my face and then on my back and then on my face again. When I finally turn off the tap, my feet have thawed out and Lynn's calling from the next room.

"Out in a minute," I say. I wrap a towel around my waist and open the door.

"Hey," she says. She's sitting up on the end of the bed with her sweatshirt on and a lot of nice leg showing. Normally, I'd make a pitch for cutting the Donut Shack, but I don't trust myself at the moment with anything too intense.

"How you doing?" I says.

"I'm going to go home with money in my pocket," she says.

"This sure is the right casino," I say but my voice sounds feeble.

"You okay?" she says. "You're looking kinda flushed."

"My stomach's a bit upset," I says. "I think it was that marguerita."

"Maybe the third one," she says and comes over and puts her hand on my forehead. Instantly I'm so nervous I start sweating. "Yeah, you feel clammy. Maybe you should go back to bed."

"Naw, I just got up," I says and I expect her to say, 'Liar, you've been up for hours,' but all she says is, "I didn't hear a thing until the water running." I take a deep breath and give her a hug and go get a shirt on.

"You want breakfast? I'll put on coffee," I says.

"Yeah. Got any eggs? I'm not supposed to have too many eggs," she says.

"I think so. I think there's some eggs."

She makes a face and wanders out to the kitchen to check the fridge. I'm getting into a clean pair of brown Bargain Barn jeans for work when I remember the note. I just about a hemorrhage at the stupidity of it, and I'm making up some story about getting up and going back to bed when I go into the kitchen and see she's got her head in the fridge.

"There's bacon," I say as I go to grab the note.

"What the hell's this?" she says. "Come here and look at this."

She looks around and I step in front of the table, all the time asking myself did she read the message? There's a strong smell of old hamburger from the fridge. "I'll put it out," I says, and I grab the package which is dried up and stained, stained with blood, which makes me flash on the sidewalk and starts my stomach twitching again.

"Phew," she says.

"The bacon's okay," I says. I'm still thinking, did she read the note, did she read the note?

"I'll make eggs," she says. "You wanna egg?"

"Just one," I says. I don't want an egg. I don't want to eat, period, but Lynn always makes me eggs, and I see that everything has to be as always. Normal: it's a kind of magic. If everything looks normal, everything will be normal. I grab the note as I go by and wrap it around the hamburger and take both out to the cans, going down the splintery back steps cautious in my bare feet. I drop the hamburger in and the note, too, then I think of searches and the show I just saw with the FBI going through some guy's garbage week after week. I rummage around, find the note, tear it in half and in half again, drop the pieces in the can. I think better of that as soon as I've done it, so I have to start picking up the bits and putting them in my pocket. I've got the serious shakes, and my head's in orbit. I can still make out my handwriting on all those little pieces of paper; all those little pieces of paper saying, "Going fishing", "Going fishing", "Going fishing".

I hear the door open behind me. "Eggs are ready," Lynn calls. She's added her sweat pants and her sneakers. "You okay?"

I'm clinging to the cold, bashed up metal sides of the trashcan. I let the last little piece of paper go and straighten up. I shake my head. "I just feel kinda sick," I says.

Lynn starts down the stairs.

"No, I'm okay now. Maybe that flu that's around, I don't know." And for a moment I let myself think, I'm feverish, it's the flu, I've been in bed and just gotten up. I keep thinking that until I get upstairs and look at the egg on my plate and smell the toast and feel the shock wave between what is and what might have been and realize that my only chance is to be normal and natural even if I've forgotten how.

CHAPTER 3

Lynn has to be at the Donut Shack by 9:30, and though normally I'd as soon spend time with her as anyone, I'm real glad to see her leave. I go down to open the garage door, see my waders, and worry she'll notice them dripping in the corner. That's what I mean by I've stopped being normal. It's like everything comes with a hidden meaning. I have to keep figuring out which life I'm in and whether it's okay for there to be waders in the garage and a pool of water under them and what I'll say to the Red Gal if she notices.

She doesn't, which brings me to something else I don't understand right away but catch onto only gradually: most people don't notice. I guess it's hard enough keeping one life straight without considering all the alternatives, but most people only see what they're expecting to see. Standing waving to the Red Gal outside the garage, I don't know that, so what I do is run inside and get paper towels and dry off the waders and mop up the puddle on the garage floor like some ditz in a detergent commercial. I'm swearing and breakfast is turning over, and I'm beginning to see how much has to be changed for me to have spent the morning in bed and never gone fishing.

When I'm finished, I go in and turn on the news but it's too early for anything. Maybe Michelle is okay, after all, and maybe she'll be smart and say she tripped. Or maybe there's already a police car pulling up. I'm so nervous I can almost hear the feet on the stairs. Although I know it's not cool at all, I want to get in my truck and drive right down to the park and see what's happening.

I make myself wash up the dishes, instead, and put them away. Not exactly normal behavior, but normal is way beyond me. What I've definitely got to do is get to the Bargain Barn on time, which means eleven for the start of our shift. And when Timmy asks how the fish were, I got to be ready to give him a wink and say how I had a tough night and how I'm hoping to get out this evening. I'll maybe put my rod in the cab, too, and stop on the way home, though I'm pretty sure now that I don't want to be anywhere near the river.

I get my Bargain Barn badge, comb my hair, and fart around until I'm almost late. At the last minute, I gotta go around by the park. All the way, my mind's busy rearranging things. I've almost got myself convinced it's a normal day and I'm driving to work, when I see the cop cars. There's two of them and they're not hanging at the Donut Shack with their coffees and cigarettes, and they're not up watching the road work north of the new intersection. They're the front men for a big van and some other cars that are pulled onto the grass. I slow down enough to see a loose square of yellow police tape and a sort of canvas screen and a lot of activity right at the edge of the park. Everything goes black for a second and then I'm past it and it's all true: there is no alternate life, just the one I'm in, and there's no way to get back to the river and to do it all again differently.

I expect to see troopers in the Bargain Barn lot, too, but, of course, they don't come til later. Which gives me time to get calmed down a bit and think things over. When I first get there, of course, I'm in a panic. I have to stand by my truck for a minute, thinking, be calm, be calm, everything's normal. But I don't feel real, never mind normal, til Timmy starts hollering from half way across the lot. He'd been at the stream and caught three beauties—the liar. Probably none of them bigger than my brownie, and I want to say that, but instead, I says, "I got wasted last night," and give him a wink. "I'm going to try the stream after work."

"It'll be S.R.O.," he says. Timmy's tall, taller than me, and he'd be good looking if he'd spring for a haircut and wash oftener than once a week. He's got these round blue eyes and little wire glasses that make him look more alert than he really is. "Christ, half the town was there."

"You're lucky you got anything," I says, "with all the competition."

"It's skill," he says, "I've got the touch. Like you, you've got it for other things." And he laughs and I laugh, too, and we walk in with everyday cool. Lou's leaving as we're punching in, and we stop to tease her for a few minutes, with her giving it back in Spanish and English combined. Lou's a Peruvian gal with a new green card who works the early morning shift. She's dark and built low to the ground like Danny's Chevy, but that's a bad thought, cause I see the truck and the garage and walking back from the river where I haven't been. I feel myself stop smiling, and Lou says, "You okay, Jeff?" cause she's a nice gal and knows we don't mean any harm.

"He's hung over," says Timmy.

She says something in Spanish, and I says it's maybe the flu, before Earl yells that her husband is waiting outside with the produce truck. 'Adios' to Lou. I start on orders from the Norwich branch store, while Timmy and Earl lie about their fish. It's past noon before Morrissey comes bustling back to where the Hitachi VCR's are stored. Timmy's been sneaking a smoke, and I figure Morrissey'll have a shitfit, but he doesn't even notice the Marlboro haze mixing with the usual new metal, formaldehyde, and synthetics smell.

"You seen Michelle?"

"Naw," I says. "Isn't she at the desk?"

He's not pleased.

"I punched in on time," I says. "I've been getting orders ready."

"What about you, Longdon?" he asks Timmy. "You seen Michelle?"

He shakes his head and Morrissey barrels away. "Damn," Timmy says. "She's out and we didn't even know. We coulda blown off the whole morning."

"And who'da punched you in?" I says. Timmy doesn't think more than one step ahead even if he is a college student. Me, I'm always looking down the road. Right now, I'm figuring Morrissey will piss around asking everybody in the warehouse, like we're going to know where Michelle is, then he'll call and pretty soon we'll have the cops. That's just what happens. Round about 1:30, Morrissey's back with a couple of troopers. One's dark with a yellow, kinda sunken face. He looks like he's got acid indigestion as a permanent thing and he's chewing on an unlit cigarette. He has this notebook where he's writing down everybody's name and address and did we ever see Michelle outside of work and all this crap.

The other one's Lieutenant Stankus. Now I know him so well I can even tell you which teeth are capped and how often he gets his hair cut. At that time, all I see is this big, smooth faced blond guy who doesn't look so much grown as machine tooled. He's all business and about as warm as a ball bearing. I can tell right away he's the boss and the brain and the one to watch out for.

"Water Street?" he says and he looks at his partner who's writing this down without any expression.

"Seventeen," I says. "It's a two family." Like he's interested in my living arrangements and not in the fact that I'm only blocks from the park. I feel sweat running down my back.

"Convenient for the river," he says. I know he's not thinking about fish. "Get out fishing much?"

"Yeah," I says. "I'm hoping to get out tonight."

"Not this morning?" he asks.

"Naw. I've had this upset stomach," I says, and I look at the assistant who gives a little grunt. I'm expecting more, but he just nods and takes my phone number and moves on to Timmy, who's stupid enough to want to know why they're asking. Mr. Machine Tool gets a chance to shoot him down, and I go back to work. I'm checking off another order, when I remember that all Michelle's notes and invoice copies are still in my fishing vest. My heart stops, bang, like it's on a pneumatic brake, and then it starts again so fast I'm all over sweat. I want to say I'm sick and bug off home and have a bonfire. I know that's craziness, but I don't get hold of myself til Timmy comes over to bitch about the troopers.

Course no one gets much done even after law enforcement leaves. Little knots of guys are talking behind the shelves all over the Barn. Out on the loading dock, they're asking the drivers if they've heard anything and do they remember Michelle, the gal with the pink tinged eyes who used to check the invoices. I clam up, seeing I'm barely supposed to have known her, but I'm listening a lot, cause anything I learn is maybe something that can help me.

Pathetic, huh? I didn't realize the way the universe is rigged for guys like me. It's like the trout don't know there's a string and a hook attacked to the spinner. I see that's the way life is: if it's after you, you may get some slack or you may not, but the hook's always there and sooner or later you'll get pulled up short. I was still on the slack then and thinking all the time. I learned some things, too. Like Earl had actually gone out bowling with werewolf eyes. I flash on Friendly Bowl: Michelle is carrying the big black purse where my life is crackling and rustling among the invoices and Earl—beard and flannel shirt and Pearl Jam hair—is toting two bowling balls in those new pastel colors. I can hardly believe it. Earl's the quietest guy in the Barn, yet he's got this secret life where he dates werewolves and takes them bowling. I want to lean over and tell him everything, like we've got this secret in common, like he'd understand everything.

Then I swallow hard because he's going on about her friends in Providence. "She ran with a rough crowd," he's saying now. "You know what I mean?" Earl's not big on details. He gives you the frame work; you gotta put on the siding.

"What sorta rough crowd?" I says.

"There's this guy one night when I go to pick her up. Vito's his name or something like that. Italian name." He pauses and we're all waiting.

"So what, he's Italian?" says Tony, who's Italian-Polish.

"He has a big car," Earl says, not wanting to give offense, "and Michelle tells me she never has to worry, because Vito is her friend. See, he's something in the rackets. I don't know what. Collects from restaurants, maybe, cause Michelle says he takes her to all the nice places."

We're impressed by this. As much by the fact Earl's put more than four words together, as by this evidence that Michelle, too, had another life. "Life After The Bargain Barn" goes through my mind, cause I'm beginning to feel silly and feverish. I'm in the most trouble I've ever been in, and when I'm not feeling so sick I want to die, I'm cracking up. Then

I remember the invoices. I see the machine-tooled lieutenant opening the door to my apartment and putting one of his clean, smooth hands into the pocket of my fishing vest and pulling out disaster.

Meanwhile, the others get busy pumping Earl, and Mike mentions he'd seen Michelle around town with a red haired guy. We chew on that until someone notices it's time for the local news, and we hook an extension cord into a Sony reject. We're not supposed to run the stock, but when Morrissey comes over all he does is bitch about the picture.

Earl bangs on the box, bringing up the governor shaking hands on a tax break with some executive extortionist. After the commercials, we're promised "Woman found dead in River Trail Park" like it's some treat. Earl says, "Oh, shit," and the others all start talking—of course, they didn't already know. I can't say a thing; the commercials are just a blur. You know the way people say something must be true because they've seen it on tv? That's how I feel. It's like I could almost have forgotten the whole thing; even after the cops came, I'd had hopes she'd just been hurt. Then I hear the news on tv and it's suddenly official.

When our local Action Team comes back on, we've got this smart looking reporter who acts like she's been electrified. She's got a bright red coat on and a scarf and she's holding a mike like a black ice cream cone, licorice flavor, maybe. This is her big moment with a real corpse in the background, and she's so excited I think she's maybe going to take a bite right out of the mike and short the circuit and ruin her teeth.

One part of me sees that and wants to laugh. The other part smells exhaust fumes and Michelle's body and feels the stiff wind and the cold, hard railing of just before. Just after is lying behind the tv reporter. They've got the area roped off like it's some kind of shrine, and there's a green tarp over Michelle. It kinda bothers me that they've left her lying on the walk. The stroller is there, too, tipped on one side, so I guess the kid tried to climb out after all. Lots of police and technical people are walking around, plus tv reporters trailed by big guys shouldering cameras.

"...shock to the community," the Action reporter says, then she's shoving the black, fuzzy mike in a trooper's face, and he's basically saying, "no comment". The camera swings away like it's got a mind of its own and peers down the slope. I break a sweat, thinking footprints and evidence. In the voice over, the trooper mentions "no witnesses at this time", which gets my breath back. "We're asking the community to come forward," the Action reporter says in those low, hollow tones tv people get when they're being concerned and serious.

I'm hoping they'll tell us more, but they don't know much. Michelle's dead, the kid's okay, and we'll have interviews with the families on the late night show. Morrissey gets up and switches off the set. He wants us to go back to work but his power cord's so frayed, he doesn't have the energy to say so. I wonder about him and Michelle for a moment and whether he's going to wind up taking some heat. Earl's pissing and moaning about having gone out with her—he's just understood the troopers will be back to question him sure. Timmy's saying the red-haired guy must be the one, and Morrissey is still standing there looking like last winter's snow.

Maybe he'd of said something and maybe I would of—it was that kind of moment—but the driver from the Norwich store arrived and saved my ass. He's standing on the loading dock yelling about his order and why the hell are we fucking with his schedule, typical driver's crap. I tell him where he can go and then where the order is. Like all he had to do was ask, cause it's all ready for him and has been since before the troopers came. Of course, by now the driver's got to know everything, so I tell him what we saw on tv. There's half a dozen others willing to fill in the rest with what they know and don't know, too. I hadn't realized Timmy was so creative; that's maybe how he's making it through college when he's barely got sense enough to find his way between the Sonys and the Akais.

Anyway, I say enough not to look odd and no more. I tell myself I got to make it through the shift and start watching the clock big time. The dial's like a guy with a bad hip. The second hand hitches from one dot to the next until the minute hand takes pity on it and hops to the next number. By quitting time, I'm about crazy between watching that damn clock and thinking about the invoices in my fishing vest, the troopers coming back, and the late night news show.

For one thing, I know Mom will call as soon as the Bargain Barn is mentioned or maybe before, since it happened near where I live. That's the kind of thing will get her fussed. I'll have to say how Water Street is a safe neighborhood though, no, it's not as safe as hers and Dad's. They live out on the other side of town where the lots are bigger and the houses are all single family. They have a big field next to them and the community college, making it one of the nicer parts of this deadass town. Mom gets it in her head periodically that I should come home and live for a spell to save up money so I can get out of renting once and for all. Lucky my Dad is all for having me "be independent" as he puts it; I encourage that. I'm not bothered by renting except for the money involved, and going home would mean giving up nights with the *numero uno* Red Gal and certain other things.

Now, of course, I'm really thankful I'm not living at home. I may get by lying to Mom on the phone but never in person. And it would be worse for them if I got caught there. You know how the news is; it would be like it was their fault, because I was still living at home and all that. I think again about Seattle or L.A. or Chicago or somewhere. And soon. But not too soon. A month maybe. I'm wondering if a month is too soon, when Timmy comes and says he and Earl're going to stop at the Little River. I find myself saying my rod's in the truck, and I've got no choice but to follow them as soon's we're punched out.

We're on the river til dark. A couple of other guys leave just as we arrive, so we've got room to pull Earl's truck and mine and Timmy's junker Chevy in by a farm gate. Right there the river's not much bigger than a good sized stream, but it's swift and carries a lot of water. The fields one side belong to a sheep farm and several dozen woolies with bare faces and yellow snake eyes are tanking up on grass. Some have new lambs with them, light and frisky looking without their mother's thick coats.

The farmer's got an electric fence strung up for them, so we work the other side, climbing over big fallen trees and looking for good spots on the muddy bank. We stopped at the package store on the way, and I've had a couple brews to take the edge off. I'm basically just going through the motions, which the fish must know cause I don't get even a nibble. Timmy's the only lucky one; I guess Earl, like me, has got things on his mind. Finally, the light starts to go, and I climb back onto the road to try my luck casting off the bridge on the sheep farm side. The sun's already behind the dark hills, but overhead the clouds are pink and the west is pink, too, and the stream is reflecting pink all through the little marsh and the darkening pasture. I wish with all my heart it was yesterday, though I know that yesterday I would of just said it was a nice night. I wouldn't have had any sense that here is something important, something I could lose, something I've already lost.

Minutes later the stream goes dark, the April night that's been turning cool goes cold, and we pack it in. First, though, we gotta sit on the back end of Earl's truck to finish off the beer. Earl and me, we're pretty quiet, but Timmy talks enough for all three of us. He's got the touch with trout, he's got a paper due, his chemistry course's a ball buster, etc. etc. Finally, Earl says he's hungry, which is the first sensible thing I've heard in half an hour. Since Timmy's paper's due the next day, he goes home to eat cold pizza and write. Earl and me wind up together at the country store, ordering meatball grinders just so's we don't have to face our own apartments. We sit outside on the store porch and work our way through big soft rolls with meatballs and red sauce. I'm glad it's Earl cause I don't feel like I have to talk.

When we're almost done eating, he says, "They're going to question me again, aren't they?"

"I guess so," I says. "Maybe. They may find who did it quick."

"I hate talking to cops," he says.

"You'll need an alibi," I says, "for—this morning." I can feel my gut tighten. I'd almost mentioned a time. Earl does that to you. He never asks questions but you're tempted to tell him things just the same.

He doesn't say anything for a minute. Earl's thought processes are slow but sound. "The pisser is I was on the river," he says.

I feel myself getting nervous. The big silence Earl carries around with him is suggesting bad things. "So was half the town. Timmy said."

"Naw, I mean the river through town."

"Yeah? See anyone?"

"That's just it. I went early. It was pretty quiet. A few people out, that's all."

There's no way to ask, "Did you see me?" so I don't say nothing and try to keep a grip until Earl gets ready to say whatever it is he wants to say.

"I was pretty far downstream," he says at last.

"By the trout hatchery?" I asks, forgetting Earl lives north of town.

"Naw, not that far. Above the bridge."

"Well," I says, "the park's below the bridge. You weren't down by the park, were you?"

Earl takes so long to answer that in the normal course of things I'd of fallen asleep.

"Not til later," he says. "I was going along, you know, trying some of the pools when I heard the sirens. I didn't want to get mixed up with anything."

"Anyone see you?" I asks again.

He shrugs. He looks worried and miserable—about like I feel. "I don't know. Who's to say it was someone from the river?"

"No one at all," I says. This is an idea I definitely do not want to plant in his mind, cause Earl holds an idea like superglue. "But still, it might be better if someone saw you fishing."

"That's what's bugging me," he says. "I'm coming down stream, right, and I see this guy going up the bank."

"Well, then," I said, "they'll find him. You heard them asking for people to come forward."

"What's bugging me," Earl says, "is I don't think he noticed me. It was foggy as hell this morning and he was in a hurry."

"Where was this?" My mouth's gone dry right down my throat.

"You know where the fence is broke by the feed store?"

"Is there an opening there?" I says. "I'll have to remember that."

"Yeah," he says.

"Anyone you know? You could call him."

"Naw," Earl says.

"Know him again?" I asks.

He shrugs and gives me a look. "Naw," he says, "I didn't see his face. Too foggy."

"Tough," I says.

"Yeah," he says now, "cause first I thought it was you. If it'd been you, I sure wouldn't have to worry so much."

CHAPTER 4

It takes a while to get Earl straightened out. I'd wanted to delay getting home before, but now I'm panicked to get back. Of course, I can't. I have to tell him about meeting the Numero Uno Red Gal and just enough about subsequent events to stimulate his imagination and convince him that I'd been in bed til nearly nine a.m. Earl sits there looking like I'm discussing nuclear physics, and I can imagine him telling the troopers that yes, he'd seen someone up north on the river, someone who looked just like his friend, Jeff, but wasn't. I flash on dead meat and expand on the Red Gal's attractions.

"It's like a hangover," I tell Earl. "Total Sensory Overload."

I can tell by his expression this is another new concept, but after he struggles with it for a while, he gives me a sly little smile. I clap him on the shoulder, chuck my grinder wrappers in the trash, and head home, the meatballs churning cement along the way. When I get out in my garage, I spot the waders in the corner and I go upstairs quick to avoid thinking about soil samples and also so I won't have to see George, who's always got his nose in my business. What I've got to do is handle one thing at a time, the invoices first and then probably a call from Mom. Soon as I get in my apartment, I grab for the fishing vest and the papers. Out the corner of my eye, I see the light on the answer machine winking.

"It's Mom, Jeff. I just saw the six p.m. news. Wasn't that terrible? That poor girl! I said to your Dad, 'Jeff's always out there alone along the river and who knows who's around these days with that new highway.' Vi saw someone in the parking lot when she was hiking up in Furnace Brook; she said he was just sitting in his car and didn't look right at all...."

I take a deep breath. I'd been shitting Earl with Total Sensory Overload: Total Sensory Overload is sorting the werewolf's invoices while Mom worries in the background.

"Call," she says. "Call when you get in. Just thinking about you. Bye."

I could cry, I really could, but I figure I'd better see what I've got. I start laying shit out on the table, original yellow and pink invoice sheets, photocopies, a little leatherette notebook. What I really want to do is to crumple them up, put them in the trash, and never think about them again. Sorry! Garbage collection isn't til next week. I start to tear the sheets up, but that makes little bits of tell tale confetti. The whole thing's like some eco-freak's nightmare: the Garbage That Can't Be Destroyed. I finally decide the best thing's to burn everything. I should of come straight home and used the invoices to light the barbecue and cook up some burgers. And I could do that tomorrow, if I could stand to wait. But I want rid of the stuff pronto, and I'm carrying the whole heap over to the sink when there's this knock on the door.

For a minute I freeze. I feel like some poor dumb possum smack in the middle of route 6 with lights coming both ways. I see Lt. Machine Tooled and his dyspeptic partner and newspaper headlines and being caught red handed with a bundle of evidence.

"Hey, Jeff! You home?"

It's fucking George! I'd like to stay right where I am until he gets tired of banging on the door, but he maybe has a key from his brother and he's noisy as hell. "Just a minute," I says. I stick the invoices and papers under the sink and close the cabinet. I grab the fishing vest, hang it up, and open the door.

"So, Jeff!" He swivels his head around like it's on casters. I figure some new disease before I realize he's looking for the Red Gal.

"I just got in from work," I says but George can't take a hint.

"Surprised you made it to work," he says.

"Some of us have stamina," I says. Which is stupid. I should have said I was wrecked and was going to bed.

"I can believe," he says and laughs. "Got any beer?"

"Naw," I says.

He goes over to the fridge and opens it. "Don't you have any Coors?" he says. "I gotta have a Coors."

"So buy some," I says.

"You kept me awake last night," he says and helps himself to the last of my Rolling Rock sixpack.

What a cretin. I know he wants to talk about the Red Gal, but even though he's part of my alibi the whole idea turns my stomach. George is like a kid who wants to play doctor.

"Well I won't be making a sound tonight," I says. "Today's been a bummer."

"Yeah, that's right! We gotta catch the news." You'd think he didn't have a tv of his own. He walks into the living room and switches on the set. Leggy babes are dancing around a couple smiling guys hoisting brews. Behind them is this full band and a beach just as the sun is setting. The whole thing probably cost more than I'll make if I live to be a hundred.

"Whooo," says George, making with some dance moves. "Ooooh!" Somewhere somebody must of studied George before deciding what beer commercials ought to look like. They must of recorded his brain waves and matched up the music.

"Don't spill my last Rolling Rock," I says. Next time I rent anywhere I'm going to make damn sure the landlord doesn't have cretin relatives.

On screen, the party fades into the sunset with nobody getting drunk or barfing on the sand or trying to take out the musicians. I'm still thinking about parties and sand and dancers with three foot thighs when the anchors come on. He's old and reliable looking and she's young with glamour hair; they're both light orange cause the color bars are off. I focus on that and try not listen too much to what they're saying which is that "...tonight's lead story is the killing in River Trail Park..."

"We're famous," George says. "Hey, right there. I was right there on Sunday." He actually gets up and taps the screen. "Me'n Pete and Fern. Remember Fern Bailey?"

"Why don't you listen?" I says. I never planned to hurt Michelle, but I feel I could murder George without regret. On screen is the park, "the murder site", and they've got a good shot of the police at work and of a big rolling stretcher with a blue body bag on it. We get a reprise of the afternoon footage before Lt. Stankus comes on and says how they're "following up every lead and interviewing the deceased's friends and co-workers".

"They talk to you?" George asks.

"Yeah. They talked to everyone."

"Shit!" says George. He's impressed by the reality of it, like it's on tv and it's real, too. I'm trying to go the other way; I'm trying to see everything as just another news story, just a lot of motion on the screen. Hell, we handle bad stuff every night; it's just a matter of focus, and, in some ways, I'm glad George is watching, cause he helps keep me from being back at the river and feeling all the things I need to forget.

"...any suspects?" the reporter asks. This is a blonde version of the electric gal from this morning.

"I don't have any other comments at this time," Machine Tool says. "We're in the initial stages of the investigation."

"Do you have any advice for the community?" she asks. I'm still trying to digest his last answer. Do they have a suspect and aren't telling? Are they clueless and trying to hide it? Initial stages means they'll be back at the Barn. Maybe my apartment, too. I think of the invoices stashed under the sink and start to sweat.

"...caution but no need to panic..."

I wonder what it would take to make Machine Tool panic. I focus on his mouth opening and closing like some complicated engine: "...asking the community to come forward....a major road...anything unusual... river...."

"Well, you've heard it here, Dean", our reporter says, all teeth and intensity. "The police are continuing their investigation, but the public can help. If anyone has information...."

Up comes a special police number and also the Action Team's Special Alert Number before the anchor returns. He's so serious he doesn't look real. He and the co-anchor are shaking their heads to show they're people of feeling and then nodding to show they agree with their buddy out along the cold, windy river.

"Thank you, Kim. And now we go to Caroline Steele for the good news of this story. Caroline?"

The screen splits and there's this black gal with dainty features and two inch nails. "That's right, Dean. And it's very good news, indeed, for Jessica Simeone and her son, Leon, who was found beside Michelle Portinari in the park this morning.

"Shit," says George. "That's Jess Portinari. She was in my brother's class. Wasn't it her husband..."

"Shut up!" I says, still riding the shock wave. Jess Portinari of all people. That was Jess Portinari's baby. I suspect right there what I come to know later on: that the universe is crazy, then I'm noticing that Jess's still got lots of dark brown hair and nice dark eyes. She's dressed in an old pink sweatshirt and jeans, and she's holding the fat faced little kid I last saw screaming his lungs out in the stroller. Kiddie's got a bandage on one cheek and he's sucking his thumb and scowling at the microphone like he's getting ready to howl again.

"Is Leon all right, Jessica?"

"Yes, he is." She brushes the hair back from his forehead. "Just a scratch."

"He wasn't attacked?"

"The police think he tipped over the stroller. I had to go into work at the last minute, and Michelle was taking him to his sitter." Jess sounds semi-frantic.

The reporter makes a sympathetic face, but she's moved too close, and little Leon starts to scream.

"He's been frightened," says Jess. "He's still frightened."

She wraps her arms around the kid like he's all she's got in the world, and right then I'm afraid reality may get through to me after all. Lucky for me, the reporter starts talking into her mike with that super alert reporter look, and George starts in about school and did I know Andre,

Jess's husband, who got killed, didn't he, in that helicopter accident just before the Gulf War?

"I don't know," I says. I just want to get rid of George before he can start rehashing the story. I switch off the set.

"Hey," he says. "I wanna get the scores."

"Watch downstairs," I says. "I worked with the woman, for christsake."

"Don't take it personal," says George.

"I'm tired, that's all." I don't say anything more, cause he's part of my alibi, but I think I really will move to Seattle.

Soon as I hear George downstairs, I open the cabinet, take out the invoices, and put them in the sink. I'm set for the bonfire, when I notice they aren't all for my shipments. Whoa! I stop right there. My first thought is that the whole thing was pointless, totally pointless, that Michelle and I both got screwed but good by whoever's in charge. My next thought is so why the hell was she carrying this stuff around?

I sit down at the kitchen table, and I no sooner get the carbons spread out than the phone rings. I'm up like a shot, but I gotta wait two more rings to get my breath again before I answer.

"It's Mom," she says. "How are you?"

"I'm kinda tired," I says. "Long day."

"Did you work late?"

"Naw," I says. "Some of the guys went to the Little River after work. We just wanted to get out for a while. After everything."

"It's a terrible thing. And right here. You don't think of anything like that happening here. Which is silly because there was that shooting just last year."

"It happens everywhere."

"You're all right?" Mom says. She's got a trouble detector like you can't believe.

"I think I'm getting the flu," I says.

"Going fishing's not the best thing for flu," she says. "You stay off that river, all that damp, and you never know who's going to be along there now."

"You used to be pretty fond of fishing, too," I says, trying to kid her along.

"That was years ago. That terrible thing this morning. You just don't know."

You can maybe see how I couldn't tell her even if it was mostly an accident. "Let me speak to Dad," I says. "How's he doing?"

"These damp days are bad," she says. She doesn't need to say anything else. When he comes on, I can hear his chest wheezing all the way across town.

"You know that young woman?" he asks right off the bat. Dad watches all the news shows now that he's home on disability. Mom picks up the gossip at the Discount. Between the two of them, they've got the town covered.

"She was invoice control checker on my shift."

"Troopers around already?"

"After lunch."

"You'll lose a lot of time with them," Dad says. "The place of business is one place they always look." He says this with enthusiasm, like it's something I'll be taking an interest in. Dad doesn't pick up vibes as quick as Mom.

"Yeah," I says, "so I've noticed." My eyes keep straying back to the invoices and photocopies, little orders—too little—from the big regional depot, and large orders—too large—from the Norwich and Worcester stores. Between the two, big time opportunity for shrinkage, for stock that gets conveniently "lost" or "damaged".

"You get out this morning?"

"After work. I slept in this morning."

"You missed the start of the season?" Dad can't believe it. He never missed an opening; younger generation's gone soft and the world's coming to an end.

"I got up and didn't feel so good. I thought I was getting the flu. Not much in the river anyway."

"You're right about that," he says. "Now you'e talking." We get right into stocking trout and lawn runoff, which is one of Dad's big beefs.

"Next Saturday," I says after a few minutes. "Want to go out next Saturday after I get off work?"

I hear his chest laboring away like a leaky accordion. "We'll see," he says, though I can tell he's pleased I asked. "We'll see. If it's not too cold. I can't take the damp air anymore."

"We can go midday," I says. "Way the fish're biting, midday's as good as any time. I can go out early by myself, first."

"Don't worry your mother," he says which can mean half a dozen things. I figure he means be careful with the early mornings. It's fucking too late now, but I says, "Sure thing."

"And Grampa," he says. "Call him."

"I'll call him tomorrow," I says. "He all right?"

"He'll bury me," Dad says and says good-night.

I hang up the phone feeling wasted. I'm fine so long as I don't care about anything. If I don't care about anything, things are as close to normal as they're ever going to be. It's when I worry about Mom guessing

I'm in trouble, or think about Dad's emphysema, or see Jess holding onto her son that I remember the park and all the bad stuff gets real.

Michelle's collection's almost a relief. Though it takes me a while, eventually I figure out what's coming down. Michelle caught me ripping off the Barn and she had me cold, all right. That's one thing. Then I give up larceny, but I've already given Michelle an idea, and her invoice collection continues. No business of mine, except there's my name on the sheets, and they aren't any orders I ever filled. I take a closer look at the signatures and, though they're pretty good, they're sure not mine, either.

Well, I sit there for a minute, feeling as stupid as George and Earl combined. After all that's happened in the last sixteen hours, I oughta be shock proof, but, goddamnit, somebody has re-started the racket and set me up. That's what it amounts to. I got the proof right in my hand and the only problem is that it provides a helluva good motive for taking out Michelle.

I start swearing, which doesn't do much good, and then I start regretting Michelle a little less, which makes me feel a whole helluva lot better. I've still got to get rid of the papers, though, and when I figure I've learned what's what, I carry the invoices to the sink and set them on fire. Course, they flare up like a blowtorch. Pretty soon I've got ashy gray bits of paper floating around the kitchen and a smell like polymer city cause the notebook isn't leather, it's plastic, and it's melted all over. I turn on the water and open the window and spend the next twenty minutes scraping red plastic goo outa the sink cause I'm getting compulsive in a big way. It's midnight before I'm done, but the evidence is history. All my adrenalin is gone. I stand under the shower for a minute, then fall into bed and pull the covers over my face. I wish I was dead.

That's Saturday night. I sleep most of Sunday. Monday, I wake up at four a.m. to throw up everything I've eaten for the past three months. Maybe I really do have the flu. I'd like to think that everything that happened is just a fever dream, but of course it isn't. And even if I feel like creamed shit, I've still got to get up like normal, which, this time of the year, means five-six o'clock to get on the river. I lie in bed for close to an hour before I get up and put on my thermals. After I make a pot of coffee, I load my gear into the truck. I drive to the north of town and park smack out in front of the electric supply firm where anybody who wants to can see I'm down checking the river. I pull on my waders, clomp across the sidewalk, and scramble over the low fence to the rocks. Making like an every day good guy, I wave to some fishermen trying their luck toward the bridge, then I open my fishing box and start tying on a spinner. At that moment, everything contracts and darkens; the rushing water fills up my ears and I think I'm going to fall. That's how it hits me. I'm shaking so much I almost put the hook through my finger, and then, just like that, I'm back standing on dry land, so to speak. The river stops being some dangerous subterranean current and is just greenish water bubbling white over the rocks; the mist, not so thick this morning, is lifting; the April sky is blue over town. I know just what I have to do and I do it: I cast the line out across the pool and start practicing fishing as a normal activity.

I get a couple nice trout, too, which I can take round to my folks later. Back up on the walk, I jaw with a couple of late arrivals, night shift guys just rolled out of bed, and I go out of my way to say hello to an old lady who's out every year with an antique kit and a big labrador dog. Then I go home with river mud on my waders, leaving behind a lot of folk who know I've had a touch of flu and didn't get out for the opening morning of the season.

I feel only slightly sick by this time and that's lucky, cause work isn't much fun. No one's in a good mood. Heavy events have sunk in over the weekend, the troopers are expected, and Morrissey is running around like a head case, fussing about the stock and trying to sort out shit he's neglected for months. If I'd been able to take a detached view, I'd of kinda enjoyed that, especially since I got him picked as my replacement in the shrinkage department. Him—or maybe Earl, who's gone from quiet to silent. He dated the werewolf, after all, and he was nearly as nervous as me yesterday.

Round about 11:30, the troopers roll in for their second visit. It's understandable, since Michelle worked our shift, but I don't like it cause it narrows down the field too much. Machine Tooled and the Indigestion Special commandeer Morrissey's office. Course Morrissey's running his mouth with "anything we can do to help" and "every facility" and "complete cooperation" and talking about the "terrible loss to the Bargain Barn family". It's such a crock that everybody but me's wondering about him and Michelle, and I'm wondering about him for the losses. But he's got me set up for that. He'll maybe get away with it and I'll maybe get stuck for everything. With thoughts like these, you can see why it isn't such a great day at the Barn.

The troopers are in with Morrissey for over an hour. I figure they're going over the inventory and rechecking invoices, and I'm getting sorrier by the minute that I didn't buy that Harley 883, cause if I had, I'd be out the door and heading west pronto. Anyway, by one, I can't stand anymore. I got a problem with a shipping order and I go round back to Morrissey's office. They're still talking away. I don't like to interrupt anything useful, so I wait just outside the door for a minute.

"You're sure?" That's Machine Tooled himself.

"Lieutenant, some shrinkage is normal. It's part of the price of doing business." That's Morrissey, sounding like a sales manual.

"You'd complained to the warehouse staff," says Stankus.

"You have to keep them on their toes," says Morrissey. "We cut our losses by even one percent, that's money in the bank."

"You were up to what—maybe 5%?"

"It averages out," Morrissey says. "Couple weeks in there, we're down to two-three percent."

They can thank me for that, I think, and I'm waiting for him to say he's had his eye on someone, and I feel my muscles getting tense when I hear a step and all of a sudden the door opens. He musta heard something. Morrissey looks like a cup of yogurt, chalky white with a bit of blue around the edges. I'm betting he's up to his eyes in trouble.

"Need your signature," I says and stick out the invoice.

He takes the paper and runs it through his field of vision without reading it, then signs real quick.

"Okay," I says. That was when he ought to have had me in. Said "Maybe Jeff can help us out on these discrepancies", that's the kinda word he uses, "discrepancies", and let the shit hit the fan. Nope. He closes the door fast like he doesn't want them to see me. Which tells me he really does want to keep everything quiet. The Bargain Barn version of virtual reality: I'm pretending to be normal, Morrissey's pretending to be smart, and both of us're pretending to be honest.

I think about that as I go back to work, rolling out Toshiba VCR's for a big special down in Norwich. I guess that Morrissey's had his hand in the stock and he doesn't want anyone looking at invoices. Or, alternately, he's set to bust me, but he doesn't have enough evidence. Maybe Michelle kept all the records, which I've now burned. Was he that dumb? I believe it but then I can't believe it. I can't make up my mind, though it somehow seems important to decide before I talk to Stankus again. I haven't gotten fatalistic yet. I still think it's all logic and using your head and keeping your eyes open—as if you ever could see what's really coming after you.

Anyway, I put on such a burst of busyness that I'm almost the last to be called. Timmy gets me just as I'm finishing my lunch break.

"You're next," he says. "Morrissey's office."

"What'd they ask you?" I says. I wouldn't risk looking interested with anyone else, but Timmy's a gabber.

"Where I was early Saturday morning. Seven to eight-thirty. Establishing time of death is tricky," he adds like he's some kind of coroner or something. "With the cold."

"Yeah," I says before I can think. "It was windy. It's been windy and cold every morning." Christ, I sound like the weather channel. Don't volunteer, I think. Don't volunteer anything. But don't be too quiet, either. Just act natural. As I open the office door, I realize I'm absolutely clueless.

Inside, Stankus and partner are sitting behind Morrissey's desk with a stack of papers on one side of them and some coffee cups and a couple of styrofoam containers on the other. There's a strong smell of french fries and onion rings. Goddamn! Talk about offensive. They've brought their lunch! My whole life is at stake and these guys are having french fries and onion rings.

They don't say anything right away. The assistant is studying his notebook like he's sorry he's ever eaten anything, while Stankus stares through me like he's got X-ray eyes and is really more interested in what's going on out in the corridor. I decide right then that Morrissey hasn't said anything. I decide that and figure to relax, but though you can tell your emotions stuff they don't have to listen. When the Machine Tooled one tells me to sit down, I feel my heartbeat go crazy.

"Jeffrey Woodbine, 17 Water Street, Slatertown?"

"No change," I says. Like I've moved since the weekend. He gives me a look. Stupid, I think. Don't volunteer and don't say anything you don't have to say.

"Where were you Friday night?"

"I was at work. Then I went to The Kitchen for dinner."

"When was that?"

"I get out of work at seven. I musta got to the restaurant seven-twenty or so."

"How long were you there?"

"Knicks were still in the first half when I left."

The assistant looks like he's got gas. "You don't remember a time?" he says.

Who's watching the clock with the Red Gal? I just shake my head.

"Where did you go after you left The Kitchen?"

"I went home."

"You went home alone?" Is that a natural question? Does this guy routinely pick people up in bars? Or has he already been poking around my life?

"No," I says. "A friend came in while I was there. We went to my apartment."

"Who is this friend?"

"Her name is Lynn Santorini. We went to school together."

"S-a-n-?"

"S-a-n-t-o-r-i-n-i."

"Address?"

I take a breath. I should of called Lynn and warned her. "She lives on Cedar Street. I forget the number."

"And when did Ms. Santorini leave your apartment?"

"Nine-fifteen, maybe. She works the morning shift at the Donut Shack."

"She left at nine-fifteen Saturday morning?"

"Yeah. Right around then. She's gotta punch in by 9:30."

Stankus looks at his pal like it's a federal offense. What is this? Or maybe they'e pissed cause now they'll have to check me off. That's right, they're disappointed, cause I musta looked right to them.

"What time you get up?" he says then.

That takes me by surprise. I'm kinda impressed by how thorough he is.

"Maybe five, maybe five-thirty. Opening of the season," I says. "I get up, but I feel lousy. I go back to bed til 8:30 or so."

"And Ms. Santorini can vouch for that?"

"She woke up when I got out of the shower. We had breakfast, she left. I went to work twenty of eleven."

"So you didn't get out for the opening of the season?" the assistant says.

"I went out with a couple guys from work that night," I says.

We go through this. Where I went fishing and what time, but I feel somehow that their hearts aren't in it. I'm finally beginning to relax when Stankus says, "Ever talk to Michelle Portinari?"

I might have expected this, but I still don't like it. "Sure, every day," I says. "She was the checker for our shift."

"I mean outside of work."

"Naw."

"In the parking lot, maybe?" You never know what people see—or what they'll remember.

"I gave her a lift to where her car was parked one night. And she'd sometimes make a comment or ask something in passing."

Stankus raises his eyebrows like he's amazed by the range of my social life.

"What sort of comments or questions?"

But I've been thinking about that. Like I say, I'm quick off the mark. "She stopped one night and asked me how I liked my truck. How it ran."

"Was she thinking of buying one, maybe?"

I shrug. "She didn't say. She never had much to say to me."

CHAPTER 5

You think 'No way': situation impossible. But before you know it, you're still alive and the landscape's been altered beyond anything you'd imagined. That's just the way things are. The pisser is that just when I figure, okay, I've got this under control, I can live with this, events twist like a game fish, and I'm caught a whole different way than I'd expected.

Like time. You know how when something terrible happens, you feel, this is it. And it is and everything's different, yet it's the same, too. Like when Barry got so sick and we first found out it was Lou Gerhig's disease. I remember standing out by the swings Dad built and knowing my big brother, who could do anything, anything at all, was going to be crippled and then he was going to die. That may of been the first idea I put together entirely out of hints, cause nobody had told me. I just knew, that's all, even if I was too young to understand what it all meant.

Mostly I thought how amazing it was that this was happening to me: I was the kid whose older brother was dying. Standing in the back yard sunshine, I was sure my life wasn't ever going to be the same. I'd gotten different, somehow, special, I guess, and I was surprised when I had to go off to school as usual. I thought, see, that the whole universe had stopped and then restarted in a different course. But it hadn't, and I still had to get on the school bus. Same thing now, I still gotta get dinner, lug laundry to the machines, stop by and see my folks. Nothing's ever in isolation, though I keep trying to seal off Thursday morning. I'll think I've gotten it buried pretty good when, whammo, there it is again screwing up the rest of my life. Thursday morning is never over, that's the bottom line, and I kinda understand people who confess, even confess to stuff they haven't done. They confess cause shit's been dragging on too long.

I can understand that now, cause speaking personally, I was tempted. I was. I was. I almost tell Morrissey that very first morning, which is as near crazy as I ever hope to get. And Mom—I almost tell her when we're alone in the kitchen the night I take them the trout. Dad's gone in to talk to Grampa for a while. He's into politics, and Grampa's gotten to what he calls the listening stage, meaning he's learned enough, as he puts it, to keep his damn mouth shut. Silence is the beginning of wisdom, he says. Grampa has a collection of phrases like that. When my mom's in a good mood, she'll say he's our own guru, and when she's in a bad mood, she'll say he's an old fool.

Anyway, Dad's occupied. He may be gasping, but he'll work his way through the whole town from animal control to first selectman. Grampa will sit nodding his head and chewing on his pipe, unlit cause of Dad's emphysema. At the end, Grampa will say it's all graft and they're all crooks, and Dad'll agree except for a few favorites, who he'll defend until Grampa falls asleep in his chair. Then Dad'll come back and say how the old man's failing. Which he's been doing ever since I went to elementary school.

So Mom and me are in the kitchen. She's washing the dishes and complaining I'm not getting them dried right. She takes these funny spells and right now she's so nervous she's making me jumpy, too. It's like she's got this emotional radar that keeps sweeping round and round and picking up unidentified flying anxieties. For a variety of reasons, her radar's always focused pretty heavily on me.

"Things all right?" she asks.

"No worse than usual," I says.

"How's work going?"

"Cops were there again today."

"No, not that cabinet—next one over. You'd think you'd never lived here. What did they want?"

"I've been on my own for four years," I says. "They wanted to question everyone."

She gives me a look like I'm maybe leaving something out.

"Yeah, you know, the usual. Where we were Thursday morning, did we know Michelle, that sort of stuff."

"Are you feeling better?"

Now there is a good example of how Mom's mind works. This simple question really includes a, my alibi, b, the Red Gal, who is my alibi, and c, my health.

"Yeah," I says cause after all I've been out fishing. "I thought it was flu but it was maybe the margueritas."

"I wish you wouldn't drink," Mom says. What she really means is she wishes I wouldn't drink margueritas with the Red Gal.

"You like Lynn," I says, "and Lynn likes margueritas."

"You're not ready to handle a family," she says.

Privately, I gotta agree, but it's easier to get mad and rattle the plates around and complain that she's treating me like a child. Not smart, cause, bang, the radar picks up on it. She stops washing the dishes and looks up at me. Mom's maybe five feet on a good day, though somehow she's always seemed bigger. She's got a solid frame and a round, candid face.

Standing there with the dishtowel in my hands, I realize all of a sudden that she's thinner, that worry's making her smaller.

"Something's wrong," she says just like that.

"Aggro at work, that's all," I says.

"Not trouble with Lynn?"

"Lynn's a friend. I've told you that."

She doesn't say anything for a moment, and I have this sick feeling that she suspects, followed by an awful temptation to tell her, to say, "You know that woman that was killed? It was really an accident, just an argument, she just fell. I never meant to hurt her."

Then Mom says, "I'm sorry to be picking at you. With work and all." She puts her head down and starts scrubbing a pan like mad. "Don't say anything to him, but I've been worried about your dad. The weather up here isn't good for him anymore. We should move, I know we should, but unless I can hold on for my pension..." She shrugs, and for a minute we're both thinking will the Discount stay open, can they get enough for the house to move the three of them south, can Dad make it?

When she looks at me again, I can see she both does and doesn't want to know. Always before she's wanted to know no matter what: the time I took the car when I wasn't supposed to and piled it up in Plainfield; the time me and some other Red Men sneaked a couple beers on the team bus. This time, she's got too much on her hands already, and she knows it. "I worry sometimes," is all she says.

When I put my arm around her, I feel a big empty space opening: I've been left alone with Saturday morning. This is an unexpected part of the price, and I feel angry at Mom and Michelle and the world, and sorry, too, and careful, like I've been handed something delicate. "I'm a big boy now."

Mom smiles for the first time that evening. Maybe the radar's gone off on her or maybe she's so tired she's pushed the switch, herself. "I know," she says, "but you were always my baby. Barry and Mary were so much older. I've always though that was hard on you."

Actually, I was fussed over and nothing too much was expected of me. It was only after Barry took sick that I got promoted to a whole new set of expectations, and family life got complicated in a way I never fully understood. But maybe that would of happened anyway. If I'm going to blame anything, it's got to be Michelle's greed and my own stupidity. That and the bad luck that goes fishing for us the way I go up the river after trout.

Course, what turns out to be bad luck I mistake, at first, for good: subsequent events, for example. For starters, the coroner's report comes out: Michelle died because a blow to her face caused her to fall onto one of the big bolts holding the park bench. News reporters backpedal on the "brutal beating death" kick. The town parks department issues a statement that the same benches and fastenings are 'used by municipalities across the country', and Lt. Stankus takes to the air waves to ask guys with information to step forward. Far as I know, nobody does. Which is fucking amazing, when you think that for five minutes or so right on the edge of a major road, right in the center of town on a work day, nobody's around, nobody sees a thing—except a little kid too young to talk. What are the odds of that? Then there's me, worrying about evidence and witnesses and not understanding anything, least of all how events were going to take me where I am today.

Anyways, a day after the report, the body's released to the family. Morrissey calls our shift together pronto and says that we're all to go to the funeral. The Portinari family've set the service for 10:30 a.m., and the Barn management's going to allow our shift to come in a few minutes late so that the "Bargain Barn family" can be represented. He goes on about this, about "showing the community we care", til I think I'm going to puke. Michelle wasn't a werewolf, she was a vampire, and she's going to be on my case forever. But since everyone's nodding their heads and saying how it's a great idea, I try for normal and do the same.

That's how come I'm sitting in one of the back rows of Our Lady of Lourdes the next Monday morning. The air is cold and smells like a better grade of pot; incense, Earl tells me. There's bunches of pastel gladiolus around the altar and big wreaths propped up on easels so we can get a good look at them. I feel like a fool in my brown Bargain Barn uniform; I gotta remind myself we're not there to grieve but to show how we're working for "an enlightened and caring company"—to quote Morrissey. I may be the only one of us who really feels the occasion, and I sure wouldn't want to exhibit <u>my</u> emotions. But maybe other people have mixed feelings about Michelle, too. Maybe other people feel remorse and sorrow and hatred and, I gotta admit it, a kinda grim satisfaction.

Stankus and the Indigestion Special show up, too. They stand toward the back in proper dark suits, looking us over like well paid bouncers. I don't want to attract their attention, so I concentrate down front where the Portinari relatives are arriving. There's some smart looking young women in short skirts and long jackets—the various Portinari cousins and daughters. I think I spot Jess Simeone, but I'm not sure cause the women have mostly got these big dark hats on. They're escorted by the sons and sons-in-law, their faces scraped red by Bics and bad weather. Other young relatives are bringing in tiny, stooped men and women almost as old as Grampa. They're dressed in black coats and gray suits, and they look surprised and foreign and a little bit lost like they didn't expect to be going to anybody's funeral except their own. One couple comes in after everyone else is settled. From their brave, frozen expressions, I figure them for the parents, and I feel my gut seize up. I know I gotta detach myself or I'll be in major trouble, especially since I can feel Stankus' X-ray eyes boring into my back.

Beside me, Earl's going through the prayer book in a knowledgeable way, but I can't focus. I start studying the big stained glass windows that show Jesus and some saints in a perpetual twilight of purples, greeny-browns, blues, and golds. With the organ wheezing away behind us, the windows on each side, and the crucifix up front, the whole place is depression city. I wish I'd cut the damn service or told Morrissey I was an atheist or something.

Then the organ shifts a gear. Everybody stands up, as the altar boys march in with these smoking silver balls on chains. Behind them are the priest and his backup and the pall bearers guiding an enormous coffin covered in a blanket of red roses. I start to think how I caused all this, how one second on opening day produced church, priest, flowers, coffin, and I feel the way I did along the river. Only instead of the sound of water, it's the organ mooing like a crazy cow, and instead of the morning mist, it's incense billowing up to take my breath away. I'm actually getting dizzy, and I have to hang onto the pew in front of us until the service starts and I find the right distance again. I tell myself it wasn't just me; it was Michelle and the C of F—who screamed, "Jesus, don't ever call me again"—when I phoned afterwards, and Morrissey, too, if I'm right, and Frenchie and the proprietor of Dougie Donnelley's. Now you may look at it differently, but that's how I see it at the moment, and I hang on to that cause if I don't I know I'll fall, not into the pew in front of me, but into the river and the mist.

Maybe I'm not cut out for funerals. I've only been to two. My brother's is just a blur; I was only ten and too scared and confused for anything to register. I remember the other one better, the one for Chad Boysie, who drowned swimming drunk junior year up at the reservoir. This one's much the same, though being Catholic, there's a mass, and at one point everybody turns and shakes hands with the people on either side. Earl's all shook up, I see, and I pat him on the shoulder, thankful that Morrissey is several rows away. Stankus, too. The priest prays for a bit out of a little book and does complicated stuff with the altar boys and the cups and plates he's got to work with. I'm detached now and going with the flow. At one point he asks for "eternal light to shine upon her", Michelle, that is. I wonder about that. Whether any of us, being what we are, could take eternal light, or if, as Grampa says, this is just one of the many queer things Catholics believe. I have this odd image of Michelle, her werewolf red eyes gleaming in the eternal light, opening the purse that's stuffed with her life and mine and Morrissey's, and maybe Earl's too. But before I can get in trouble with this, the priest starts the benediction and asks for our peace. I ask for that, too; then the organist powers up and Michelle rolls down the aisle on the big trolley covered in red roses.

The closest relatives step out behind, remote in their thoughts and griefs, and, soon as they're out the door, you can feel the atmosphere change. Men straighten their jackets and check their ties; women gather their purses and fumble for their coats. People start talking in normal voices about normal things. Michelle's dead now, the official property of the family, the church, and the grave. Since the police have zilch, I have a hope that maybe I can get on with my life like the rest of them, who probably have better reasons to remember her than I do.

"Nice service, Father," says Earl, shaking the priest's hand. That seems to be the thing to say, and I say the same and shake his hand, too. Then there are the relatives. I don't want to shake hands with them, but I've got to, cause they're thanking us for coming and jawing to Morrissey about how much they appreciate the gesture. "I'm very sorry," I say to each one, and I feel kinda better, cause I really mean it, and kinda worse, cause it's all under false pretenses. But I've decided to do it this way and now I've got to go through with it. I've got to. So I say I'm sorry for the fifteenth time or so and start sidling over to the big front steps. Not to seem rude, but I'm anxious to get my truck and leave. I'm wishing I could keep going all the way to Maine or the West Coast or somewhere, when this low, kinda husky voice comes right outa the crowd and hits me square in the solar plexus. I stop dead and hear her say, "I gotta get back, Brenda. I can't leave Leon with Holly for too long."

"You've got to go to the cemetery! It won't be that long."

"I want to go home now." Her voice starts rising like she's seriously upset. I turn around to see two women standing at the top of the steps. The tall one is Jess Simeone; I recognize the straight dark eyebrows, the high cheekbones, and square jaw even under her big hat. She looks very pale and she's rocking nervously on her high heeled shoes.

"What will Aunt Lillian say? They expect everyone." The second gal's shorter with reddish hair and a prissy manner I dislike even at a distance.

"If I go, you know they'll expect me back at the house, too. Please, Brenda, they'll never miss us. I gotta get back."

"You shoulda brought your own car if you wanted to cut the cemetery. Everybody's going to the cemetery."

Christ, I think, Michelle reincarnated.

Jess looks nearly in tears. "I'm worried about Leon," she says. "I've not left him alone since. You know how frightened he is!"

That hits me about as you can imagine, and I start angling down the steps. This isn't my problem, and I can't afford to make it my problem.

"He's gotta start getting readjusted," Brenda says.

Jess mutters something, and I hear her heels rapping angrily on the stone, before I'm nearly knocked flying. I reach out a hand to balance myself and catch her arm and keep us both from bagging an insurance claim.

"Oh, Christ!" Jess says, "I'm so sorry." I can feel her shaking. She's as tall as me in those high black shoes and twice as unsteady.

"You all right?" I says.

"You're Jeff Woodbine."

"That's right. You wanta ride home?"

Her face is white and strained and her dark eyes are focused else-where, but she still gives this funny little smile. "Yeah," she said. "Yeah, I'd like a ride home." She looks over her shoulder. "But quick. Holly's nice and all, but I don't want to leave Leon any more'n I have to. Mother keeps him while I'm at work; that's okay, he knows her. But Holly's just a neighbor, you know what I mean."

She says all this in a breathless rush.

"My truck's just over in the lot," I says.

She starts down the steps with long, prancing strides. I notice she's got these beautiful beer commercial legs, really special. Someone's call-ing from the church, but Jess never turns her head. When she hits the drive, she pulls off her wide brimmed hat and shakes out her long, untidy hair like she's finished with church and Michelle and Aunt Lillian, too. I unlock the door of the truck for her, and as she climbs in, I get a glimpse of a long, slim thigh and feel an irrational surge of lust and sorrow and longing, all hopeless. It's the effect of strain, I guess; being under pres-sure and moving careful makes you rebellious. I understand that now. At the time, I'm so busy fighting off an attack of craziness that I almost scrape a big Caddy that's angled out into the drive.

"Helluva great way to park," I says, wrenching the wheel.

"That'll be Vito's," she says. "A sleezeball friend of Michelle's."

"I'm sorry about Michelle," I says. "And your boy. But he's okay now?"

"Okay and not okay. He got a real fright. The doctor says he'll be okay but he may regress a bit. You know, wet the bed, delay talking, that kind of thing."

I nod like I understand this, but I don't know squat about kids.

"I was trying to make Brenda understand that."

"She doesn't seem too quick to understand anything," I says.

"Totally thick. Like Michelle but not so bad tempered. I shouldn't say that day of her funeral, but why she took him along the park's more than I know."

She's tapping her fingers along the edge of the door.

"I thought the news said she was taking him to day care or something."

"Right. I figured she'd put him in her car and take him to Mom's on the way to work. Instead, she takes him out along the river before eight o'clock. In the stroller. Normally, Michelle wouldn't walk across the road if she had a car."

"No?" I says—I'm thinking all kinds of things.

"I didn't want her to take him at all. I was going to walk him down to Holly's instead, but Michelle called me and said how she was talking to her mom who'd been talking to my mom, and she was coming by to pick Leon up for me. Just like that. That was Michelle wanting something. I knew it and I shoulda said 'no' right then and not let her bully me. You got a cigarette?"

"Maybe one in the glove compartment. It'll be old, though."

"You gave it up? Smart. I hadn't had one in over two years, then I'm at work, the police call me about Leon and Michelle, and I just freak out. I gotta have a cigarette." She rummages around until she finds a crumpled pack. I pull out the truck lighter. She lights the cigarette and opens the window for the smoke. Thoughtful, you know. I remember she was always nice.

"So when were you appointed to be my guardian angel?" she asks after a minute. Her voice is normal now. She's going to pick up Leon, she's had a hit of nicotine, she's beginning to relax.

I look at her. The color's coming back into her face, and she's damn nice to look at.

"This is the same truck, even."

"That was some night," I says. I suddenly have this vivid—not memory, it's too vivid for memory—sensation, I guess, of a warm summer night, of sitting in the truck with the radio off, hearing peepers calling, feeling the faint breeze from the river. I'm taking a drag on a cigarette and trying to be totally cool, while Jess Portinari, who I don't know well, just from school, and who's supposed to marry Andre Simeone, the best shooting guard the Red Men ever had, is sitting beside me with an untouched cigarette and a stack of balled up kleenex, trying to decide what to do with her life.

"I've often thought about that," she says.

"Me, too," I says, and I realize it's true. Sitting in a dark truck along the river with Jess Portinari's been a kind of benchmark. Only Lynn, sometimes, brings on the same mind blowing desire. I momentarily wonder if there's something seriously wrong with me, cause that was a sad night, a complicated night. A night I behaved pretty well. I decide to remember that part of it.

"You gave me good advice," she says now. "Things just worked out in a different way altogether."

I wonder if, after all, I should of done things differently. Made out with her in the truck. Advised her to cancel the wedding and go visit her cousins in California. Told her she'd gotten hold of the wrong guy. "Yeah. I heard about Andre. I was awful sorry."

"He was a good guy," she says after a minute. "But maybe not a good guy to be married to. With the air force and all. I think I wasn't cut out to be a military wife."

"I guess it's a hard life."

"You gotta love someone a whole lot but not necessarily want him around all the time. Then it works okay," she said. "I guess I had it backwards." She doesn't explain this; she takes another drag on the cigarette then rubs it out in the ashtray. "Next right," she says. "Holly's this end of Vine Street."

She stops me in front of a little one story cape with pinkish composition shingling. "Thanks so much," she says.

"Want me to drive you and Leon home?"

"No, that's okay. Leon's funny now with men."

I musta looked surprised, cause she says, "He screams and cries. The police sure haven't helped. Coming around all the time like they have been."

"To question him, you mean?" My gut seizes up so fast I'll be lucky to have digestion at all if this keeps up.

"Yeah. The big blond hunk and Benny."

"Lt. Stankus?"

"That's the one. Benny's not too bad with Leon but Stankus is terrible. Leon screams as soon as he sees him."

"I thought Leon couldn't speak yet."

"Oh, he's right on schedule," Jess says proudly. "He says 'Mama', 'doggie', 'yes' and 'no'. A few food words. They're convinced he knows something about the killing but he hasn't got the words yet. I tried to explain that to the police, that they're making it worse, that they've got to wait a few months, but they won't listen cause he's their only hope."

The door of the house opens, and a woman comes onto the step with the little boy. He's in the same blue sweater, and he's got his thumb in his mouth. Jess leaps out of the car and so misses my expression.

"Take care," I call.

She's already halfway up the walk, but she turns with this thousand watt smile. Then the child runs toward her and as she scoops him up, I slip the gear. In my rear view mirror I see a dark woman with beautiful legs and hair, a woman who's a whole other level of experience, a woman who I would risk craziness for, holding the fatal baby in her arms.

You tell me the universe isn't malicious.

CHAPTER 6

After the funeral, I can't focus on anything. I screw up a shipping order, pick a fight with a guy at The Kitchen, and work my way through a six pack before it's time to turn on Letterman. This is like the new routine; I'm waiting, as Grampa puts it, for "the other shoe to drop", a phrase that suddenly has meaning, cause I can't seem to get on with everyday life. I try. I buy a bunch of flowers from the guy who parks near the airport and take them to Lynn, which works out semi-okay, though she's still not happy about cops coming to see her at the Donut Shack. I keep my rod in the truck and hit the river every morning and some days after work, too.

So you see I'm going through the motions. My mind, meanwhile, is on other things. I keep seeing Michelle charging out of the mist, her head down, full of greed and bossy stupidity. I wonder what she was doing barreling along with the stroller and whether she was meeting someone. Someone who was maybe interested in her records. That's one thing that's taking up a lot of psychic space. The other is Leon. I don't know much about kids. I was the baby with a much older brother and sister. The only time I've ever paid real attention to a kid was those few minutes with Leon, and the other thing I keep seeing is his alien baby eyes, very large, very dark, very undecided, like he's soaking life up but hasn't reached any conclusions yet. One of the first things he'll have to decide is whether to tell or not, unless the memory's gone, scared out of him or irrelevant. Maybe I'm worrying myself into an ulcer, while he's thinking doggies and bunnies and where his next jar of mush is coming from. You can see the possibilities.

Elsewhere in my mind is Jess. To be accurate, in my mind and in my body, too, cause Jess is definitely a total mind-body experience. Before it's been one or the other, mostly the other, starting with Amanda Beck who opened my eyes, literally, when I squinted through the partition in the lake changing rooms and saw her take off her top. I was thirteen, and I felt this big light of awareness and some other things, too.

But Jess is in a whole other catagory and extra-special because absolutely impossible; impossible, that is, in the opinion of logical, smart guy Jeff. But he's not all of me, not by a long shot, and, especially after a few beers, I can look at the phone and think of lots of reasons to call her. Perhaps I will, too, cause nothing's happening. People at the Barn have stopped gossiping about Michelle and returned to the Knicks, the Celtics, and the Bosox. The Action News Team has left the park to report on killings in Hartford, a fire in Willimantic, a toxic spill in Naugatuck. Stankus and Benny, the Indigestion Special, have returned to their barracks.

All in all, we have a no-sweat situation—til Thursday, that is. Thursday I'm on the river with Earl and a friend of his from the hardware til dark. We get a pizza from the general store, and I'm rolling onto my street with Travis Tritt going full blast, when I see a dark car parked out front of my apartment. Right away I get this bad feeling. I'm basically thinking one of Michelle's heavy connections like Vito, the sleezeball. My impulse is to keep going when I register the light stuck in the rear window. Stankus and his pal are outa the car before I have my motor turned off.

"Looking for me?" I says, though it's pretty obvious they haven't been sitting there for the view.

"We thought we'd missed you," says Stankus. "With your busy schedule."

What's with this guy? He lives for work, maybe. For crime solving like some tv detective. I reach into the back for my fish, and Stankus freaks out.

"Hold it right there," he yells and reaches under his jacket. The Indigestion Special drops his notebook and gets into a low, stable crouch with this nasty looking pistol. "Get away from the truck! Move! Get your hands up."

I jump back so fast I nearly fall over. I put up my hands and feel the blood draining toward my elbows. "Christ," I says. "Can I get my trout?"

Stankus huffs and puffs and yells for me to stay away from the truck. Then his pal sidles over ultra-cautious and checks the bed: a rod, waders, tackle box and a plastic bucket with two rainbows. "Fish're biting," I says.

"Hey, those're nice trout," Benny says. He's human, see what I mean. I can see how Leon prefers him, but it's dangerous to think about Leon or Michelle. Stray thoughts give off vibrations, and I gotta keep my mind blank and alert.

Stankus clears his throat, pats me down, and makes a show of putting away his pistol. "We want to talk to you for a minute," he says. Or course, he's got no time for small talk or an apology or anything like that. He's all focused and important and intense, like maybe he should be on tv.

"Fine," I says. I'm agreeable, sure thing. I've nearly had my head blown off. "Can I get my fish now?"

He gives a grunt like I'm not worth talking to and we go up the back stair. I unlock the apartment and hit the switch: hard yellow light reflects off black windows. I smell the musty, closed up odor of mildew and old garbage.

"Sit down anywhere," I says. "I gotta put away my fish." As I open the door of the fridge, awareness hits me: they've come to arrest me; they've found something important; they've got a witness. Why the hell else are they here?

"Good sized apartment," Benny says from the other room.

"Yeah." I close the fridge. Stankus is looking around like he wants to buy the place. I step into the living room and look around, too: a third hand tv, a brown tweed thrift store couch, a couple of flower print chairs my folks threw out, and two wooden pallets with a sheet of ply on top that serves as a coffee table. Only there's never been much coffee on it; right now there's the week's newspapers, a couple magazines, half a dozen empty beer cans, and two library books. Stankus picks the books up and looks at the titles. I can see he's not happy with Fine Woodworking and Cabinets. What did he expect? How to Defeat Police Interrogations, maybe, or Spontaneous Murder—You Can Do It? I gotta watch myself, but the guy's so chilly-creepy he's an inspiration.

"Been here long?" he asks, though what business of his I don't know—unless he's looking for an apartment.

"Two years in July."

He thinks about this and the silence gets so long that I can hear the kitchen clock ticking. I want to say something just to hurry things along and get them outa my place, but I think Grampa's right, "Silence is the beginning of wisdom". I focus on the ramifications of that until eventually Stankus gives up.

"Wanted to ask you a few questions," he says.

I sit down. Am I being too quiet? Is this quiet natural? "I've told you what I know," I says.

"Just routine," says Benny, but I suddenly don't find him sympathetic. I want to know 'why me?', 'why routine?', and besides, I'm sure he's lying. "After we've talked to people's alibis we like to double check."

"Go ahead."

"Ms. Santorini," Stankus says. "You've known her long?"

"Sure thing. Since junior high. Junior high at least."

"She confirms that she spent the night here," Stankus says. And he looks around again like he can't believe it. In other circumstances, like if I weren't so shit scared, I'd be offended. Then it strikes me that he's disappointed again. He was maybe expecting a big screen Jap import, lots of expensive audio equipment, fancy stuff. Here's a guy on salary, benefits; he hasn't a clue how fast hourly money goes—even with a larceny garnish.

"Yeah," I says. "We're old friends."

"Something more than friends," he says.

"I guess."

"She says she didn't hear you til," he opens his notebook, "eight-thirty or so."

"That would be about right."

"Correct me on this," Stankus says, "but didn't you say that you were up earlier?"

"It was opening day. Like I told you."

"But you were sick." He says this like I'd claimed to fly or read minds or something.

"That's right. I thought it was flu but it was maybe just too many margueritas."

He raises his eyebrows again. I wonder if he's taken vows: no drinks, no women, no fishing. "How many margueritas?"

"I remember one. Lynn thought maybe three."

"But you clearly remember getting up and going back to bed?"

"I got up and started to get dressed like I told you. I'm in the john and I get so dizzy I gotta sit down." Had I added that detail before? Be consistent, I think, don't volunteer. There are so many possible ways to screw up that my stomach starts wrapping itself around the pizza like a boa constrictor.

"And then?"

"I decide to go back to bed. I'm dizzy, I lie down and I go back to sleep. That's it. I wake up near 8:30, get up, and shower."

"Ms. Santorini sleeps fairly soundly then?"

Now I see what's coming but there's nothing I can do about it. I might as well be standing midfield again, watching a ball come across that Porky Rebol is too far out of position to keep from the back of the net. In some situations, you gotta appreciate inevitability. "Pretty soundly, I guess."

"She didn't wake up when you went back to bed, did she?"

"Not that I know of."

"I wonder," Stankus said, "if she'd have heard you if you'd gotten up and left the apartment." He looks at me and, just for a moment, he's transparent like the special windows I saw at the home show. Switch the current on and they cloud over; switch it off and you got normal glass.

Just for this one minute, Stankus is clear to me: he's convinced I'm the one and he knows how it was done. Though, of course, he doesn't know why and he hasn't a fucking clue as to how irrational and accidental and unpredictable the whole thing was. Maybe machines can't understand irrational and accidental. I think that's maybe his limitation, but there in the living room, I'm not capable of taking a detached view. "I don't know," I says. "How could I know that when I'm asleep myself?"

"If you were asleep," Stankus says.

My old fear of witnesses comes back. Have they found something? Has Leon suddenly begun talking in whole sentences: "See the man. See the man punch Michelle. Run, man, run!" Am I maybe up the creek? "My truck's noisy," I says, forgetting Grampa and everything else. "Start that truck up early morning, everyone on the block knows."

Stankus mouth twitches like he'd smile if he was capable of it. "Maybe you got up and didn't start your truck," he says. "Maybe you walked to the river."

"I always take my truck when I go fishing," I says. And I wait, all of a sweat, for him to pull a witness out of his hat.

"Maybe you wanted to be extra quiet," Stankus says instead.

"Why was that?"

He doesn't answer, just starts pacing around the apartment. I smell fish and stale beer and feel depressed. What have I gotten out of all this but a load of useless shit?

"You ever see Michelle Portinari outside work?" Stankus says after a minute or so.

"No," I says.

"You didn't arrange to meet her before work on Saturday April 20th?"

"No. Why would I meet her when I saw her every day at work?"

Stankus gives that excuse for a smile, which just about freaks me out, but nothing happens. Nothing fucking happens. He knows but he can't prove, that's the deal, and I'd better sit tight and say nothing. So we talk about the Barn for a while, about was there much stock loss and about 'employee relationships', as Stankus puts it. I shrug my shoulders a lot and try to look helpful. Stankus isn't deceived, but since he hasn't gotten the full picture yet, he keeps throwing things out to see how I react.

"So," he says finally, "you never went out with Michelle Portinari?"

"No," I says.

"Didn't like her?" he asks. You can see how his mind works: I gotta be guilty of something.

"She wore these colored contact lenses," I says. "I didn't like her red eyes."

Benny kinda smiles then kills it off, cause Stankus is pissed. "I know there's something," he says, leaning up so close to me that I can smell the chili dog he had for dinner, "and you can bet I'll find it. Understand that. Sooner or later, I'll find it."

Benny stands up, too, and I wonder if they're going to try to pound that something outta me. No, they're public servants, all by the book, and they're going to leave now. But they'll be back. Stankus makes that very clear. They'll be back. Although I don't realize the implications right then, what they're going to do is nibble me to death. That's in the future; in the present, I'm beginning to breathe normally. I'm opening the door and saying good night and listening to them pound down the outside stair. I wait until their car starts up and they're really gone. I feel fucking relieved; at the same time, I could puke, cause they're in my personal space which is ten times worse than an interview at the Barn.

And they're coming back. I believe Stankus on that, absolutely. And correctly, cause that's part of the new routine, too. He and Benny make a habit of stopping by couple of times a week. Sometimes they stop by between 9 and 9:30 a.m., just in time to ruin the day, and sometimes they come late, 8:30 p.m. or so, to give me something to think about all night. There's no pattern that I can see. They show two, three days in a row, and I see disaster coming down, then four days, five, a week'll go by, and I'll get to thinking I'm home free. I start hoping they've given up or gotten another case or something, when, bang, there's the car again.

Some days I plain can't face them. I get out in the morning, hit the river, and go straight to work. Or else I'll drive home from work along French, park the truck on the street, and cut through the yards, avoiding both law enforcement and George, who often follows up the troopers' visits with one of his own. The only possible good thing in this would be if George persuaded his brother to let me break my lease, but there's no sign of that. Things are getting as bad as when I was roofing; my stomach's in knots and my beer bill's getting outa hand.

At the same time, the troopers don't have squat. Jess was right: Leon's the only witness and Leon's their only chance. Otherwise, it's just Stankus and me. He knows and I know he knows, and he figures sooner or later he can break me down. He doesn't factor in luck and universal malice any more than I do.

The second week in May, after a long break that raises my hopes, Stankus and Benny show up one evening. I'm out in the little backyard with my grill, some burgers, and serious thoughts of calling Jess Simeone, when I hear footsteps on the drive. By this time, I recognize their tread.

"Smells good," says Benny like he hasn't eaten in a month.

I'm not in the mood for conversation.

"We need to talk to you," says Stankus.

"Fine," I says, "but I want to watch the grill."

He doesn't like this but what the hell. Everyone on the block already knows I'm their favorite person. I know cause some talk's already filtered back to my folks. Mom calls every two, three days to see 'how things are going' without ever mentioning Michelle or the case directly, and every time I'm over at the house, Dad worries at the topic worse'n the national debt. Most of the time, the whole business is so miserable, it doesn't bear thinking about.

Stankus opens his notebook and takes out a pink invoice sheet. It's like I know what it is even before I see the thin carbon backed paper: I missed one; this is it. They've found another cache of Michelle's souvenirs, and the damn werewolf's back from the grave. I feel myself start shaking—they've got to notice, got to—then Stankus holds out the paper. "Recognize this?"

I reach for it, but he just moves the paper so I can read it. It's got the Bargain Barn logo at the top and all the usual data. This order's for a shipment of VCR's and tv's to the Danbury showroom, and I'm hearing the river and wondering how to tell Mom and Dad, when I check the signature at the bottom. It's "Jeff Woodbine" all right, but I never wrote it. The river recedes, and I feel confident enough to look at Stankus. He's as focused as a cat under a bird feeder.

"No," I says, "I don't recognize it. It's not my order and it's not my handwriting."

He gives me a look. I'm not sure yet if he knew it was a phony and thought he'd bluff me—or if he was really surprised.

"Look at the signature," I says. "It's like me writing your name. The 'f's' are wrong and the 'i'. They can tell, can't they, about signatures?"

"Why would someone else sign your name?" he says.

This is something I'd like to know myself, but I'm not going to speculate. "Someone neglected to sign a sheet, maybe, and she'd forgotten whose it was. I don't know."

He stands like he's thinking this over, and other stuff, too. Like why Michelle kept invoices, phoney or otherwise. "You'll need to give us a writing sample," he says.

"Sure," I says. I scribble a note and sign it. "Give it to the pros," I says. I feel like dancing.

From his look, Stankus feels like hitting me around a bit. I think he would of if he'd had even a shred of evidence. Even a shred. But I'm still just an innocent citizen, one of the werewolf's helpful co-workers, someone who would have a helluva police brutality suit.

"We'll be in touch," he says. "When we get the graphologist's report."

"Any time," I says. "Glad to help."

"Sooner or later," says Stankus. Neither he nor Benny says good night.

I return to the burgers which are raw on one side and getting little bumps of char on the other. I'm hungry, yet I don't feel like eating. Too many emotions are hitting me all at once. With all the eddies and cross currents, I can't feel anything clearly, not even relief, though I'm sure that was the Machine Tooled One's best shot. Without a witness, I'm outta the mix. I can wait a month or so, leave town, and let everybody forget. Maybe check with Jess first to see how Leon is doing, to see if Leon is talking. Or maybe not. Maybe better not give baby any reminders.

I think this over so hard I lose my appetite entirely. I eat a burger and a half and feed the rest to Ralph, the skinny shepherd cross that lives on a tether in the next yard. Then, cause I can't face an evening alone, I hop in my truck and drive over to see Grampa. It's Mom and Dad's night to do the week's food shopping. Dad'll have all the coupons organized and the store battle plan worked out, and they'll be gone for a couple hours at least. With luck, I'll miss them entirely.

The homestead's an old cape with a breezeway skewed off to an even smaller house. When Grampa came to live with us, he wanted to come independent and what he did was have a foundation put in and one of those kit houses set on top. It's not much bigger than a two car garage, just one good sized room that has his bed, a couch, a couple chairs and a tv, with a bathroom at the back and a big closet. He's got a microwave set up on the book case now, so he can make himself tea and coffee—soup, too, if he doesn't feel like regular supper—and a big low table where we used to play checkers and two handed poker. Round the walls are all his pictures: photos of winning horses white eyed over their collars of flowers, or posed like statues, clean and strong without any tack. Yellowed newspaper clips preserve headlines and result tables or press snaps of grinning trainers and jockeys.

I haven't looked at the pictures for a long time, and while Grampa totters around making us tea and finding some biscuits, I study his days of glory.

"Getting near Race Day," I says. This is strictly a Woodbine family holiday, June 25th, commemorating the day Grampa rode 5 winners at Belmont.

"Ach, too long to be remembering now," he says.

"I used to love these when I was a kid." I mean the big, noble horses with their bony cheeks and sweat glistened coats, but also the impassive face and taut body of my grandfather, and even the beefy owners in their fedoras and dark suits. The harshly lighted news photos always suggested a life of glamour, excitement—even danger—to me.

"It was a great life," Grampa agrees. "A great life." He comes over to the couch in a half crouch. "Have your tea, lad."

"Sit down. I'll get the rest."

"If I didn't get up to eat, I wouldn't get up," he says and shuffles away again. He's got arthritis in the spine and in one leg, courtesy of his last fall, when a mare named Tropic Baby snapped her right fore in a race at Hialiah. Half the field went over Grampa. He was forty-five then, and when they picked him up, he had a couple of cracked vertebrae, a broken leg, smashed ribs, and a mangled wrist. He worked for a time as a bookmaker, then went legit and got a job supervising the stables at a riding school. He worked there til he was nearly seventy, and his arthritis got so bad he couldn't sit on a horse.

"Nice colt, that," he says, following my eye toward a nervous gray prancing in the winner's circle. "That was Algonquin. A nice, nice horse for distance."

"He was one of the five on Race Day," I says.

"Right you are. Fifth race, fourth winner. It was a hard life but I wouldn't trade it."

"What I never figured was how come you were small enough for a jockey." I'm looking now at a sepia photo of Grampa standing between his older brothers. They're maybe six footers and he's like a child between them.

"Wasn't fed, lad. Simple as that. They were pre-war babies, when we was on the estate with plenty to eat. Comes the war, my dad has to go and the stables close down. Mum and all of us go to Dundee so she and the older ones could get into the works. She ruined her health in the munitions, she did."

"You were quite young then?"

"I didn't grow at all between time I was 5, and the war started, and the time I turned eleven. That was when food started to ease up again and my dad was back and working. See," he holds out his large, square, still powerful looking hands. "I have the hands and feet of a big man like my brothers. Hunger took care of the rest."

"You wouldn't have made a jockey, otherwise."

"That's a consideration, that's true. You never know what life's got in mind for you and that's the truth. When I first come here, I had to pretend I was Irish to get mounts. I'm not kidding you; they didn't think

Scotsmen could ride. I used to say my name was Paddy Woodbine. Had one of the Irish chaps teach me the cross, you know"—he crosses himself quickly—"so I'd look right before my races. Oh, it was great days," he says. "Course, lots of things are better now."

"You think so?"

"Lots of things worse, too."

That's so evident I don't say anything.

"World's always been in a mess," he says.

We chew on this melancholy idea for a few minutes.

"Like Canada," he says. "Remind me some time to tell you why I left Canada."

I smile at this. Although it's one of Grampa's pet phrases, he's never told anyone that story. It's the great untold story of his life, the one he's saving up for last, like a singer who holds his best number for the finale. I know all the others, most of them by heart. Some're true, like Race Day, and the stories of his boyhood in Fife and Dundee. And some are either not true, or, like a Scots verdict, not provable. Our Spanish ancestor, Don Alonzo, fits this category, I figure, along with those bold horse and cattle thieves that Grampa calls "our piratical ancestors". Perhaps I should promote them all to reality and blame everything on my larcenous inheritance. I'm thinking about this when I glance over and see Grampa's looking at me in this sharp, interested way like he sees something new he hadn't noticed before.

"Why not tell me now," I says to break the mood.

He shakes his head, but slowly, as if he's thinking it over. "Not quite yet," he says. "Though you're maybe the one to tell."

I understand this. We're a lot a like, Grampa and me. I don't know whether it's something in the genes or just lots of time together. Grampa came to live with us the year Barry started to show the first bad symptoms, and Mom went to work full time at the Discount so there'd be extra money for the doctors. I spent nearly all my free time with Grampa, going to the races up at Rockingham or hanging around the stables and the University horse farm, or just sitting in his room with the racing form between us figuring out the day's bet. The racing form taught me math and probability and took my mind off my brother's disaster. And mine, too, cause that was when I lost my faith in a future and in planning.

Maybe I've carried that too far. As Grampa says, it's hard to know what's in store, and no matter how you play your hand you can get caught out somewhere. I don't say this, though, cause Grampa has started to nod his head and doze off. He went through a period where he didn't sleep much at all. I'd see his lights on even if I came in at two, three o'clock from a dance or a concert. He still kept horseman's hours, too, up and dressed every morning by five at the latest. Now, though he's still up early, he naps a lot—with one eye open, he always says. Sure enough, when I get up to leave, he sits upright.

"Go back to sleep, Grampa. I'm on my way."

"I wasn't asleep," he says. "I was catnapping."

"I'd better go anyway."

"Wait and say hello to your mother and dad. What time is it anyway?"

"It's twenty to ten."

He stretches his neck toward the window. "They're not back yet?"

"They're doing the week's shopping. They're never back much before ten."

"I wish Andrew wouldn't let your mother drive. There're some good women drivers, I mind that, but your mother is the worst driver I've ever seen."

"She's not that bad," I says, though it's true we've never had a car without crumpled fenders and scratched body work. Mom never does anything catastrophic with the car, but she does a lot of little stuff, like backing into the garbage cans, scraping the sides of the garage, or nicking fenders in parking lots.

"It's the only thing I'd ever say against your mother," Grampa says. "Your mother should never be behind the wheel of a car."

"She'll be all right," I says. "Just going to the store with Dad. She goes that way every day to the Discount."

"Too much on her mind is part of it," Grampa says now. "Take care how you worry her."

"I'll leave them a note," I says. "I've got to be into work early tomorrow. I'll leave them a note and you tell them I said 'hi' and that everything's okay."

"And is everything okay?" Grampa asks.

"Yeah, great. It looks like they're finally wrapping up the investigation. You know, that woman at the Bargain Barn they've been asking us all about."

Grampa nods his head and begins to slide down into sleep again. I rinse the cups and plates in the bathroom sink and set them to dry on top of the microwave. Then I stick a note in the breezeway door and hit the road.

CHAPTER 7

Just like I told Grampa, things should be all right. Should be. Stankus and Benny back off. George from downstairs is living with a woman in Wauregan Mills and outa my face. Bargain Barn talk shifts between Wade Boggs and Roger Clemens and the best spots for bass. With the warmer weather, Dad's feeling better. We get out a couple times to the lake, where we rent a boat and talk politics and fish for a few hours until he gets wheezing. Everything's fine, and I have no worries except that I feel awful.

It's a delayed reaction. I wake up in the morning and want to stay in bed. I get home at night and don't want to sleep. I go out fishing without enthusiasm and stop calling the Red Gal and start serious drinking with Porky Rebol and Binkie Liss and a couple of burnouts I know from school.

The new program is that I meet them at The Kitchen or the diner or Excelsior Pizza and wind up two, three, four hours later completely wasted. One morning I wake up in my truck on a side road and nearly freak out cause I can't remember anything. I don't know where I am or who I've been with or even what day it is. I'm on a gravel road somewhere facing a fucking blank cause my mind's hit a faultline and time has dropped out the bottom. I smell of whisky, which I don't like and can't afford, and I'm wearing a t-shirt I've never seen before. I sit there twisting it around so I can see the design which is a woman with long black hair that bleeds away under my armpits. Her face is white against the gray fabric and she had a big red mouth and red eyes. I let out a scream and bang my fists on the dash and generally lose it for a few seconds, before I fall out of the truck and heave up a lot of nasty smelling brownish fluid.

So there I am, leaning against the truck, tasting crap and dying for water, when I notice the gravel road and, click, life comes back into focus. Saved from terminal psychosis by a weak stomach. I'm in the state forest; the sun's in my eyes and, yes, I still have my watch. It's 6:30 a.m.; I'll make work easy. I feel relief for just a moment before the terrible weight of indifference drops back onto me. I don't want to start the truck or drive anywhere or do anything but maybe get another sixpack and see if I can lose some more time down the fault line.

Other days, I feel different. Not better, just different. I don't want to be alone, so I run out to the lake or up the river with Earl. Some nights, me and Timmy hang at the seedy club near the university where we drink lousy beer and dance up a frenzy in front of the stage. Music opens a different kind of fault line. What you need is a steady rhythm pulsing from shoulder to thigh. Then guitars to jangle the nerves as they slide up the spine. Under everything, you want the bass, moving up and down the chords, upsetting the heartbeat, altering time. That's the ideal situation.

Course, the musicians at the club aren't much, all this yelling and dancing and flipping their hair around like beauty queens on acid, but you can ride the percussion, thump, boom, thump, boom right outa there. And sometimes the sound man gets the screaming guitars mixed just right so I can feel their twanging whine coming outa my throat, louder and louder, bursting over the rocks and scouring the stream bed and clutching my legs so that I almost fall. I can almost feel myself falling and the water closing over my head.

Basically, I'm outa the zone and finding it hard to stay detached. I got Michelle safe in St. Benedict's, and mice are enjoying the police files, but that's just the physical evidence. There's this whole other side that can't be buried, or if I do get one part buried, another pops up like a balloon full of air. I mean stuff like Michelle coming suddenly out of the mist, and the stiff way her mom and dad walked into the church. Or Leon's camera eyes, and Jess's long untidy hair and beautiful legs. Or the awful noise and worse smell and the rattle of loose stones down the path towards the river. That stuff's always there, and it's not only incompatible with normal, it's made normal, abnormal. I gotta create normal fresh every day. Look, there's Jeff, washed and dressed and punching into work on time and loading up the fork lift and checking his invoice sheets like everything's ordinary. But underneath is the river and screaming insanity.

I suppose you'll say it's a bad conscience. I don't know. See, this is the thing: I've got regrets, sure, but they're not personal. I'm sorry Michelle's dead, but I didn't like her. I didn't care about her, and her absence doesn't bother me. That's the truth. What's really bothering me is the craziness, like my brother all over again. If everything's craziness at bottom, does anything matter? See, that's the question I'd like to get answered: does anything really matter? Or is it just that you go along, imitating sanity as best as you can, so as not to hurt too many people's feelings? That's what I've been doing, protecting myself and minimizing the damage, but it's bleeding off a lot of energy, and I don't have enough left to keep up.

On top of everything, there's Jess, who's like the other side of Michelle in that my idea of her is so much bigger than what I really know. I remember her from school—four, five years ago: a pretty girl who dated Andre Simeone, flunked algebra, and went to study cooking at the Tech School. Then there's that night when I hung around at a school dance and saw Jess Portinari standing at the back, looking wild eyed and sad and gorgeous, and said 'hi' and wound up sitting with her in the truck with my throat aching and my heart pounding. I know that and how she holds Leon like he's her own life, and the way she takes a quick, anxious drag of a cigarette and opens her window to get rid of the smoke. I've seen how she moves in high heels like a racing filly and heard how she thinks Michelle was a bully and a bitch. That's all I know about Jess, yet she's expanded somehow, so that I feel her, too, under the percussion and in the guitars.

Half drunk that morning in the forest, I realize I'll never have her this way. No way. But still, when I'm sitting at The Kitchen's bar with Porkie and some of the guys, I check my wallet and put yet another beer between her and me, cause everything's screwed up.

Then something happens. Make that two things. First of all, I'm leaving the Barn one night, when I see this car running its motor. No big deal—most of us have cars that need warming up—but this one's a late model Honda, expensive enough so I take a good look at it. I look again going down the access road when the car floats into my rear mirror: a dark Accord driven by a big guy wearing shades. He hugs my bumper all the way to The Kitchen before roaring east toward Providence: confirmation that Rhode Island has 50% of the world's lousy drivers and Massachusetts has the rest. I spring for a burger and a brew and benefit from Jon's wisdom for a while.

When I come out, the street lights are on, although the west still has a smudge of pink-gold like a rainbow's belly. There's the usual row of pickups and vans in front but no dark Honda. No Stankus and no Benny, either. I tell myself that my nerves are shot and get into my truck. I've just crossed the bridge and turned off the main road into town when the Honda shows again. It's the same guy, kinda hooked nose, small mustache. He follows me through the intersection, down Main, and onto one of the dark side streets that lead to Water.

Lots of apartments along here, I tell myself, but I don't buy it. I hang a quick right without signalling and then another. Across Main Street on an angle, bump over the old rail tracks by the bicycle shop. In my mirror, the lights disappear as the Honda dips at the tracks. He's after me for sure. I floor the accelerator up the steep little hill that rises past St. James' and bounce over the crest. In the few seconds that I'm out of sight, I peel into the lot beside a defunct appliance store, kill my lights, and slide up the alley behind the building. If he's police, he'll know this is the only open lot on the street.

The Honda goes on by, but there's nothing, no squeal of brakes, no sound of a fast car accelerating out of a U-turn. I start the engine, ease across the ruined asphalt with my lights off, then cruise down the hill. At the bottom, I switch on the headlights, take a side street that runs parallel to Main and drive north until I can pick up French. I come into Water Street the back way and circle the block. When I'm sure there's nothing suspicious, I run the truck in the garage and lock the door. Upstairs, my apartment's hot and still. I walk through the rooms just to be sure, then I carry my tv out to the back porch where I sit in the dark and watch the ball game.

So that's the first thing, and it's pretty minor, considering everything. Hardly worth mentioning except I keep seeing the Honda—in the back of the Bargain Barn lot, parked at the Kitchen, cruising along Water Street. I stop eating at The Kitchen; the Honda shows up outside the diner. I pick up a pizza at the Excelsior; the car's parked half a block away. All this attention gives me mixed feelings. Since I can't afford trouble, I ignore the guy and start taking weird routes home, snaking down along the river and cutting though parking lots; going all the way up to the interstate and coming into town the back way, that sort of thing. At the same time, I feel strongly like hauling the guy out of his car and punching his face in.

I finally get so antsy about the whole thing that I call the C of F C, Arnie, and, when I don't get him at his apartment, I leave a message at Dougie Donnelley's. Still nothing. I figure he's avoiding me, and I'm plenty pissed, until one Saturday when I see Frenchie at the hardware. After I give him a hand with some boxes of nails and cans of roof cement, we stand beside his truck bitching about the heat and the drought, the lack of bass, general misery. Then he says, "Hey, you knew Arnie, didn't you?"

"Arnie. You mean your friend's cousin—runs a delivery truck or something?"

"Yeah. Worked with some electronics shops up in Providence. But, shit man, he's not going to be working for a while."

I feel a concentration of forces, like the whole sweltering lot's suddenly been packed into my stomach. "Too bad," I says. "Accident with the truck?" Don't I wish.

"Naw. Couple guys beat him up pretty good. He's been in Hartford Hospital over a week."

"Ke-risht!" I says.

"Head injury and broken leg. First they thought he wasn't going to make it. Then they were hopeful. Now they're not so sure again."

"So what was it?" I says. "Robbery or something?"

"Not a clue. But you know Arnie. Always finding an angle. He'd been doing real good, too. I heard he'd bought a condo."

"You been to see him?"

"Naw. Family only. As I was saying, they're not so sure he'll make it."

"Goddamn," I says. We talk about this for a while. About the surprises of life, about the general unexpected shittiness of existence. Frenchie says how they need a helper—with the last bad winter everyone's getting into home repairs and new roofs. I tell him I'm strictly low altitude work.

"Keep me in mind if you start doing ranches," I says, and he laughs and climbs into his truck.

I ride home through an alien landscape. The town's been undergoing this weird evolution ever since Michelle hit that bolt. Everything's started looking a bit odd. Some stuff that hadn't any meaning before, like the feed store lot and park benches, now has a big significance, while ordinary things like the river or a dark Honda can suddenly turn life threatening. Living here's like being on spring ice with cracks running straight to deep water. Or like walking on old rotten planking where you never know if you're safe on the first floor or about to wind up flat in the basement.

It's sure changing me, I can feel it. I go around for days, smooth and careful, avoiding trouble, until the wind shifts or the humidity rises or something strikes my mind, then I say the hell with it and begin bouncing the boards. I'm sick of the goddamn suspense, and I'm dying to hear them crack.

Earl knows the feeling, too, even if he never says much. We don't talk about it directly, but we talk all around it, it being the hole in the flooring, the cracked ice, the trapdoor that has opened directly underneath our feet. I think that's how come we wound up at the dam that day, and that's the second thing that happens.

All week, the weather guys bleat about a Bermuda High like it's some designer drug. The Barn blows the AC full speed to keep the electronics happy, and, as a side effect, the staff've got just enough energy to bitch about the weather. Everybody's sick of the sticky heat and wishing they was in Maine. On top of everything, we're a man short, so Earl and me fill in the early shift Saturday morning and collect some overtime. Comes Saturday afternoon, we feel like we've been humping boxes forever. We stop off for a burger at The Kitchen, where we sit around drinking Rolling Rock and Sam Adams until the AC no longer feels cool. Earl suggests a swim.

"Naw," I says. "Too hot to go to the shore."

"I know a place," he says.

"No pond weeds," I says. "I can't stand wading in pond weeds."

"Naw, nothing like that," Earl says. "Absolutely clean and A-OK."

So we go. We pick up our suits and towels and a couple six-packs. I leave my truck in the garage and hop into Earl's. Right away, I know this is a bad idea, cause Earl's driving ultra-cautious, looking four, five ways at every stop, creeping along route 6 at 40 mph, studying every light like it's the secret of the universe. At the same time, his hair is all over his eyes and he's clearly not focused. To tell you the truth, old Earl is wasted.

"So where we going?" I says.

Earl thinks a couple minutes. "Up the dam," he says.

"Can't swim at the dam," I says.

"Not at the dam. Further on up. Real nice," he says. "Too hot for anyone to bother us today."

"You're kidding," I says. "What other sort of day are they going to be out?" The dam, see, is part of the water supply, and the park is patrolled.

"Naw," says Earl, "not where we're going."

"All right," I says. I'm going to see the other side of silent Earl, the side that dates werewolves and takes them bowling. I feel myself start to giggle. I'm not in the best shape, either, and I'm in worse shape after we finally park the truck and hoist another couple beers in the lot.

Where we are, the artificial lake's crossed by the roadway, and there's water on both sides of us. The air's like wet cotton; the sun's blazing hot. If I close my eyes, the parking lot begins to revolve. When I open them, everything's outlined with white glare and kinda indefinite.

Boomboxes are going hard up in the shade by the picnic tables, and a few boats are trolling slow and silent with their electric motors.

"Let's jump in," I says. Pond weeds or not, the lake looks pretty good.

"Naw," says Earl, "cops come along here. We gotta take a hike." He grabs his towel and a couple beers and crosses the road. The other side is a steep gully that reminds me of the park along the river. Earl goes skidding down, the beer cans glittering in one hand, his towel flying in the other. Half way down, he slips on his ass, swearing and laughing at the same time, and I slide down into him, coating my boots and jeans with dry yellow dust and sending us both into a mess of weeds.

The path cuts away from the water through scrubby woods and brush. Tangles of blackberry bushes, burdocks, and weeds fill the open patches and a little stream runs along the low places. There are a million mosquitoes and nearly as many flies, and they've all been on a starvation diet. Earl's in some other, better world, cause he's started whistling.

We pass sweating hikers and an exercise freak on a mountain bike. The biker's red in the face like he's on the verge of heat stroke, his eyes don't focus, and he's humping his damn machine up a slope so eroded it drops off nearly straight. Tell me fitness is good for you. Then there's a couple of big slobbering dogs too dumb to sleep in the heat. They run in circles around us, barking the whole time, before loping off to see if they can find someone to frighten. Over in the west, the sun's dropped down without the heat letting up one bit, and the whole afternoon has a kind of surly edge, like a quarrel waiting to happen. I walk along behind Earl, thinking that he's a dumb fuck for coming up with this idea, and that I am too for going along with it.

Finally, we reach a grove of hemlocks, very dark and shady. The lake glitters below and the opposite shore is just haze. Three or four guys and as many girls are sitting on the little strip of sand, their shorts and tops drying in the sun, but when I start to go down, Earl waves me on.

"What's the matter?" I says. "I thought we came to swim."

"Little further," he says.

More sun, more brambles, more gullys cut by mountain bikers. Behind us, we hear the swimmers scrambling back up from the shore, getting ready to leave. The girls are laughing. "That's normal life," I says to Earl. Why the hell hadn't I called the Red Gal? Even the beach with her kids doesn't seem so bad at the moment. "We oughta of called up some girls."

Earl gives me this funny look. "Girls are nothing but trouble."

"You're forgetting Total Sensory Overload," I says.

He just grunts. It always was a difficult concept for him. He doesn't say anything more, just goes into that maddening silence he's patented, and finally I says, "They still bugging you?"

"Who?"

"The cops. That Lieutenant Stankus and his assistant."

"Not much," he says. "I see them occasionally. What about you?"

"Same here. Not much lately."

"No," he agrees.

"I've seen this Honda, though. You notice that Honda in the Barn lot? An Accord. A '90 maybe?"

Earl thinks this over. "Maybe internal," he says. Meaning Bargain Barn security.

Another joyful idea. I hadn't thought of that, though on consideration it doesn't seem likely.

The sun explodes between the trunks of the trees in dazzling interrupted bursts and the air's so heavy we're practically swimming already. The dusty trail turns stony, with rocks and boulders of all sizes and shapes laying about like a dry stream bed. The cold wind's gone and the river's solidified into heat and boulders. I wonder if Earl's thinking the same things, thinking about rivers and cold winds, but, of course, he can't be, because he was at a different place. Earl was just that lucky few minutes earlier or later.

Up ahead is another hemlock grove, and Earl starts whistling again and turns off the main trail. I hear water running loud and clear, and my first thought is that it's the river come to life. Then I see a mess of big rocks and a pool beyond them, and cold, fast water bubbling black and white.

"Whooo," says Earl, sticking his hand into the stream. "Cold as ice."

The stream pours in at the upper end of the pool and spreads out black, deep, and calm, before rushing away over a steep jumble of rocks. Earl sits down and pulls off his shoes and peels off his shirt. He gathers up his long hair and ties it back, then drops his jeans and flops into the water. His legs look white and skinny and froggish and his red trunks are very bright against the gray bed of the pool. I watch him sink down like a big catfish before he pops up, blowing water out his nose and shaking his thin, wet tail of hair.

Meanwhile, I'm standing there, uneasy at the way the lake turned into a dry river, and the dry river's come to life.

"Hey," says Earl, and he slaps up a sheet of water that chills my midsection.

"Shit, man!"

"It's great," Earl says. He starts wallowing around in the water, threatening to soak me. I feel kinda stupid standing there sweating in the heat, so I sit down on the rocks and start undressing, but slowly, cause the afternoon feels different again, like everything's sliding toward another sinkhole.

Meanwhile, Earl's doing somersaults in the deep end of the pool where the current isn't so fast. Every now and again, he'll get too close to the rocks. The current will start to pull him toward the white water at the edge, and he'll splash into an awkward crawl. I'm sitting dangling my feet by this time and either the beer's just hit me or it's the sudden cold, cause I'm reaching a high degree of detachment. Old Earl looks like a big water strider caught in an eddy, and I'm watching, without worrying a bit, to see if he'll get himself onto the rocks.

"Great, isn't it?" he says.

I slide in and lose my breath. After the close heat of the woods, the icy water closes around my chest like a vise. I jump up and gasp and feel the furnace air and flop down again like Earl and drop underwater. I can see the sky and Earl's pale legs and the dark rocks and some fine wavery patterns on the sand. Everything's a bit disjointed, shifted off center, if you know what I mean, but I can handle that.

We float around in the pool for a while til we're both shivering then clamber onto one of the big rocks and sit in the sun. I'm staring downstream at the drop from the pool to the swift water and the rocks below, when outa the blue, Earl says, "They think it's one of us."

See, this is what I mean by saying that Earl and me, we're on the same wavelength. I don't have to ask what "it" is. "Who thinks?" I says.

"The police," he says. "Some of the guys at work."

At work! How does Earl hear these things? But I do know how: old silent Earl attracts talk like a magnet. Still, this is tricky ground. "I haven't heard anything like that," I says quickly.

"Well," he says, "maybe they're afraid to bring it up with you."

Things are refocusing in a new and dangerous way. Maybe I should dive back into the water and try to come up in another situation. "Meaning what?" I says.

"Meaning nothing," says Earl.

"No," I says, "what do you mean?"

"The police are still talking to you, aren't they?"

"Not for a while," I says. "Three, four weeks."

"I haven't seen them for six," Earl says. I wonder if he's lying.

"That's only natural," I says. "I live along the river."

"I was sure I saw you that day," Earl says now.

"Well, you were wrong about that," I says. "You didn't tell the police about that, did you?" Christ! No wonder they've been after me.

"Naw," he says without much conviction. "They laid offa me."

"Oh, great," I says. "Otherwise you would of."

"I was pretty sure," he says stubbornly.

"You gotta be absolutely sure in these cases," I says. "I've told you where I was. Lots guys fish along the river. It was fucking opening day."

"He hada blue cap. You know, like your Sox cap."

"This is Bosox country," I tell him. "Half the guys at the Barn got Bosox caps."

Earl thinks this over. I begin to wonder if Earl just wanted to talk. If this whole stupid swimming thing was so he could talk. "So what about that car you've been seeing? What about that?"

I realize mentioning the car was a mistake. To Earl's mind, it's evidence, it's a sign. "Christ, I don't know. It could be the Red Gal's ex for all I know."

"You'd know him," Earl says. "Wasn't you in school with him?"

"It's been years," I says. "Look, Earl, they're just doing their job. Following up, you know. It could of been anybody."

"They think it was us," he says. "And I think it was you."

"Earl, you're kidding me. You're joking, right?"

Maybe it's the beer, maybe the heat, maybe he was just joking, but old Earl starts to laugh. I'm not sure how to take this. "Christ, don't kid like that," I says. I grab one of his bony ankles and start shaking it. "You're kidding, right?"

When he doesn't stop laughing, I give a jerk, and he loses his grip and splash. The next thing I know, he's got ahold of one of my legs and I'm sliding down the wet rock. Then water, colder than hell, colder than before, and I've got no air, 'cause Earl's on top of me, holding me down. There's no time to think anything but disaster, surprise, and panic, before my feet touch bottom, a shallow spot. I stand up, throwing Earl back into the pool. A mouthful of water's making my nose and lungs burn, and I'm choking it out, when Earl jumps up, big as a manta ray, water pouring off him like wings. I feel his arms around my shoulders, and it's pure reflex: I hit back with my elbow and catch him just right. As he's dropping away, he catches my arm, then the waist of my trunks, then we're both in the pool with no idea which way is up.

The current takes us by surprise. It was waiting for us to be occupied with other things, like breath and survival, so it could catch us broadside and spin us around and start sucking us toward where the flat rocks turn up jagged edges and the pool narrows and spills in five and ten foot steps to a lower pool and then into the fast and stony stream.

There's a moment when we're floating, Earl and me, floating and struggling and under our own power, then we're underwater and thumping against rocks and feeling the numb burning of flesh rubbing stone. I see the sky, gulp air, and hit bottom again before the water opens. I'm high up, higher than I'd imagined, and when the current hits me between the shoulders, I tumble forward. I hang at the edge just long enough to see the wet boulders below, but even as I start to yell, the water smacks into me and I'm falling through air, through water, down rocks. I thump into the lower pool right to the gravel bottom where the current slams me into the slimy side of a boulder. I come thrashing up, scraping my hands, back, and shoulders along the way, coughing and spitting into the hot brightness.

My feet start to go again and I grab hold. I'm right at the edge of the lower pool. My back's been scoured, my chest's on fire. I'm gasping and wheezing and thinking of nothing but breathing, not even seeing anything, when suddenly I know something's wrong. It takes me a minute, hanging onto the rock, before I realize I don't hear Earl. I don't see him, either.

He's up in the pool; the shit pushed me over. That's my first thought.

I start yelling, but when there's no answer, I let go from the rock. That's when I see a flash of red and white downstream and start plunging through the water, running and falling, half swimming, half crawling, the rocks leaving thin trails of blood on my arms and legs.

Earl's lying face down in the water, caught against a big ledge that's sticking out into the stream. I grab his hair first then get one arm around his cold, slippery chest. I fall twice with him before I can prop him up. I'm up to my knees in icewater and my hands are going numb. I can't feel his chest, never mind a fucking heartbeat, and my voice calling to him is far away, a stranger's voice. For a minute, I'm in danger of getting permanently detached. Then his eyelids kinda twitch. I get my arm around his shoulders and drag both of us onto the ledge. I put Earl on his back and lean on his chest the way we learned in Lifesaving I, then take a deep breath and blow into his mouth, one, two, three times without even thinking once how basically disgusting it is. He gives a grunt and his chest starts heaving. I turn his head just before he pukes up half the stream and starts coughing, I collapse beside him. I feel can't do any more, but he lies there groaning so long, I wonder if he's got something broken. I start patting his legs and arms but he seems same as me, just all bruised to shit with blood running into the water from a lot of white and red scrapes.

"Earl," I says, "can you sit up?"

There's this long moment while I think paralysis and concussion and the impossibility of explanation. Then it's like Frankenstein's monster. Earl seems to move in pieces. His head first, then his chest, and then he kinda bends at the waist and he's sitting up, yes, indeed, kinda like a soft doll, but he's sitting up.

"Your legs," I says. "Can you move your legs?"

He lifts one and then the other and for a minute I'm crying, then Earl lays back down and opens his eyes.

"Where the hell are we, man?"

"Below the pool. We went over the rocks."

"I coulda drowned," Earl says now. He's got this stunned look of revelation.

"Yeah," I says.

He goes quiet, busy catching his breath, assembling his thoughts, finding the words. Finally, he says, "I won't forget that." And just for an instant, we're in complete communication, sci-fi stuff with thought transfer or something: he knows, he really does know, but now he's gotta set knowing against the chute down the rocks and the stupidity and terror and water closing over his head and me hauling him out.

"Thanks," I says, cause, while there's no guarantees, I got this conviction old Earl's gonna keep his mouth shut.

CHAPTER 8

So there's me and Earl, beat to shit, sitting on a rock way out in no-where with a damn hot walk ahead of us, and we've nonetheless come to an understanding. An understanding! Course by the time we've dragged ourselves to the truck, we're both feeling woozy and a bit sick between the heat and the bruises and the fact that every fly, tick, and mosquito in the county's had a piece of us. We're all over in dried blood, and by the time Earl gets the truck unlocked and climbs in, he's too bushed to start the engine. That's the shape we're in.

I mention all of this as preliminary cause subsequent events would sound pretty stupid otherwise. I don't mean driving back and getting in the shower and eating dinner and all that. I mean the next afternoon, Sunday, when I get myself upright and check out the multicolored mess that used to be my back and shoulders. I've hurt muscles I never knew I had, and I feel so crappy I don't even want a beer. What I'm doing is lying on the couch with the Mets at Chicago, when I stick my hand out, pick up the phone, and dial Jess Simeone's number.

Three rings, four rings; I'm about to hang up, half disappointed and half relieved, when the receiver clicks and she's on the line, a little breathless, like she's come running in from the yard. I hear this vibration in her voice, an extra deep string I hadn't noticed before.

"Hi," I says before I can get appreciating her vibrations too much. "It's Jeff Woodbine. How're you doing? I just wanted to see how you and Leon were getting on."

"Oh, Jeff, hi. Oh, I appreciate this. We're doing real good. Well, pret-ty good. Just wait, I gotta get to the door."

"I can call you back," I says. "I don't want to bother..."

"No bother. I got this extra long cord. Leon length," she says with a little laugh. "He's out in his kiddie pool."

I hear footsteps and the sound of a door opening and closing and her saying something to Leon.

"Okay now," she says. "I had to take the phone outside so I can watch him. You can't take your eyes off kids in water."

"That's for sure," I says. Boy, do I know that now. I suddenly want to tell her about the dam and about Earl and me. About being stupid and lucky and semi-heroic. Particularly the latter.

"He just loves the water," she says. "I keep thinking I gotta get organized and take him to the beach."

"Me and Earl were thinking about driving to the shore yesterday," I says, "but it was too hot."

"You're not kidding," she says. "And a small child's exhausted before you get to the water."

"So he's doing all right?" I ask.

"Better. Thanks. Yes, he's doing better. Still some nightmares and he's not so good with strange men. But otherwise okay, thank God. We were so lucky."

So there we are on the phone, chummy as hell. I find out that Leon hasn't started talking yet—in fact, he's stopped saying anything, not even individual words. That's the good news. The bad news is that Stankus and Benny are still visiting regularly. Which sends up a red flag, a big STOP sign with a flasher on top. Which I ignore.

"I'm glad you're doing good," I says finally. "I'd like to stop by some time just to say hello."

"Great," she says. "That would be fun. With working and not wanting to leave Leon, I haven't seen anyone in ages."

So we gotta discuss the way you stop seeing school friends, and how it winds up is that an hour later I'm washed and dressed and driving over to Jess's house for a little cookout. I got some cans of Rolling Rock in a bag and a couple frozen trout, and I'm nervous as hell. I'm tempted to stop for some flowers but decide not to over do it. I hit the bake shop instead and buy some nice cookies to a bribe Leon. Just in case.

The heat's still coming like a blow torch, and Jess's street's worse than most. Those boxy capes and two families on Vine are jammed in so close there's no room for trees. She's up at the far end in a little buff house with composition shingles. I see right away that the chimney needs work and the gutters are sagging. But Jess's put some pots of geraniums out front to brighten things up, and, round the back, where I can hear kids playing, she's growing tomatoes in tubs.

"Hey, Jeff," she calls like she's really glad to see me. She's wearing little white shorts that do a lot for her legs and a blue and white t-shirt that doesn't hurt the rest of her. When I hold out the trout, she sweeps her hair back just the way I remembered, and I see she's nervous, too.

"I hope you like fish," I says.

"I love fish. Especially trout. I'll put it right in the fridge. Keep an eye on Leon, would you?"

Leon's sitting in his wading pool under a big ragged silver maple, the only shade around. He's got sand all over his back from the sand box next to it, and he's kicking his feet and splashing water at a little girl standing in her underwear, holding a beachball.

I'm not sure I'd have recognized Leon. Even in a few months he's changed. His hair is bleached with the sun, and his face is tanned. He's all busy kicking and splashing, then he takes a look at me and goes real still.

That's when I should of known. I should of seen everything in that one look and understood how things would be, but I'm thinking of Jess's smile and the way she fills out a t-shirt and the husky vibration in her voice. I give Leon a little wave like he's an ordinary kid. He throws back his head and starts to howl. I don't mean a whimper, I don't mean a cry, I mean a pure scream of outrage, hate, and anger that makes my heart jump.

"Oh, Leon, Leon," Jess says. She's out the door and over to the pool and scoops him up, water, sand and all. She shoos the little girl home and towels Leon off, talking to him all the while, and, all the while, he's staring straight at me and shrieking. I feel like that woman in the story we read in high school, the woman with the big red letter, and I'm sure as hell glad Stankus and Benny aren't cooped on the next block.

"Maybe I should go," I says.

"No, no," says Jess. "He'll settle down. He was like this even with my brother for a while."

And she's right. After what seems like a twenty-four hour tantrum, Leon changes to sobbing and then to sniffling. He accepts a cookie and eats it slowly, flashing me these sullen looks the whole time. The kid's destined for the F.B.I., maybe, or the troopers' barracks.

Finally, Jess ruffles his hair and comes over to the back stoop. She gives me a lopsided smile. "I may have to take the veil," she says.

"Naw. But you'll know when guys are serious."

"That's true," she says and laughs.

"Nice tomatoes," I says now. You can see I'm on edge. Garden produce isn't usually one of my convesational lines.

"Have one. You like them with sugar?"

"Salt," I says.

She goes into the kitchen and comes out with the shaker. We each pick a tomato, warm skinned and smooth and sprinkle it with salt.

"This is great," I says, wiping the juice off my chin.

"All Italians are gardeners. Didn't you know that?"

"No, I didn't. So what else do you grow?"

"Geraniums. Marigolds. Basil. You want to see my basil?"

"Sure," I says. We're both laughing now. We're going around the little yard looking at stuff in pots. "Soil's all clay," Jess explains. "Tree roots, too. Containers are the only way to go."

She's got all this stuff for cooking—thyme, basil, dill, oregano, and marjoram. Of course, I don't know squat about herbs at the time. They just look like weeds, but she keeps breaking pieces off and I can smell the differences. Basil and oregano are spicy and good on the tomato. Dill smells sour; thyme, clean and nice.

"What do you do with all this?" I says.

"Cook."

"Naw," I says. "You work at the school, right? No gourmet treats in the lunchroom."

"I'm not going to be in the cafeteria forever," she says. "Boring as hell. Though the kids are okay. I like kids. Some are a bit bratty but I don't have too much trouble."

"The boys will all be in love with you," I says. I'm kinda working without a net.

She gives me a look like that was outa line, and I see how come she has no trouble with the kids. Then she decides I'm joking, which she likes, Jess likes a joke. She pokes me in the ribs with her elbow to show she understands, and I go pale and nearly puke.

"Jesus, you all right? What's the matter?"

"It's a long story," I says. "I've maybe got a cracked rib."

"Oh, God! I'm so sorry. Sit down. Wait, not in the sun. I've got a chair." She runs to house and comes out with two folding chairs and sets one up in the shade. "What happened?" she says.

I tell her about the dam and swimming and being crazy. Which I can see she kinda understands, like she hasn't been in the same place but maybe next door to it. That's the thing with Jess that's different. We don't waste time on small talk but get right into what really matters to us. Even the Red Gal, whom I gotta say means a lot in a certain ways, never gets much beyond school stuff—like "do you still remember so and so", or when this or that happened.

What I'm talking about now is another sort of conversation altogether. And though I gotta leave out some stuff, pretty soon I'm telling her about how Earl and me started fooling around in the pool and how we got pulled over the fall onto the rocks.

"I know that place," she says. "I don't know how you weren't killed."

"Just half way," I says, and I pull up my shirt. "I feel like chopped meat."

She winces like she can feel the bruises herself. "You were awfully lucky," she says.

"Yeah," I says. And I suddenly do feel lucky, like an exception's been made for me, personally. Michelle's gone and a whole lot of shit with her. Earl's breathing; I've been spared a broken neck, and I'm sitting talking to Jess Simeone with only a bad rib and a mess of bruises out of the whole deal. That's lucky.

After a little while I start Jess's cooker. We get the burgers and buns from the kitchen, and she fixes corn on the cob and more tomatoes. Leon won't eat with us, so she sets up a little tray for him under the tree. Jess and me sit near the stoop under her beach umbrella.

The sun starts to go down; the sky fades to pink and then to lavender, and big dark shadows skim out from under the silver maple and darken the yard. The day's still throwing heat like a furnace that's been turned off, but you can feel the difference. We have a Rolling Rock each and it's a nice evening, real nice, that leaves me happy but restless, so that I call her up to say good night again when I get home. Between the bruises and the vibrations, I have a hard time getting to sleep, and I'm stiff as hell in the morning, but that's okay, too. I'm prepared, see, to be happy. Even when Morrissey gets on my ass for dogging it at work, I don't lose my cool. I've got everything in hand.

That's Monday. I talk to Jess on Tuesday. On Thursday I take over a couple bass I've caught and we cook them out. She fixes the bass with stuff from her backyard garden, and they're damn good. Everything's fine, except Leon gives with the five minute siren when he sees me and won't sit at the table. Jess isn't fazed. He took weeks with her brother, she says, but he still makes me uneasy, and I don't stay late. I get home early and happy and cold sober and careless. That's what happiness does; it makes you careless. I don't see anything, cause my mind's on other things, and it's only later that I remember an unfamiliar car parked up the street, a shadow under a tree, the red pinpoint of a cigarette.

At the time, I hop outa my truck and unlock the garage. I'm climbing back into the cab, when I hear a step on the drive, and then it's too late, cause there's an arm around my neck. I try for an elbow in his ribs, but I'm way off balance. My next idea's the steering wheel. I hit the horn, like the idea, and hit it again. When button sticks, someone starts swearing in my ear and I wind up on the asphalt with all the wind knocked out of me.

The basic situation is that there's two of them and they intend to beat the crap out of me. I'm trying to get some air in my lungs, protect my head, and kick back with my feet, and I'm pretty much failing at all three. The result is some serious pain, and I might of joined Michelle if the stuck horn hadn't set my pal Ralph barking. The pissy next door neighbor can't stand dogs, and he starts hollering about the goddamn racket just as a boot connects with my jaw. My mouth fills up with blood, woosh!, but the frantic pummeling and kicking stops. I'm left lying on the drive listening to the horn blaring, the neighbor yelling, and Ralph barking.

I haul myself up on the door of my truck—like this guy's complaint is really important—and flail away at the horn button. A sudden silence. My hand drops down and I manage to turn off the truck motor and the lights. I'm just hanging there, holding the wheel and bleeding on the upholstery for Christ's sake, but at some point I musta let go, cause next thing I know I'm back flat on the driveway.

I try to sit up, whang my head on the open truck door, and flop back, ready to die. Except this time, there's blood running into one eye and more is dripping from various interior passages into the back of my throat. My stomach can't take blood, and sure enough I puke up a mess of blood and dinner at the edge of the lawn. I wipe off my hands on the wet grass and rub my face against my sleeve. More red stuff. Though I feel strongly like I wanna lie down, I have this sense of urgency. Like I oughta get up and clear the area and get in behind a locked door soonest.

That's the program, but my legs haven't gotten the message, and the muscles that have hurt like crazy. What I do is I get my back against the truck and kinda slide along until I can grab the door and shut it. Right then, I remember my keys and have to wrestle the door open again. I grab once, twice, third time lucky for the keys, then kinda bounce off the door and push it shut. I resume maneuvers along the side of the truck.

The garage is five, six feet away. I launch myself toward the corner post and catch hold and stand there shaking. I don't even think about trying to pull down the door. But I've got the technique now. I hit the wall with my shoulder and put one foot in front of another and edge along until I reach the rear and have to go solo to the back stair of the house. Clutch time, as the announcers say.

I don't know how long I stand there. Time's been altered in so many different ways I can't be sure. It's all quiet, anyway, by the time I find myself on the stairs. Half way up to be precise. I'm crawling step by step, listening to a waterfall dropping into a chasm. I'm hearing water rushing and bubbling and I'm scrambling over wet rocks lit by the neighbors' security lights to a big ledge, to a platform of boards, to the worn, chipped paint of the second floor porch.

The moon's come up, taking the air from hot to mild. I take the opportunity to lie down and watch the thin disk sail across slate colored clouds. One cuts in front so that the moon face goes dark and the edges of the clouds turn silver. I don't remember anything, not even the fact that I should be afraid. I don't have anywhere to get to; I don't have anything to do. I'm fully occupied looking at the moon.

When I wake up, the sky's a gray blank and the security spots and street lights have fuzzy halos. It's started to rain and little drops are drifting onto the porch, wetting my jeans and my shirt. I put my hand down, expecting my mattress; the wood floor of the porch brings me back with a lurch.

By the time I make the door of my apartment and get inside, it's three a.m. I figure I've done a whole day's work already. I drop my clothes and stagger to the shower. Water makes the bruises better but the cuts worse, and I can't take a deep breath without my ribs hurt like hell. When I step out, I don't even dry off; I just find the bed and collapse. Whenever I wake up, I get a drink of water and sometimes an orange juice before staggering back to the mattress. That's how I spend Friday.

There's not a lot of variation to Saturday and Sunday, either, except for an emergency trip to the dentist to get a couple of broken teeth seen to. Normally I hit the folks for dinner, but I call and tell them we're cooking out at Jess's. Not exactly a lie, but a rearrangement. Though I can tell Mom is dubious and Dad's disappointed, they don't say much. Mom contents herself with a half dozen questions about Jess, and Dad gives me the rundown on the zoning board deliberations on the Lopes subdivision plan. I agree that the septic fields are sure to pollute the brook, and we agree that him and me're about the only sensible guys in town.

What I really do is stay in bed, eating canned soup, and jumping every time I hear an unfamiliar noise. My face is still a mess on Monday, but I get myself together and tell anybody who needs to know that I got pitched off a friend's dirtbike when it sideswiped a rock. That seems to satisfy everybody except Earl, who's maybe not quite as dumb as I thought.

Anyways, I got more immediate worries than Earl's IQ. Like everything hurts. It hurts to write on the clipboard, to push the hand truck, to sit on the fork lift. Picking up stuff is pure torture, and I basically survive the week by dogging it. I hang out in the Korean isolation wing with the Daewoos and Goldstars, loiter in the john, and get friendly with the drivers. Whenever Morrissey's looking, I'm double checking my inventory sheets, busy, busy, busy, cause he was pissed when I didn't show on Friday.

By the end of the week, I'm beginning to breathe okay, and I can pick up lighter stuff if I do everything with my legs and protect my ribs at all times. Three-thirty on Friday, I'm easing some boxed tvs off the shelves in a complicated maneuver with a board and a hand truck, when Morrissey appears.

"Gotta talk to you," he says.

I sliding the tv down. The shape I'm in, a no-sweat thirty-eight inch job's become the original 800 pound gorilla. Finally I get fifteen hundred dollars worth of chips and transistors parked safe on the hand truck and turn to Morrissey.

"What's the problem?" I says. I just assume that anything with Morrissey's a problem.

"Come into the office," he says.

"What'd you want me to do with this?" I says. "They're waiting for it out on the ramp."

"Just put it back on the shelf," he says, "and give Earl your sheets."

I look at him a minute. I see he knows I can't no more lift that tv than I can fly. Not without wrecking myself. I realize he's been waiting for this. He was probably watching from the back room until I tackled something big enough.

"You can stick it up your ass," I says and I crumple up the invoice sheets and drop them at his feet.

Then he gets going and I give it back. He tries to block my way, but I'm still strong enough to shove him into the Hitachi VCR's.

"You're fucking fired!" he keeps shouting. I'm walking through the warehouse, heading out the door, and he's screaming,"You're fired! You're fucking fired!" I think he's going to run all the way to the front and keep me from walking out til he can fire me officially or something. I punch out on my time card and go downstairs to payroll, where there's more yelling. Stella's already cut the weeks' checks. She's flipping though them with her three inch purple nails, showing them to Morrissey. And Morrissey's screaming that it's four o'clock and Jeff's fired so, goddamn it, he can't be paid for eight hours.

Stella shifts her cigarette from one side of her mouth to the other and back again and says for the fifth time, "The checks is all cut. What you want me to do? Recut the whole payroll for three lousy hours? You coulda fired him at ten to seven, you know."

So Morrissey gets yelling at Stella. I'm just standing there, cooling off now and feeling a bit better and beginning to enjoy it. Stella's older than Morrissey and me put together and she thinks payroll's the key to the universe. She understands checks and finance, see, and nobody gets paid unless it goes across her desk. That's the bottom line for her. Morrissey's a dick head, that's the bottom line on him, and he's dumb enough to try to pull this "I'm the manager" shit on Stella.

"You give him notice?" she says finally. "He's been here a while; he's entitled to notice. He'll put in for unemployment, too. They don't like that at the management." She means the main office, the honchos.

Morrissey goes ballistic. I think he's going to fire Stella, too, but at the last moment he pulls back from that cause he realizes he don't know shit about payroll. Finally, Stella pulls out the check, her long purple nails like plastic wrapped pliers, and hands it over.

"Don't spend it all in the one place," she says and winks.

I stick the check in my wallet, shake hands with Stella, and give Morrissey the finger. Two minutes later, I'm in my truck and free for the evening. I've got two temporarily capped teeth, a black eye, banged up ribs, and more bruises than I can count, plus big time enemies and my last ever check from the Bargain Barn. A terrific week.

The whole thing gets me so far down that come Monday I'm sitting around watching storm footage from the big hurricane that's slamming Dade County. The situation's kinda unreal. We got overcast and a chance of rain, while, on the tube, the storm's going like a wind tunnel. The Sunshine State's ash gray: storm skies, dirty looking surf, blown out windows, shattered roofs. Junk's flying everywhere, cars and boats and trees and front porches and trailers, tumbled by the wind like so much paper. I sit there, thinking of large and small storms, and watch people's lives being blown away.

For the next couple days I can't get enough of the coverage. It's like trouble made visible, and I feel like if I can see enough of it, I'll maybe figure out some things I didn't understand before.

I'm still tv side on Thursday when Frenchie calls. "Hey Jeff," he says. "Ready to go?"

"Where?" I says.

"Land of flat roofs," he says. "They're gonna need every roofer they can get down in Florida."

I wait a minute, while thoughts of my folks and Jess and screaming baby and midnight visitors and Bargain Barn grief flash through my mind quicker than an MTV video. Big psychic winds are blowing, and I've lost my grip. I want out.

"We'll take your truck," Frenchie says. "So Dad and Bernard can finish the fall jobs up here. I'll bring the tools, the generator, and some ladders. Man, there's gonna be money laying all over the ground."

"Give me an hour," I says. "I'll be ready to go."

CHAPTER 9

Though it's a different story altogether, I could tell you a lot about my adventures in the Sunshine State. Cowboy City: guns and crooks and insurance fraud and five dollar a bag ice and fifteen dollar a gallon water. Yellowing plastic sheeting, endless chow lines, boiling tent cities, overflowing Portasans. Men shouting, women crying—and vice versa. Kids jumping on cars, kids hiding under cots. Sulphur stink in the air and outdoor fires, sewage, and rotting meat. And everywhere, stray dogs, stray families, stray bullets: enough misery and heat to do me permanently, a circus.

Course, we don't see south Florida at its best. Or so I'm told. At its best, this is vacation paradise with fun under the palms. Not at its best, the real estate's hotter than hell with one hundred percent humidity. The palm trees are broke off about hip height and underneath's a rustling mess of fronds full of rats. We got storm water standing all over, and the mosquitoes come in clouds like fog.

The main thing, though, is that ordinary life's been recycled into garbage and disruption. You can't count on anything. Boats are laying on front lawns; houses are floating in marina slips; trailers are crumpled like beer cans, and every car's a junker. Neighborhoods are so messed up that people paint their names and insurance company numbers on whatever's left and hope the right folks find them. Sidewalks are iced with glass; lawns splotched with wallboard. The housing's totally trashed, and, after drinking water, the two top commodities are the tarps and plywood that go up in price every day regular, so that lumberyards gotta keep a guy going constant with a price taper.

People've gone crazy; that's the truth. They see a truck with tools and supplies, they come running out, fighting over whose job is first. They want their lives fixed and the job started, even when you can see that they don't need a roof, they need demolition and maybe a ticket back to Milwaukee.

But it's work and it's money—if you can get the supplies in the first place and keep them from getting stolen in the second. First week we're there, we invest in a shotgun and a .38 and that helps somewhat. The second week, we take on Courtney and Lucien, and then we've got the manpower for efficiency. We've always got two guys searching for supplies and two on the job, plus a split shift guarding the truck, tools, and material at night.

Course neither Courtney nor Lucien knows squat about construction. All the skilled and semi-skilled are in business for themselves already. Courtney'd been working sugarcane, and Lucien'd been picking vegetables: minimum wage stoop labor in crap conditions. Now they're taking turns sleeping in a truck, but they're all of a sudden worth near $8 an hour, and folks who wouldn't give them the time of day are falling over themselves begging for help.

That puts Courtney in a happy frame of mind. He's a big, tough Jamaican with a gap between his front teeth and a king sized laugh. He's illiterate, but since all the street signs are down, Courtney finds his way around no worse'n the rest of us. I don't think he's driven before, either, but he loves everything mechanical, and he doesn't grind the gears more'n a couple times.

Lucien's his exact opposite, a tall impassive Haitian, who's so thin I figure he won't be much use for heavy lifting. He talks a form of <u>francais</u>, though, making him an honorary Canuck, and Frenchie says he'll do. Lucien is indifferent to heat, bugs, and pleading homeowners. He works slow but he works steady, and he can do great things with chicken and beans. We soon get it fixed so Lucien stops work an hour or so before the rest of us and forages for dinner. Round about sunset, he's got something ready, and we camp out at the jobsite, eating great food and drinking Courtney's rum.

That's the okay part of the deal. The bugs, the heat, the hassles, the grief; the ten to fourteen hour days, the seven day weeks; the surly lumbermen, the gunshot ridden nights, the psychopathic population are just so much misery. The thing is, we're making too much money to quit. At the same time, it's costing us so much to live that we're all the time feeling we're falling behind: post hurricane Dade County is basically an irrational state of mind.

On the positive side, some of the bad stuff lurking between my ears gets wiped. I stop hearing the river running and the bubbling water of the falls above the dam. Park benches start to lose their meaning, and Michelle's red eyes fade out until I can't clearly remember what she looked like. My bruises fade away, too, and pretty soon the Bargain Barn and serious enemies and my old life seem pretty distant. Working in the hot sun all day accelerates the process, and if I'm not quite sane, I'm too busy to notice.

I might of stayed there, I suppose. I might of been like Grampa and "left Canada" and forgotten everything and had a whole different life.

I might of. Sure, I sent Jess a couple cards—and some to the Red Gal, too. I sent Mom and Dad money every time we got paid and called them whenever we had job site with a working phone.

But one day flows into another and different things happen and before you know it, you're not the same person anymore. You have different friends and a different job and you're seeing different things and you're doing things differently. By winter, I'm getting used to the place. There's a lotta sun but less heat, and even the middle of the day is pleasant. I don't mind the roofs anymore, either. Two stories up's as high as we go, and, most of the time, we're working safe on a flat surface, mopping on tar and dumping down gravel so white it about blinds us. We start taking a day a week off, and Courtney and me go fishing along the Tamiami Canal with a couple improvised poles.

I have some days of thinking about Jess. Up on a roof, laying down new ply, maybe, or holding a rafter in place for Frenchie, I'll see a girl passing below with a mass of dark hair and slim arms and legs. Or maybe it's just a gesture, a woman waiting for a ride or toting water bottles, who pushes her hair back the same way or picks up a child that looks like Leon. But there's always distractions, frantic homeowners, mostly; folks whose roof's gone and who're holding off the heavy Florida rains with deteriorating plastic or folks who've lost windows and doors and are holding off looters with semi-automatics.

With one thing and another, I don't even think about going north until the weather starts getting hot again in March. We've acquired a couple tents by then, cause the jobs are beginning to be less like disaster relief, where you camp out in the ruins, and more like normal work, where you're expected to disappear at night.

That's when Frenchie and me start thinking about the future, the heat, the high cost of doing business, the trout season up north. Then I get the phone call about Grampa, and suddenly everything's settled. We sell most of our equipment to Courtney, who's bought himself a truck, and Lucien takes the lumber to fit up a storefront restaurant in Little Haiti.

So there we are, standing out in a pink evening on the dead brown lawn of our last job. The beachball sun drops below the horizon as we pass around a bottle of rum and shake hands. Two and a half days later, me and Frenchie roll into Slatertowm where it's still gray and cold and threatening rain. I drop him off and head home to see my folks.

They're outa the house soon as they hear the truck. Mom throws her arms around me, exclaiming, "You're so brown!", "You're thinner!" "And your hair!" She looks eager and anxious, and smaller than ever.

"No time to get it cut," I says.

Dad puts his arm around me, too. He looks kinda pale and I can hear him breathing. "You shoulda been down in Dade," I tell him. "Hotter than hell and sun every day."

"We've about forgotten what sun looks like," Mom says and Dad agrees it's been a dreadful winter.

"How's Grampa?" I says. "I'd better look in and say hello."

"We couldn't get hold of you. You were already on your way," Dad says. "He's had to stay in the hospital."

I'm not functioning up to speed. "I thought he was to get right out. I thought—"

"We'll go see him tomorrow," Dad says. "First thing." He shakes his head and turns away like this is something he doesn't want to discuss. Mom hugs me again and says, "It's in his spine. There's nothing much they can do. Not at his age."

"What's in his spine?" I says, but I kinda know it isn't just arthritis.

"A tumor," Mom says quietly. "They've done some chemo—but he's tired of it. You know what he's like."

"They need to leave the old man in peace," Dad says like he's angry. "He's had enough. It's not as if—"

"Can't they do anything else?" I ask. "Operate? Radiation?"

"We'll see him tomorrow," Dad says. "You'll understand the situation then. He's been looking forward to seeing you."

Mom gives me this look which I know means to shut up. I'm still digesting this when we go inside. The old house looks small, dark, and orderly, and I suddenly realize I haven't been inside an intact house since I left. "That meatballs I smell?"

"They'll be ready in a minute," she says, and I says, "Great," cause I'm overtired and a bit disconnected. Grampa, home, orderliness and the smell of meatballs are getting mixed up with white sun glare on the glass, highway wind roaring through the truck, a thousand plus miles of asphalt, and the various irrational states of Dade County. I can't focus, and it's not til I've had dinner and told stories about Frenchie and collapsed into bed and slept for twelve hours straight that it really registers that Grampa's house is empty and that we're going to see him in the hospital.

By then, it's eleven o'clock, and Mom's gone off to work. "A bit disappointed she didn't see you this morning," Dad says.

I pour a cup of coffee and sit down without saying anything.

"You want something to eat? We've got bacon, eggs; Mom bought your favorite cereal."

"Maybe after," I says. "I think we oughta go see Grampa first."

"You should have something," Dad says. "Toast, maybe?"

"Yeah, maybe toast." I'm beginning to feel like a guest at home, and

I realize this is the longest I've ever been away. Dad makes the toast and has a piece himself. We sit there crunching brittle, well-buttered slices, thinking our own thoughts. Mine keep wavering between Grampa's empty room and the sunny, wrecked yards and houses of Dade County, as if I'm here and there simultaneously. I'm wondering how Lucien and Courtney are doing and whether the Alvarezs' got that plumber they were waiting for, and, at the same time, I'm wondering about Grampa and what kinda shape he's going to be in. With all this thinking going on, we have a pretty quiet breakfast and a silent drive to the hospital.

We don't go in the main building. We go round back of the oncology section and park next to a two story addition. "They've moved him to the hospice," Dad says, which is the first definite thing he's said about Grampa and the only thing that's crucial.

I wouldn't have known him. That's my first thought when we finally get inside and upstairs and into the room Grampa shares with an emaciated young guy and a curtained off bed with tubes and oxygen tanks everywhere.

"Both real bad," Grampa says. "Young fellows, too." He's not looking so great himself. His skin is thin and yellowish, and there's not much of him left except for his square jockey's hands, immense with every bone and joint and ligament standing out sharp and clear. He takes my hand for a minute and doesn't say anything. Dad whispers that they keep him doped up so he doesn't feel the pain.

"You shoulda told me sooner," I says. On the way home I quarrel with Dad about that. All in all, it's a lousy visit, so I think here I'll skip up to a later, more important, day that's somehow become the visit.

Grampa used to say that there's a time and place for everything—I guess that's it—and one day in April, couple weeks after the visit I've been talking about, was the right time for Grampa to tell me about Canada. I remember it as if he told me the story the day he died, but that's not true: he died after being unconscious for most of three days. This particular day was the one we talked, the last day he had anything important to say to me. Course, "Hand me the can" or "Let me have a drink" are important, too, but not memorable, if you see what I mean.

Anyway, it's one of his good days, and they have him sitting up in bed. Herman, the emaciated young guy, is sitting up, too, watching the afternoon cooking shows. The lung case is back behind the curtains with his tubes and his oxygen tanks.

"You find a job yet?" Grampa asks, quite chipper. His mind's still fine at this point, though he loses whole days, even weeks, to the morphine.

"I interviewed with the lumber yard," I says, "and I should find out about the siding company this week."

"Siding?"

"Yeah, new outfit up the industrial park. Cedar clapboards. They sell and install. I'm trying for installer."

"Good experience in Florida," Grampa says.

"You bet. I did a little of everything in Florida."

"I thought you might stay in Florida," Grampa says now. "I'm glad you come home, but I thought you might stay. Must be opportunity down there."

"More work but lousy wages. I couldn't take the heat."

"Not much for you here, though."

He's watching me with that funny, interested look he sometimes gets. When he sounds and looks so much like himself, I sometimes think he'll get better. I sometimes fool myself and then I go home feeling bad and angry at the world, and at Grampa, too, for getting my hopes up. I shrug my shoulders.

"Well, you don't always have as much choice as you think," he says now. "Like when I left Canada. I'd figured I'd be there the rest of my days. But there you have it."

Although I've been teasing Grampa for years for that story, I suddenly don't want to hear it. I know it's the last one and I want to put it off, but now Grampa's got it in his head to tell me. He's leaning back on the pillows with his eyes half closed, and he says, "...Hamish and me came out in '25. Easier to get into Canada so that's where we come. From there we figured to go to Brooklyn where we had an uncle. Met him, finally. A tight old coot. In the meantime, I got a job mucking out at the old racecourse. This is up in Toronto, now, mind. Hamish went to work in construction. He was big, like you, Hamish. With a good head on his shoulders. Always figuring how to make a dollar. He died a rich man, your Uncle Hamish did."

I says I knew Uncle Hamish had money and let it go at that. Grampa's eyes are closed now and he's slipping into a druggy sleep. I'm getting ready to say good-bye, when he starts talking again in bits and pieces. What I'm telling you here's been straightened out, without all Grampa's little side stories and remarks. Otherwise, it might not make sense to you. It just about made sense to me and I'd known him all my life.

"It should of been his idea," he says now without saying what idea. That's what I mean about bits and pieces, but I pretty soon get the gist. "The tracks in those days were full of characters. The Canadian bootleggers was making money faster than they could spend it. That's a fact. They and their families and their girlfriends, all together, they couldn't have spent it if they'd lived to be a hundred. Not that they weren't always trying; they hung around bookies thick as raisins in a fly cemetery. One guy specially."

There's this long pause, and I shoulda said, "Go to sleep, Grampa," but I didn't.

"Billy," he says after a minute. "Billy, that was his name. Funny how I forget names now. Billy was one of them. Oh, a sharp young guy. Suits, shoes, hats—all the best. Gold watch, too. He come up with the idea and he broached it to me."

He kinda nods his head, which since he's lying down means he sorta wobbles his chin. I make a sharp young guy in my mind. I give him knickers like Payne Stewart and a gold watch chain, but I'm stumped on the shoes and thinking them over when Grampa starts again.

"And I pass the idea along to Hamish, cause I was young and green and Hamish was my older brother. And big. They always liked the big guys, you know, in case there was rough stuff and trouble over the shipments."

"Shipments?" I says.

"Canadian whisky, bourbon. Rum up from the islands. All sorts of booze."

"You were a bootlegger," I says, getting the picture.

"I was the driver," Grampa says. "See, I could drive a horse van— with or without horses. The revenue boys was used to seeing horse vans going back and forth between the tracks in Toronto and Detroit and Buffalo. Pretty safe. I never mixed horses and booze, though. No, no. They used to want to stick some in with the horses, but none of that. Though I did take some with a stable pony once. What was that pony's name?"

There's another long pause. Not that the pony's name matters, but he won't go on until it comes to him.

"Deaf, he was. Could of set off a cannon next to him. Great for big races and nervous colts."

We wait. Grampa's face—that's nearly unrecognizable what with all the bones and no blood—takes on the meditative expression he always gets talking about horses. Like he's not seeing the white ceiling and the big eye of the tv and the bed rail with the urinal dangling, but horses milling about behind the starting gate or a long curve down the backstretch or colts driving hard toward the finish. I start to feel real bad, cause this is Grampa. It's not the sickly stranger who doesn't always know me and who drools and mumbles in his sleep. It's Grampa, and I'm already missing him a lot.

"Clambake," he says finally. "That was his name. Clambake. I did a run with Clambake once cause we'd been stopped going north and I knew they was suspicious. So there's old Clambake packed in with a fortune in the best Canadian whiskey. Never so much as stamped a hoof."

"You musta made out all right."

"More'n all right." He gives a little laugh. "I'd of owned horses if I'd stayed. I reckon I'd of owned the track, too."

"Why'd you leave?" I asks. I hadn't wanted to know, but now I do.

Grampa's not to be rushed. "There was a nice little girl, too. Lizzie was her name. A really nice girl. Relative of Billy's, she was. They was cousins of some sort."

"I'm not sold on cousins," I says, thinking of the C of F C and Dougie Donnelley's.

"No? Well, Lizzie was a fine lass. The rest of them," Grampa makes a face, "a rough crowd. City boys, mostly, Glasgow, Dublin, Liverpool. A Mick-Mac mob. The Micks was mostly on the Detroit side. The Canadian side was more Scots and English. The Italians and the Jewish boys were just coming in at that time, and things was starting to get nasty. What with one group shooting up the other's shipments."

I remember FBI movies and old film clips of Al Capone and all those beefy, hard faced owners in Grampa's pictures.

"There was this one night," Grampa continues. "They'd stashed the booze near the border at a broken down old farm house, and we was to pick it up and take it across in the van. They had several pick up spots, but for us, the farm was the best, because it was quiet and there was room to turn the horse van. Hamish was with me in the cab with the machine gun, and we had two new guys Billy'd found riding in back to help with the loading."

"You were fifteen? Sixteen?"

"Near seventeen by that time. Didn't look it. Which helped with the cops. We pulled in the way we always did. I backed the van up to the old barn. Only it had been improved a bit with locks and a good door and such. Billy come out and gave the orders as usual. I was supposed to stay in the cab to be ready to roll in case of trouble, but him and Hamish jawed for a bit. Then, cause it was a quiet night, Hamish left the machine gun on the front seat and went to help the others. They were almost done when I heard a car coming long way off. I knew it was trouble. I could always feel trouble. I could feel a horse going lame. I'm telling you the truth. I always knew the moment before a horse started limping."

He tells me here about his great aunt who was a speywife in the Old Country and had second sight. This is a story I already know. He wanders on about her for a while and then dozes off for five minutes. I'm about to leave, when he picks up right where he left off.

"That's the feeling, I got. The feeling of trouble coming," he says. "Right away, I started the engine. I yelled to the others, and I expected

Hamish to come get the machine gun. Instead, I heard shouts and a scuffle."

He shakes his head.

"We'd been set up. It was them new guys—maybe Billy, too, though I'd rather not think that despite the way things turned out. They figured they'd pull a fast one: load up the booze and take both shipment and van. They hadn't figured on how quick and strong Hamish was. He grabbed one guy around the neck and dragged him back behind the open door of the van. The other fellow hesitated just that minute too long to fire. Or maybe it was Billy; maybe he was the one who didn't want to shoot. I'd already picked up the machine gun. It was about as heavy as me—I don't exaggerate. I saw how things was going and, no time to think and scared as hell, I put my finger on the trigger and fired off a round. They weren't expecting that. I swung that damn gun across the yard from one side to the other, firing all the time. There were screams and the barn lights went out. Hamish let go of the guy and jumped in the cab. I handed him the gun and put her in gear. Maybe fifty yards down the road, he told me to stop and hopped out. I was pretty nervous cause I could see car lights barreling up the road. Hamish banged the doors of the van shut and then he was standing on the running board, yelling for speed. 'Where's Billy?' I said. 'What about Billy?'

"'Never mind!' Hamish shouted. 'They'll kill us both, ye wee idiot!'

I hit the gas and started going through the gears. Mind you, I never expected to see Detroit that night. Lucky I was small. I kept my head down and floored the van. Them vans were like tanks, you know. The cars, too. None of this plastic and aluminum junk they make now."

"You're right," I says, cause I'm thinking about Dade County and modern recyclables.

"It was a narrow track; we was doing maybe thirty, and Hamish was firing away like to wake the dead. I could hear bullets whizzing and the windshield went and I figured they'd hit the radiator and we'd be sitting ducks. I had to swing the wheel to avoid them head on, but I musta caught the side of their car, because there was this awful screeching and banging and then we was by them and going like hell. I don't know how long it was before I realized Hamish was shouting. I'd left him on the running board, hanging on for dear life."

"You didn't get hurt?"

"Naw, though Hamish had a bullet in him. Probably what shortened his life. He was only just past seventy when he died. All I had was a bunch of cuts from flying glass. Oh, we were lucky. There were dead men that night, but we was lucky, lucky."

I'm trying to associate bootleggers and shootouts and wild rides in horse vans with Grampa.

"Later, I thought we should go back. I felt awful about Billy. I musta thought about it a thousand times, and I still can't decide whether I hit him or not. I can see the yard and the light and the flash of the gun plain as you sitting there, but I can't quite make Billy out. He may be standing, he may be on the ground, he may be the one with the gun in his hand. I don't know yet, and, at the time it about drove me crazy. I wanted to know what had happened at the barn, because I was worried sick what Lizzie would think. Hamish knew better. He told me to drive south and not look back, and since he was sitting there with the machine gun in his hand and blood on his face, that's what we did."

"We sold the booze cut rate to a couple roadhouses we knew, ditched the van, and bought a second hand Lincoln. A lovely car, like riding on a sofa. We left the same day, even though Hamish was bleeding; he bled half way to New York. That's how I left Canada and come to the United States permanent."

"You were lucky," I says. "Lucky you weren't killed."

But Grampa's not up for reflections. He looks exhausted. His head's sinking right into the pillows and his eyes are closed. Then they open and he gives me that sharp look for the last time. "It was part of the cost of doing business," he says. "See you be careful and don't get into one that's as high priced."

CHAPTER 10

Grampa dies soon after I start at the siding place. I go to the worst funeral yet and come out feeling kinda like I did just after Barry took sick, like I've been moved up a grade unexpectedly and before I'm ready. Everything feels provisional, even though I'm working steady and getting near $8 an hour—and off Stankus' list, too, near as I can tell.

First I figure it's missing Grampa and then that it's getting spooked by baby and giving up on Jess. Finally, I decide it's not having my own place. I start reading the rental ads serious and go look at a couple dumps that remind me of Dade south without the sunshine. I try an evening down at the casino with the Red Gal, too, hanging with the high rollers and slot junkies in the Pequots' smoke filled palace. We drop forty bucks at the slots, have ourselves a decent dinner, and spend a couple of hours up in a room overlooking the woods at the resort hotel. A lot of fun and Total Sensory Overload, you bet, but different somehow, too, in a way I can't quite put my finger on. The Red Gal knows, though. We're on the way home. She's already replaced her evening out lipstick, and she's fixing her hair, moving the rear mirror around and checking the 'do and looking in her eyes the way she does, when she says, "You've changed, you know that?"

"Yeah?" I says. I reach up and turn the mirror back so I can keep an eye on the line of cars and tour buses carrying gamblers and funseekers back to normal life.

"It's like your mind's elsewhere," she says.

"Well, it wasn't on the slots," I says. Her thigh has a nice solid feel that makes me think we could of stayed a half hour longer.

"Naw," she says reflectively, "it's like with Buddy. The motions were real good, but I could tell his mind was elsewhere."

I'll never understand women. "I thought you'd like a night out," I says.

"A lifesaver." She gives me the big grin.

"So what's the matter?"

She shrugs. "Christ, I don't know. Maybe you're in love. You meet someone in Florida, maybe?"

"I met a million people in Florida and they all wanted their roofs fixed." I'm getting annoyed. Dinner, the slots, a room at the hotel and she tells me my mind's elsewhere!

"Maybe it's me," she says in this conciliatory voice. "I haven't mentioned I'm getting married in July."

"July!" I says. My first thought is that I could of used this information sooner. The second is this crazy image of the Red Gal sweltering in a sweatsuit and a bridal veil.

"Yeah." She sounds, not sad exactly, but reflective, melancholy. Maybe that's the word, 'melancholy'.

"Well, congratulations."

"He's a nice guy," she says.

I look at her.

She shrugs again. "He's great with the kids," she says.

Funny thing is I understand that now. So I look back on the scene a whole different way. At the time, I'm thinking this is a crazy reason. "You know him long?" I says.

"Long enough. Sean Conklin. Remember him? He went to the parochial school. Mom's not too pleased cause he's Catholic, but the hell with that. We gotta grow up sometime, right?"

"Yeah," I says, cause this I understand.

"It's been fun," she says. "You're a real nice guy."

"But my mind's elsewhere." I realize it's true; there's always Jess, the elusive image of Jess, taking up the background. At the same time, I'm gonna miss the Red Gal. "Though there's no one quite like you," I says and she smiles.

"Hey, hey, hey," she says softly.

I reach over and take her hand like a kid on a first date. We're riding along, I'm steering with one hand and holding hers with the other, when she starts to sniffle, which isn't the Red Gal's usual MO. I wonder if there's something with me that makes women who're getting married start crying in my truck.

"World's all fucked up," she says after a bit.

"You know it," I says. I put my arm around her and that's the way we get to her place. The lights are all out except for the big security spot at the back, and I feel funny, like I've missed something, like something is happening all around me, and I've missed it. What I realize now is that moments like this is when guys get themselves married.

"Be happy," I says.

"We're going to go to the Justice of the Peace in July," she says as if she isn't sure it'll happen.

"Be happy," I says again, and she kisses me and for a minute my mind isn't anywhere but right there in the truck on Cedar Street. Then she's out the door quick before she can change her mind or I can change mine.

By June, it's sauna time at the warehouse, and I'm plenty happy when Dave tells me I'm going to get a trial as an installer. After that, I work with Tom, one of the regulars. We go all over the area. This part of Connecticut's old farmer construction, and their handiwork's always needing repairs. What they did, see, is dig a big hole in the ground and use the local rocks for a foundation. They didn't take it up more'n a foot above grade, which, when you see the size of the stones, you can understand. Then they run chestnut or oak boards across and threw up a frame, mostly without benefit of a level or anything. They slapped on wide spaced sheathing and heavy claps, and it's a good thing chestnut resists rot, cause most of the property's so low to the ground the first courses are practically sitting on dirt: carpenter ant banquet and pretty agreeable for termites, too.

Summertime along the back roads and village centers, every fourth house turns piebald with new siding or new roofing or new trim. Old farmer houses have kept Frenchie and his dad in work for thirty years plus, and they're pretty good for us clapboard guys, too. Repairs is what we do, mostly; ripping off claps—but saving the good ones—and filling in with new stuff that's a bit thinner and probably won't last a hundred years like the old wood.

Anyway, we're out every day, benefiting from amateur construction, and it's not until we get a week solid of rain and drizzle that I'm back around the warehouse, getting our supplies set for the next installation. Comes eleven o'clock, the warehouse guys start thinking lunch orders, and since I'm just killing time, I volunteer to go out with Gil to the food truck.

Lunch comes in an old, beat up blue van with a little blue and white awning. I'm not expecting much even though Gil says the food's good and a cute gal sells it. He ducks under the awning out of the rain, and, before I can shake the water out of my eyes, I hear him say, "Hi ya, Jess, what's on today?" There she is, great legs, dark hair, dark eyes; I suddenly know what's been wrong with me all spring.

"Hey, Jess! You got a new job," I says.

"Permanent, I hope," she says. "What'll it be?"

Gil's rattling off a half dozen orders—soup, sandwiches, chili, two burgers. Jess goes into action, flipping the burgers onto the tiny grill, filling up styrofoam cups of soup and chili and loading them into bags. She's all quick and efficient, with the wild dark hair braided behind a red bandanna.

"So how long you been running a food truck?" I says.

She gives me a handful of lunch bags, and I put down a collection of bills and change.

"April," she says. "I got the truck third hand in April."

"Runs more like fifth or sixth hand," Gil says. He's a hairy blond guy with the Superman shoulders and arms you get from humping squares of shingles and bundles of claps. He's leaning on the counter of the van, showing off the complicated tatoos on his humungous forearms. There's a scorpion on one arm and a pretty pair of fish on the other. I suddenly can't stand him, but Jess is laughing. She pats a little medal nailed to the side and says her St. Jude'll protect it.

"And Leon," I says, cause I know where her heart is and cause I really want to know. "How's Leon doing?"

Her face changes. "He's doing pretty well, thank you, Jeff," she says like she's pleased I asked. "My mom can watch him now cause I'm only out around the lunch hour. He's doing all right."

Then she's back to the grill, turning over the burgers, cutting up some onions, checking with Gil on who gets what and how well done. There are good smells of grilled meat and frying onions, of chili peppers and hot apple pie, and I'm leaning up against the wagon with rain running down the back of my neck, thinking how to see more of Jess Simeone and trying to remember why that isn't a good idea.

What saves me temporarily is the break in the weather. The sun comes out, almost July hot, and we put on a ton of clapboards and shingles, both rennovation jobs and new construction. I call Jess once, but the phone number's been changed, and I don't persist. I stop by one night, instead. The flower pots and Leon's wading pool are gone, and the skinny Vietnamese woman who answers the door just shakes her head when I ask if she knows where Mrs. Simeone went.

We're busy on different schedules until one day at the very end of June, when Tom and me finish a job earlier than expected. The sky to the west is slate colored, and the wind's getting under the tree leaves so that they turn up their pale bellies: rain for sure, Grampa used to say. We drive back to the warehouse and lock up the ladders. On the way to my truck, I notice the blue food van's parked on the far side of the lot.

Jess has the hood up, and, when I tap on the side, she looks around; she's flushed and there's a smear of grease on her forehead.

"What's the trouble?"

"I don't know. It starts and dies. I got it going, drove it this far and boom."

I look under the hood. "What about the battery?"

"Battery's new," she says and looks at her watch.

"What time you supposed to be back?"

"An hour ago."

"You want to call?" I says. "Dave'll let you call."

"I thought I could get it going," she says. "And not worry Mom. About the repairs, I mean. It's so old, there's always something."

"Why don't you call and I'll take a look," I says.

"Oh, that's kind, Jeff. Thanks." She gives a quick, nervous smile and runs over to the shop. I get a rag out of my truck and begin fiddling with the carburetor. There's rust here and there, and I can see the hoses are near the end of their life, too.

"Try and start it," I says when she gets back. "I've adjusted the carburetor a bit. Maybe that'll get you home."

The motor turns over like a cement truck but it catches, and Jess says, "You're a genius."

"Don't turn it off," I says, "not til you get home."

"I'll keep it running. Thanks so much. I owe you lunch."

"It's going to need work," I says. "That carburetor needs cleaning or maybe a new one."

"I've had to replace the alternator and buy a new battery already," Jess says. "I want to nurse it til I can get a better van. I know this one won't make the winter."

"You got a garage?" I says, cause the sky is black now and there's no doubt we're going to get rain.

"A barn," she says. "We've moved. The government settlement finally came through. A wreck but ours."

"I'm off early," I says, "so I could come by and take another look under the hood. Those hoses, too. I could pick up a couple hoses for you. Those will go next."

"They're not too expensive, are they?"

"Naw," I says. "Tell you what, I'll get the hoses and you make me dinner."

Her face lights up, giving me the sudden urge to live dangerously. "That would be great," she says. "We're just off the state road." She gives me complicated directions, and I get my car tools and stop at the NAPA for the hoses and some new connections. That's how come when the storm hits, I'm in her barn with the carburetor in pieces and hoses laying all round and Leon sitting on an old tire watching me like a little owl.

The barn's not much more than a big shed—room for couple cars with a loft above where they once stored hay. The last owner had a horse, and horses and hay have left a nice barn smell that comes on stronger when the air gets damp with the rain. From the look of the place, I expect the roof to leak in a dozen places, and, sure enough, pretty soon I hear a drip, drip towards the back. I estimate fifteen-sixteen squares to put the roof right, plus a layer of three-quarter ply underneath.

That's just for the barn. The main building's something else again, a beat up old farm house of the "handyman special" type, with moss on the shingles and nearly bare clapboards. The downstairs has three rooms and a bath, and a stair steep as a ladder leads up to four more neglected rooms upstairs. Jess has gotten herself a small library of home renovation books, and I'm betting she'll need every one of them—plus a whole lot of luck besides.

Outside, the wind's rising, bringing a clean, sharp smell, then boom, crack goes thunder and lightning. One of the barn doors slams shut in a sudden gust, leaving us in semi-darkness. I look over quick at Leon, expecting wails and shrieks, but he never moves. He just keeps watching my hands and everything I'm doing. I switch on the trouble light and hang it up, making a little yellow glow like a campfire. Leon looks at that, too, like it's some kinda revelation. I've been cleaning the carburetor components with a little gasoline and getting ready to reassemble the whole thing, and I can see how much he wants to touch everything. I give him a small wrench, instead. He turns it this way and that, struggling until he figures how the jaws open and close. He hasn't said a thing since I came into the house, unless you call a few howls a comment. Soon as I get out to the van, though, he calms right down.

"He loves machines," Jess says, apologetically.

"Longs he doesn't touch anything," I says. So there Leon sits on an old tire, and he doesn't even notice when Jess goes in to make the dinner. I ignore him first, then the silence kinda gets to me. I start holding up the different pieces and telling him what they are, and he stares at each piece with those bright, recording eyes. Leon's a bit creepy, like a clever robot or an animal that could speak just fine if it ever felt the urge.

At the moment, he's all good behavior because of the van. He's fascinated with how things come apart, and I'm okay cause I've got the tools. But also I think he's maybe puzzled. He looks different to me, like a small boy and not a baby, and I must look different to him, too. I'm tanned dark between Dade County and a summer out on the installing, and my hair's short now and I've got different clothes. So though Leon's still suspicious and quiet, his memories gotta be fading, and he's willing to be distracted by the rattle of the parts and the surprises of my tool kit.

The trouble light sways in the breeze, looping shadows along the rafters and across the floor. This is a pain in the butt when you're trying to put stuff together, but finally I get the carburetor cleaned and reassembled. I drop it in place and tighten the new hoses while I'm at it.

"Crunch time," I says to Leon, who's now standing on his tire to see what I'm doing. I open the van and turn the key and the old lemon turns over once, twice. I turn it off and open the carburetor up a little more and try again. She catches the first time, and Leon makes a noise I've never heard before, a crowing, cooing sound of pure joy. He's still at it when Jess blows in the open door with a raincoat over her head and big yellow rubber boots on her feet.

Leon runs to her and begins jumping around in a circle, hooting and crowing. I give her the thumbs up sign.

"You've got it running!"

"For now, anyway."

"Yes, yes," she says to Leon, "yes, it's running. Isn't Jeff clever?"

She picks him up, dropping her raincoat on the floor. Her hair is all wild and her eyes look black in the dim light. With the storm behind her and lightning flashing across the purple sky, she looks like the most beautiful witch imaginable. I close the hood and reach in to switch off the engine. "Do you a while, I hope. Otherwise, I can maybe pick up a second hand carburetor."

She gives with the mega-watt smile and says dinner's ready. I turn off the trouble light. For a moment everything goes dark; then the sky comes up greeny gray and we're dim shapes in the barn. Jess holds out one end of her raincoat, and I put it over my head, cause the rain's coming down like a car wash. We count, "One, two, three..." and break for the house, the raincoat flapping over our heads. Leon clings onto his mother's shoulder like a monkey; rain splashes up our jeans and soaks my sneaks. We stumble up the steps, Leon still crowing, Jess and me laughing. Wet gusts follow us onto the porch, which lists badly and creaks underfoot, but, through the screen door, the kitchen is yellow with light, and I can smell some kind of good chicken and curry, too.

Leon scrambles down, opens the screen door, and hot foots it to the kitchen.

"Your hands," Jess calls, but he clambers up into his chair anyway. She shakes her head and smiles. "You can see he's better," she says.

"He sure loves tools and engines."

"Unreal, isn't it? You can wash up in there. Leon, Leon, come on."

I can hear her talking to him from the bathroom, which is a large, dark, unsound looking room with ancient fixtures and worn linoleum. The kitchen's definitely better. It looks pretty square except for the un-even floor, and Jess has it painted up with an odd peach and dark green combination that looks surprisingly good. The dinner smell doesn't hurt, either. She's a hell of a cook, that's the truth. There's chicken, curried vegetables and rice, a fruit salad, and muffins; everything's delicious and she's made plenty of it.

"Sell this at your van and you'll make a fortune."

"I'm working on it. The tricky thing is figuring out how much of each new thing so you don't have waste."

"Warehouse'd clean this up."

"I've some good customers there."

"Where else do you go?" I says, and we talk about her route for a while and then where I've been installing and whether any of the big construction firms are a possibility. "Rockwell's putting up a lot of houses off 97," I says. "Eight, ten guys every day I was there."

"Maybe," she says. "I've gotta figure distance, too."

"Especially with that van."

"I'm saving for a new one. But the best thing is to be in one spot. I know a couple people who've gotten in at the University. Drive over, park, start selling, home by 2:30. That's what I want. I'm going to talk to the community college. There's no one there yet. I'm going to try to get in there."

Her face is serious for a moment. "It's all timing," she says. "I just need a couple breaks and we'll be okay, Leon and me."

At mention of his name, Leon begins to fidget. He's been playing around with the remains of a chicken leg and now he squirms to get down. Jess gives him a banana and lifts him out of his chair. He runs noisily across the bare wood floors and installs himself in front of the tv in the living room.

It's quiet for a moment; we both start talking at once, and then both stop at once and laugh. "This is nice," I says, which isn't really adequate but means the dinner, the room, the yellow light with the storm dying down outside, her sitting across the table, a general air of adult relaxation.

"Work like you can't believe," she says, running her eyes around the room as if she sees wallboard and peculiar piping and accumulated filth.

"I can believe," I says. I mention Dade and hurricane cleanup.

She's interested in that. In what I learned with the tools, in how long things took. She's thinking roofing and maybe simple plumbing and lally columns to shore up her sloping floors. I tell her about Lucien, the only one besides her to give Mom's cooking a run, and Courtney. But gradually we drift onto other things, to the brittleness of housing and domestic arrangements, to luck, to folks sweeping up rubble and starting over. Topics, I suppose, that are naturals for both of us.

"You sent me some cards," she says as the conversation is dying down.

"No time to write," I says. "Not many cards to buy, either."

"I didn't know you'd come back."

"You'd moved," I says. This isn't the reason I didn't call, and she knows it, though I hope she'll never know the real reason. "The Vietnamese woman didn't know where you'd gone."

She nods like it's all right since I did try and says, "I wanted to start again. Too many memories. Andre liked the town—near his folks, his buddies." Her expression changes. "That was another thing. Some of his buddies thought I must be lonely."

I can see how that would play, even though Leon must be better than a guard dog.

"Plus I hated paying rent. I wanted a home of my own."

It suddenly hits me that she's the only person my age I know who has a house. That's part of the charm of the thing. She has her own house. Course Andre had to go up in a fireball to get it for her, which makes you wonder just how things are organized. I don't mention that, though.

"And space for a garden," she adds.

"You've got that. What's the lot? Couple acres?"

"Nearly four. More than enough. I want to get a dog for Leon. And chickens. I'd like to raise some chickens. You can't make real mayonnaise anymore, you know that? I mean from scratch with an egg. You can't trust the eggs for salmonella. And real chicken—there's no comparison to the battery raised ones."

"That one was pretty good tonight."

"Just you wait. When I get my chickens, I'll cook you up the real thing."

"A lot of work," I says, cause I can see how much she's taken on just in repairs alone.

"I'm a good worker. I'll learn. And you can see it's been good for Leon."

"Way he pays attention, he'll be fixing your van before long."

"His dad was like that." We've cleaned up the plates and she's setting out some slices of cake. "Left over from the van, I'm afraid."

"I didn't know Andre well," I says. I remember him as a fast, angular basketball player and left fielder, one of the guys who hung around Potvin's Garage, pulling engines and transmissions and tuning old V-8's. "I knew he liked drag racing."

"Anything that ran. He was happy flying, running around the country, going places. I didn't see the disadvantages of that at the time."

"No?"

"Well, maybe a little. Maybe that night."

Funny how we always touch on that night, the cornerstone of our ambiguous relationship. That night is the reason we can sit and talk like old friends and maybe partly the reason things have never progressed.

"Maybe I worried a little," she admits. "But at 18, 19—other things are important, aren't they?"

I agree. I feel grown-up but I'm not sure I'm ready. Sitting there, enjoying her company and her cooking, I've got two contradictory impulses. I think I ought to buy that Harley after all and take off for the West pronto. I also think maybe I'll go with the flow and hope my luck holds out right here.

CHAPTER 11

Pretty soon we fall into this routine where, couple times a week, I make it back to the warehouse for lunch. What this means is that I bust my butt getting ahead on the job, then put some serious speed on the truck so I can roll in casually around noon. I hang out at the van, eating soup and sandwiches and trying out the new cookies, while Jess describes her latest troubles with the carburetor or pumps me for advice about renovations. She's doing everything in stages. Soon as she gets some money saved up, she puts it right into 2x's or wallboard or ply or whatever, and soon as she gets the supplies, she's needing advice. Some days, me and Gil and Tom, too, are standing round explaining things like how to get a contractor's discount or arguing over where you can get good lumber cheapest.

If I'm alone, I eventually says, "Maybe I should just come by and take a look," and she says, "Call your mom and tell her you won't be home for dinner." Everything's easy, and before I know it, I'm spending a lotta time and more energy on the handyman special. One weekend, I borrow a jackhammer and spend two days loosening my kidneys cutting a drain around the basement. That lets out the seepage water and dries up the cellar pretty good. The next weekend, we lug a half dozen steel lally columns down so we can support the beams and straighten out the floors. We spend the better part of Saturday in the dank and the dark, drilling holes in the cement floor with a rented mortar drill. We bolt everything down good and shim between the beams and the joists to keep the floors quiet. Then there's wall cracks, you bet, from old age and the shifting floors and our repairs down below, cause Lesson One of an old house is that everything's grown together. We use up boxes of sprackle and tubs of joint compound filling in the damage. On some walls the plaster's completely shot, turned to cornmeal, crumbled under the paper, which means whacking everything off with scrapers and prybars. We fill the dumpster with chunks of plaster and lath and messes of wallpaper. Then we slap insulation in the cavity and it's time for wallboard. Course that's really a two man job; no way Jess can manage herself. I know that, though she doesn't. She's been watching the home shows where every cut comes out perfect and they throw money around like the national debt. She's got this idea of using deadmen and braces, and I gotta tell her she's crazy. That's how come I spend an August weekend that's hotter than hell humping wallboard. Mom observes that I'm spending a good deal of time over at Mrs. Simeone's, and Dad says that investing in a house is a smart thing for Jess to do.

Anyway, being around as much as I am—too much from Mom's point of view—I can't help noticing the house roof. In a word, it's shot, worse than the barn, all lumpy and mossy and showing ribs like a skinny mutt. One evening, we're sitting out at the picnic table eating fried chicken and corn on the cob. A back door cool front's come down and a nice breeze is blowing through the overgrown lilacs. Times like this when we're sitting around tired and content, I get feeling soft about Jess. I'm about to reach over and take one of her thin brown hands—nicked and bruised and capable-looking with bits of joint compound under the nails—when Leon climbs down from the table and starts marching around the yard the way he does. Only now there's an innovation. Jess's face lights up and she nods toward him.

"Hear that?" she says.

I do. Leon is kinda humming to himself. A monotonous phrase, over and over, from one of the kiddie records he likes. No big deal, but it's the nearest he's come to talking, and I can see his mom's hopes rising. Naturally, I don't feel quite the same delight. Though I smile and nod, I want to get off the subject soonest, so I says, "I don't like the look of that roof."

"It doesn't leak," Jess says. What with the van and Leon and drainage and wallboard, she's working her ass off and I think she's getting her fill of repairs and renovations.

"Not that you know," I says. "You can't see what's going on under the shingles. And whatever it is, it's not good, since there's a pile of moss."

"I'd hoped to get another winter out of it," she says doubtful like. "What do you think?"

"I'd do it tomorrow if it was mine."

"I don't know," she said. "It's not a big roof, but Capple's told me a couple thousand."

"That's for Capple's," I said. "Do it yourself you'll need ladders, ply, 10 squares of shingles, nails, flashing—altogether do it for six hundred maybe. No more'n a thousand tops."

She thinks it over. We've spent the whole afternoon with joint compound and tape, finishing off the living room, and the inside of the house is beginning to look pretty good. Nothing's painted yet, but the rooms have lost the look of age and neglect. They smell of pine boards and joint compound instead of mildew and old dust and mouse shit, and they suggest possibilities, the way new rooms and new things do. Jess loves that. She stands in each room as it's finished and pivots around and smiles. Sure, the floors have to be done and all the painting and some of the trim, but the shell is there, and she says over and over, "This looks so good. I can't believe we've done it."

That's what she says, but I know what she means. What she means is that she's starting over and everything is hopeful again. I understand that and there are times when I feel the same way; when I think I can "leave Canada" and never go back.

I look over at Jess and smile. Her hair's still damp from the shower, and something about the way it curls back from her wide, smooth forehead leads me to say, "I could borrow a couple ladders from work for the weekend."

"Could we do it in a weekend?" She's alert all at once. I gotta say she's not afraid of hard work. Jess goes at everything with a great, untidy rush, and she knows what she wants. I almost think it's her hopeful, enthusiastic energy that got me. Though she's damn pretty and cooks like a chef, maybe chow and aesthetics wouldn't of been enough for me to put my ass on the line. The energy is something else. Jess is kinda like an unexpected current. If you've been making headway, you'll fight through it, but if you're drifting along, going nowhere in particular, or if you've shipped your oars and have your motor off, you're caught for sure.

"For the main roof?" I says. "Two weekends, tops. Do one half at a time in case of rain, and you'll have no problem at all—unless there's something wrong with the rafters. Did Chapple's check the rafters?"

"They're okay. We need plywood, though."

"Underlayment, sure, you need that with the asphalt shingles. You'll need help with that. But shingles are dead easy once you're shown how. I can teach you shingles. The porch roof you can do anytime. It's pretty low."

She watches Leon for a minute without replying, and I study her with lust and melancholy. I'm getting awful good at mixed emotions. Then she says, "You've been so kind, Jeff. I can't ever thank you enough."

"Naw," I says. "It's been fun. I'd just be drinking beer and messing around otherwise."

She smiles like she's thinking about that. "You've been a good friend," she says. "To Leon, too. Other guys don't understand Leon. Some of my cousins, even my brother, doesn't understand Leon."

"Leon'll be okay," I says. This is my hope and my fear. You see how things work out? There's always a pattern somewhere but it's never quite the one you expect.

"I know he will," she says. "Everyone else has doubts. We know better don't we?" When she touches my hand, I turn it over and grasp her slim, warm fingers. I can see she's come to a decision, but though I feel my heart jumping and this kinda lazy heat sliding south, everything's on hold while Leon is around.

The weekend of the shingles is different. For starters, Leon is sent to Jess's Mom's house for a sleep over. Leon's uncertain he wants this, cause my truck's already in the drive with ladders and tarps. There's a big new pile of ply and shingles in the barn, too, and Leon can see well as anyone that this is some big, interesting project. He's dancing round my truck, humming like he does all the time now, and as I'm taking out my toolbox and my work belt, I look at him and he looks back. This time the bright, empty eyes are occupied; I realize he's not just a lens anymore, and, for this weird instant, I can see that he's got himself in the same sort of bind as I have. If he doesn't talk, he's outa one sort of problem, but he's into another. Like now, he's desperate to know about all this neat stuff, but he's being packed off to his granny's.

"You'll have a nice new roof when you get back," I says to him.

He's beginning to hum louder and turn in circles, preparing to make trouble, when Jess comes out, her thick hair pulled back, her pretty legs 90% visible between a pair of work boots and her khaki shorts. She scoops Leon up and starts whirling around with him before he can work up any grief.

"Who's sleeping at Gramma's like a big boy?" she asks. She gives him his little case and she's almost sold him the idea by the time her mom arrives in the big Chevy.

Gramma kisses Leon and picks him up. "He'll be fine," she says to Jess. Then she turns to me and says 'hello'. Mrs. Portinari's not big on me. She was real partial to Andre for one thing and for another I'm not Catholic and for a third she's afraid Jess is going to break her neck with ambitious home repairs.

"You'll watch her on the ladder," she says now and Jess rolls her eyes.

"Ma!" Jess says.

"Never knew when to stop," Mom goes on. "She'd try anything, same as her cousins. You're used to heights, I know, but she isn't."

"It's not even a full two stories, Ma," Jess says.

"These are the best ladders," I says, "1-A's. Solid as a rock. Not like the ones you buy down at the hardware. You don't need to worry, Mrs. Portinari."

"Well, you know," she says, "Jess is still my baby. So you be careful with her."

"Ma," Jess says in exasperation, "Jeff's helping me as a favor. I knew you didn't want me on the roof by myself."

"There you see," says Mrs. Portinari. "There you see how I got white hair." But she laughs now and pats Jess on the shoulder, before she carries Leon away, wiggling and squirming, because he can see that, yes sir, there is going to be something worth watching.

Jess waves good-bye, and we start hauling out the ladders and getting set up. I'm up on the roof checking things out when Jess climbs up and peeks cautiously over the edge.

"You been on a roof before?" I says.

She shakes her head.

"Jesus, you're not scared of heights, are you?" I hadn't thought of that and I should of, seeing as I'm not fond of much over twenty feet or so, myself.

"I don't think so," she says, but I have to give her a hand up. She stands for a minute getting her bearings while I imagine the worst.

"Everything looks different from here," she says and then she smiles as she looks down into the green tops of the trees in the yard and in the Holbein's next door and over to the bright patchwork of corn, pumpkins, and Christmas trees in the fields beyond.

I'd forgotten that shift in perspective. "Best not to look down," I says.

"But it's wonderful," she says. "I never knew. I'll have to come up here when I want to get away from things."

That makes me laugh cause I can kinda see her sitting up here with her recipes and her home repair books, looking strange and not caring if she does.

"So what do you think," I says. "You up for scraping?"

"I think so. If I had something to put my feet on."

"Start on the ladder," I says, "til you get used to the idea."

I take a flat, heavy shovel and give her an edger. We pry up the old shingles, sending them rattling down onto the clean-up tarps in a mess of asphalt crumbs and dust. It's hot but there's enough wind to rustle the maple leaves, and pretty soon we're into the rhythm of the work, which is good because you've got to concentrate on a roof. At the same time, this isn't quite like working with Frenchie, either. There's an unspoken promise hanging over the day that I feel when I look down and see Jess's quick smile or when I look up and see the curve where her long muscular legs disappear into her rolled up shorts.

We whack through the asphalt shingles—two layers, it turns out. Underneath's tarpaper, so brittle it crackles, then a layer of wood shingles, patched and cracked and almost as black as the asphalt. The wood shingles splinter and the nails pop and screech and pretty soon we both look like raccoons from the dust round our eyes. It's eleven before we're down to the wide spaced boards that act as nailers. Through the gaps we check out old pink and yellow attic insulation gone grimy with dust and cobwebs, dead wasps, mouse droppings, and half eaten nuts.

Jess isn't sure of her footing once the roof's opened up, so I send her down to load up the dumpster. I check out the boards and the rafters and get ready for the plywood; I've got the layout already planned. With Jess doing the cuts, I muscle the sheets up onto the roof, and we get the side half covered by mid afternoon when we break for a late lunch. Jess unplugs the power saw and stretches her stiff arms, and we use the garden hose to slop water onto our hot faces and itchy arms and to wash off the worst of the dust and grit.

She's left ham and cheese sandwiches in the fridge, and we have those with potato chips and a big slab of watermelon and a jug of iced tea. Afterwards, we sit for a while in the shade and the breeze, admiring the clean blond squares of plywood against the old gray-brown rafters and blackened nailers.

"I really like this," she says. "You can see your work, know what I mean?"

"Something solid," I says.

"Cooking's great," she says, "but then it's eaten up and gone."

"Your cooking is anyway," I says.

"Like I was really happy when I bought the van," she says. "It was an accomplishment. Something solid."

"And now a house," I says, and I get up cause it's all getting too domestic and we have to get the ply finished and the roof covered.

She wiggles her shoulders; she's not used to roofing and I can guess what she feels like.

"I was never so stiff as when I started with Frenchie and his dad," I says. But Jess grins and puts her leather gloves back on and says she'll make it.

She finishes the cuts and helps me haul the last few pieces onto the upper part of the roof. I put in a few nails to hold the sheets in place and chalk snap lines so we know where the rafters are. Then we start nailing everything solid, hammers going in a steady syncopated rhythm that knocks fine dust out of the rafters and sets the ply vibrating under our feet. The sun's come round to our side now. My t-shirt's sticking to my chest, and I can see the sweat running down Jess's face and staining her back. The hammers and nails get slippery, too, and Jess bruises her thumb when she misses a nail. She shakes her hand and swears, and I reach over to take her hand and run my tongue around the chafed and swollen knuckle. I get thinking about any number of interesting interruptions, and it's just as well we're still on the roof, cause we've got a lot to get done.

The sun slides down and the grass below gets bright as a golf green before we've finished. We drag a blue tarp up over the bare plywood, then pull down the ladders and carry them to the barn. Jess staggers a little as she sets down her end. She looks very flushed.

"It's the heat," I says. "Drink some water. Or better yet, a beer. Got any beer?"

"There's some of your Rolling Rock."

I get a couple out of the fridge and a glass of water, too, and we sit down on the porch. Jess drinks the water, then a little beer and sits holding the cold can against her forehead.

"We'll go out for a burger," I says, "Or a pizza."

"I've got one ready," she says. "It's in the freezer."

"You shouldn't have bothered," I says, "when you're working all day."

"I'm never tired cooking." She pauses for a moment, then says, "Sometimes, I get worried about things, you know, or upset about stuff, I get in the kitchen and then I'm fine. I sometimes get up in the middle of the night and make cookies or soup or start bread."

"You worried about the house?" I says. "Don't be. It's going to be fine."

"No. Well, a bit about the house—it's needed more money than I expected. It's Leon I really worry about."

"He'll be all right." I hope. Whenever she starts talking about Leon, guilt comes down like a club.

"He'll be all right, but he'll be different. He's always been different," she says now, and I admit I'm surprised and interested, too.

"He was always real quiet, real watchful, different from my sister's babies."

"He's going to be smart," I says. "You watch him with tools."

"I know that now," she says. "I didn't always." She leans back against the pillar and stares up toward the top of the maple trees. She's got this almost perfect profile, except for a little bump in the middle of her nose. Even with her hair all wet with sweat and the garden hose, she's the next thing to gorgeous. "I did a lot of stupid things right after Andre died," she's saying. "Everything fell apart at once, know what I mean? My life just got outa control. I'd be out half the night drinking then have to take sleeping pills to get to sleep. Or else I couldn't get out of bed at all, wouldn't go anywhere or see anyone. They had me on tranks, too. It's a wonder I'm not crazy still."

"I know about being crazy," I says, but that's as far as I dare go.

"Worst of it was, when I started coming out of it, I panicked, thinking about birth defects, about problems for the baby." She shakes her head. "Then Leon arrived and was different." She looks at her hands and turns them over and over. "I was real nervous and impatient with him at first. I wasn't always good with him. I wasn't always good to him."

I can't imagine Jess hurting anyone, especially not Leon, but then again, what do any of us know? She probably can't imagine me popping Michelle in the jaw, and her hitting her head and everything following just the way it did, either. "You've got the touch with him now," I says. "Now's what's important."

She nods but she gets up abruptly, like she's already said too much. "I'll put the pizza in and get a quick shower."

I drink another Rolling Rock before it's my turn in the big, square, unimproved bathroom that's dark and damp and has a tub with claw feet and a funny looking shower attachment. One of the remodeling guys I know says there's cash in old fittings, and I think I must remember to tell Jess that. Also about the thick vine climbing over the bathroom window which'll rot the clapboards for sure. At the moment, the leaves give the room a kind of nice greeny light, and, through the gaps, I catch little glimpses of the back yard. I smell Jess's shampoo and the hot steam from her shower and the musty smell of old linoleum, old pipes, and old plaster.

I finally get the dirt and roof grit and sawdust washed away, and I'm cooling off under lukewarm, when I see Jess moving across the yard. Through the gaps in the leaves, she looks tiny and far away, like a sharp, clear Polaroid. She's got her hair wrapped up in a towel, and she's wearing a light blue shirt and little white shorts. She hangs our work clothes over the wash line, then takes off the towel and shakes out her hair and begins drying it in the sun. That's it right there. It's like a switch's been pushed. I'm her good friend and I understand Leon and everything's under control one minute; the next, I can hear my heart over the sound of the water, my head is swimming, and I'm right back to where I was that night she sat in my truck and talked about marrying Andre Simeone.

I reach down and turn off the shower. I grab the first towel that's handy, run it over my back and legs and step into my jeans. I walk barefoot down the wide, uneven boards of the hall to the kitchen. Jess has come back in by this time, and she's starting on salad stuff with one of her big, lethal looking knives. I can't go a step further. I lean against the casement. I feel the edge of the wood and dampness on my chest and water dropping onto my shoulders and a funny feeling in the back of my throat. Jess turns around and doesn't say anything. Then she puts the knife down and steps toward me. The moment her arms brush my sides, my heart dissolves, and I feel I'll love her forever.

Her bedroom's downstairs cause the upper rooms are a wreck. We're lying crosswise on the bed and her long, damp hair is hanging over the edge. I've still got one foot caught in my jeans and this kinda red and purple glow is fading behind my eyes. It's hot and quiet and when I move my head I can see the bars of Leon's crib against the window. For an instant, I expect to see his big, clear recording eyes, then Jess moves her head and I touch her arm and I realize the whole house smells like a pizzeria.

"Christ," says Jess, "I forgot the dinner."

She hops up and runs into the kitchen. I hear the oven open and a metallic rattle, then her feet slapping against the boards.

"A bit overdone but edible," she calls. "We'd better eat."

I don't answer. She hasn't turned on the lights, and when she comes back, she's a dim shape in the doorway until she steps right into the room and the last of the sun stripes pink over her breasts and her long, slim thighs. "Dinner will get cold," she says.

I sit up and catch her waist. "I like cold pizza," I says.

That's how we're delayed with dinner til after 9 p.m. We sit at the kitchen table, laughing and easy, then go to sleep in her bed to the sound of the tarp rippling in the night wind.

CHAPTER 12

Before I know it, I'm living in the old house with Jess and Leon. I'll skip the arguments with Mom and the silences from Mrs. Portinari and the advice from Dad, which dampen the atmosphere without changing my mind. The way it happens is that after the main roof gets done, we decide to tackle the porch. A bad move. My foot goes through five minutes after we start stripping shingles, and there I am stuck up to my knee in rotten wood and swearing like a son of a bitch. Jess stops laughing and helps me out and then starts to cry when we see the whole story, which is a couple rafters gone spongy with seepage and eaten out by ants. We make a quick trip to the lumberyard for 2x6's and use all the math we've got between us working out the pitches and getting the angles cut. Any mistake means money she hasn't got, so this is high wire stuff as well as a shit pile of work, and we're both frazzled by the time we get the hip roofs on the sides just right.

That's not the end of it, either; this project's got more legs than an octapus. With all the water that had been getting in, there's rot everywhere, so we gotta strip the fascia and soffit, then redo the flashing and basically rebuild the whole damn thing, including the bead board ceiling. That means working overhead, which is a bitch, anyway, cause your arms ache, and worse in hot weather cause the sweat's running in your eyes. By the time we're finished, we know a hell of a lot more about each other than when we started. Not all of it's good but most of it's tolerable, and we've come to an understanding.

One Saturday I buy a load of wallboard at the discount and haul it back home. We hack the old paster off a couple rooms upstairs and discover there's no insulation. Not that we'd really expected any, but what we're looking at basically is a thousand dollar-a-winter heating bill, so we gotta start pulling lath. I get a bunch of fiberglass batts cut price from a contractor with an overstock, and we have a couple weekends of breathing dust and wrestling fiberglass and feeding the semi-permanent dumpster parked by the drive. After that, the wall board takes a couple weekends of twelve hours straight, and taping the seams takes a few more. By the end of September, Leon has a room of his own with a grown up bed, and we're finishing ours across the hall. Columbus Day weekend, we're both off. We disassemble Jess's bed and take out the drawers of her big oak bureau. Frenchie comes by and after we carry everything upstairs, he calls Carla, his girl friend, a big blonde French-Canadian. She comes over with a bottle of red wine, and Jess makes a king-sized lasagna and we settle down to some serious overeating.

Afterwards, I'm sitting on the couch with one arm around Jess. The couch is a Portinari reject with a major league sag, so we're kinda balanced in the middle. The guests get the decent seats, my Grampa's old recliner and a wicker job Jess found at a tag sale. The tv's set on a rejected footlocker. The only other furniture is a cut down kitchen table in front of the sofa. There's no rug, either, but the floor's newly finished oak and pretty decent except for a few patches where I had trouble controlling the sander.

Frenchie and me're watching the Jets on tv and the women are talking about the community college. Carla's boring on about getting an associate's in dental hygiene, and Jess is asking about scheduling and the food service and trying to figure the prospects for her van. Leon's got his blocks out and is building something complicated over in the corner, just far enough away from strangers for him to feel comfortable, but close enough to the set if anything exciting happens. He's three and a half now. No more diapers. Not too many tantrums. Still quiet as a mouse, so everything's OK on that front. Anyways, I'm sitting there and all of a sudden it strikes me, I'm settled. I'm sitting in a living room where I've put up wallboard and sanded the floors. I've got my arm around a woman who's been up on a rotten roof with me and been covered with plaster dust with me and sweated over demolition with me. That's a funny feeling. Not exactly sexy, but a total mind-body experience in other ways, and as Frenchie says when he leaves, "Things are looking pretty good."

I'm happy, that's the truth, though, sure, there are awkward moments. We're at Sunday lunch at Jess's folks this one time—a big step in itself—and in come Michelle's parents, both short and kinda stout in their Sunday clothes. They're smiling at everyone and acting totally normal, but I just about freak out.

"Jeff Woodbine," Jess says, and they nod and say hello, before they roost next to Mrs. Portinari and start yakking away. They gotta remember I was questioned. They gotta know that, but they're so busy catching up on family stuff with Jess's Mom that I might as well be on the moon. Only I don't believe it. It's all an act and, soon as I relax, they'll nail me. I watch them so hard that in between the salad and the spaghetti bolognaise, I get this urge to confess. I want to stand up and yell, 'It was me. I hit Michelle. We argued about big screen tvs and the C of FC and stock wastage, but it was really just a trick of the fucking universe'. The impulse is so strong I feel my legs start to shake, and it's all I can do to sit there, drinking red wine and nodding whenever Jess says anything.

Then I start to feel I'm being too quiet. Suspiciously quiet. I gotta say something, but my mind's a blank and I don't have any breath. I can feel Mrs. Portinari watching me over the rolls and the salad bowl and the big dish of green beans with bacon. Recently she's been making an effort to be nice for Jess's sake; at the same time, she's always watching for some excuse to dislike me more than she already does. Though I feel the sweat running down my back, I give with a big smile before I turn to her husband and mention that we're selling a lot of clapboard.

"The economy's still shit," interrupts Michelle's father, who works for the state highway department.

I can't really disagree, though I gotta say we're doing a lot of installing.

"That's renovation work," he says. He's like Michelle, always got a mouth and an argument.

"Sure."

"See, economy's shit. Good economy, they're doing new construction. That right, Sal?"

That's Jess's dad, Sal. Sal Senior. Her brother, who's seventeen, is Sal Junior. He's a big kid who's starting tight end this year for the Red Men.

"Sure. But renovation or new construction, they gotta have plumbing," Sal says. This is the family motto; Portinari Plumbing and Heating is the family business.

"Thing now is septics," Michelle's dad says, and I'm glad I fought the urge to confess, cause here's a guy who wants to discuss septic systems over spaghetti. He's going on about this new law up in Massachusetts where he has contacts. Rural and shore property has gone in the toilet, he says, with this new law about septic systems.

"Trouble is," Sal Senior says, "nobody's got the answer to septic systems. There's new technology coming. Gonna have to have it, but it's not here yet."

"Integrated sewage systems," says Michelle's dad. His name, I should mention, is Louie. "If they'd get some federal money in here instead of spending it on the welfare bums, we could have sewage hookups all through here."

"Lay a hell of a lot of pipe," Sal Senior says.

"Sure. Hell of a lot of pipe. Hell of a lot of trench work and road work along with it," says Louie. "It'd be the best public works deal since the interstate system."

"You and I wouldn't make anything out of it," Sal Senior says.

Ain't that the truth?

"Sure, there'd be graft," Louie says. He nods his head which is bottom heavy with jowls and a thick lower lip. "There's always graft. There's graft at Electric Boat. Right? There's graft with DOT. There's graft with the university construction, you bet. But none of that does us any good. Pipe, sewage construction, sewage treatment works, now that's a maybe. That's highway work, sure, cause where's the piping to run? That's me. And there's piping and connections. And that's you. Am I right?"

Sal says maybe, but the strain of talking economics with Michelle's dad is kinda getting to me, so I ask Sal Junior about the Red Men's Turkey Day prospects against Windham.

"Good," he says. "Good, if Kimbo's arm holds out."

Kimbo Sloane is the quarterback. A thin black kid with bandy legs and a rifle arm.

"Christ, I've got a bet on with Frenchie. What's wrong with his arm?"

"Tendinitis," says Sal Junior. "His old man's a carpenter. Kimbo's been helping him with framing."

"He coulda waited til after Turkey Day," I says, though I know this is unreasonable, cause you wanta do framing and get things closed in soon as you can.

"Running game isn't bad," says Sal Junior, and he starts going down their ball carriers for me. But now that we're talking Red Men, I'm thinking about Lynn Santorini, now Lynn Conklin, formerly the Number One Red Gal and about her wedding in July and the little party her friends threw afterwards down at the Gaelic Club. We were invited, of course, and Jess spent a couple days in the kitchen with batter and frosting and pastry tubes, making the cake.

I felt odd about the whole thing, like life was getting unnecessarily complicated. But Jess had played field hockey with Lynn and went to her wedding shower and all, so there we are on the hottest day of the summer squeezing into the Gaelic Club. The AC's turned up full blast, which is good cause we're all overdressed, and I've about sweat through my jacket getting the cake safely out of the truck and into the hall. Inside, I see a lot of old Red Men and some guys I remember from the parochial school teams. Soon as I get the cake down like Jess wants it, I leave her to fuss with the food and drift over to where Frenchie, Binky Liss, and Porky Rebol are hitting the beer. We start ranking on the parochial school teams, and they remind us of big loses to Windham, and pretty soon we're feeling the heat less and the music more.

About this time, the best man appears, red hair, goatee and glasses, wild madras jacket. He huddles with the DJ before he gets on the mike and introduces the new Mr. and Mrs. Conklin. Sean and Lynn come in from the hallway to whistles, applause, and hoots; the music comes up, some sorta smaltzy waltz or something, and Lynn says, "I can't dance to this crap". Everyone laughs, and the D.J. flusters around until he finds a Stones number that's almost as antique as the waltz. Lynn and Sean start moving on the dance floor anyways, and we stand around clapping until Sean says, "Don't leave us all alone out here", cause he's not the dancer Lynn is and he needs support. The best man gets up with a skinny gal with a long nose and a flaming pink dress and then the rest of us hit the floor and the party gets going.

Jess says, "Isn't she pretty? I love her dress." She's looking back at Lynn over my shoulder. "You know Trish? Down at the paint store? Trish made the dress for her."

"Yeah?" I says, cause I hardly notice dresses unless they are cut low enough to be interesting.

"Got a remnant at the Mill," Jess says, so there I am dancing with Jess, who I love, and getting all the details on Lynn's outfit, details that are irrelevant to my memories, which have more to do with the Red Gal's 100% butter soft upholstery than with her wardrobe. By the time the song ends, I feel the need of another beer. Lynn comes over and kisses Jess and says the cake is wonderful. Jess went all out with enormous frosting roses and lilies and bows, and now that I'm not worrying about dropping the damn thing or squashing the frosting or having a meltdown in the truck, I've gotta admit it's spectacular.

"I hate to cut it, it's so pretty," Lynn says. And everyone's ooing and aaaing until Binky Liss, whose idea of beauty is a double cheeseburger, starts chanting, "Cut the cake, cut the cake". The Gaelic Club manager comes out with a knife big as a sword, and pretty soon the cake's in pieces and we're licking frosting off our fingers and dancing and drinking and shouting across the room. Binky and a guy from St. Tim's get into a beer drinking contest and wind up barfing off the back porch. The bridesmaids take off their uncomfortable shoes and jackets and dance in their stocking feet, and Lynn's two kids blast back and forth between the hall, the kitchen, and the parking lot until even their doting gramma begins to look frazzled.

Near five o'clock, they start to cook hotdogs out in the parking lot. The beer kegs are about done, and the Gaelic Club's waitresses are serving coffee. I could do with some. I'm leaning up against the wall just south of the beer table. That's my geographic location. Psychologically, I've backed into the comfort zone where I've forgotten everything I've wanted to forget. I'm busy watching green and white streamers bend and twist in the draft from the AC when Lynn drifts over. Her hair is beginning to fall down over her ears, and she comes with a pink haze that's either around her or behind my eyes, one or the other.

"Great party," I says.

"We haven't done too much damage."

"You look great," I says, though I still have a fondness for her old Red Gal athletic gear.

She's had a few beers, too, cause I recognize the smile she gives me.

"We gotta dance," I says. "We gotta have a dance at your wedding."

"Something fast," she says over her shoulder to the D.J., who puts on Chuck Berry's "Johnny Be Good". We head out onto the floor, my head spinning and the Red Gal swaying, for what I know is the last time. Lynn's not as pretty as Jess, and she doesn't make the back of my throat hurt, but she sure looks good in motion.

"Sean's a lucky guy," I says to her, and she grins.

"You always make me feel good," she says.

"Always?"

"Close enough," she says.

"I'll remember that," I says.

She shakes her head now. "Best forget it," she says seriously. "This is my last good chance; I'm going to do this right."

"Sure," I says but I kiss her anyway, and when she leans against me for a minute, I see how easy it would be to screw up big time.

Then Lynn straightens up and looks me in the eye. "You oughta get married. You oughta marry Jess."

"I might do that," I says. In my present state of mind this seems like a new and brilliant idea, and going home in the truck, I ask her. She's driving cause I drained the last keg after that dance with Lynn, and maybe I haven't picked the best moment cause Jess shakes her head.

"You're wasted," she says.

"In vino veritas," I says. "I love you either way. I want to marry you."

"I'm not getting married again," she says.

We've never discussed this before, so I don't know how she feels. "Not again or not to me?" I says. Like I want an argument.

"Not to anyone. You marry a guy and he goes and gets himself killed."

"That's the goddamnedest reason," I says. "Look at Sean and Lynn."

"Right," she says. I realize she probably saw me dancing with Lynn. Given the way Slatertown operates, she probably knows the whole story with me and Lynn, anyway. "Listen, I'm careful," I says, but I've suddenly got no energy for discussion. What I'm feeling mostly is sleepy, and since Jess is driving extra slow and careful, I lean back against the seat. The next thing I know I'm in the dark with my head aching and my stomach sour and my shoulders stiff. I recognize the hay, horse, and engine smell of Jess's barn, and I climb out alone into a night full of stars and cicadas. That's the end of my first proposal.

So things are on hold, and I'm on my good behavior at the Portinari's for a kinda trial run lunch. Sal Junior has finished the Red Men's lineup, and I'm making the right kinda noises, when Mrs. P and Brenda and Michelle's mom start talking about Leon, who's just been caught disassembling an alarm clock.

"...needs a father," says Brenda, who doesn't have kids and isn't married and so qualifies as an expert on the homefront.

"I could just weep," says Mrs. Portinari. "When I think Andre never saw him."

The other two pick up on this like sidemen in a band. They've each got their own riff, conjuring up Andre, great guy, good shooting guard, almost war hero. Me, I got no hope against Andre, who's dead and buried with all his faults forgotten; I'm protestant and alive and dubious in more ways than they can imagine.

"Jeff has been very good for Leon," Jess says quietly. "And the house. Having a room of his own." She brushes her hair back behind one ear the way she does when she's nervous.

"No one's saying anything different," her mother says, "but I can't help thinking about his dad when fall comes. We found out four years ago next month. I'll never forget the day."

"Ma," says Jess.

"I cried for a week," says Brenda. She's got the psyche of a pit bull but prides herself on her sensitivity.

"We've had more than our share of sorrow," says Michelle's mom. She wipes her eyes and my stomach turns over, cause this is genuine. I'm not so sure about Mrs. Portinari. Sometimes I think she goes on about Andre as a way to get at me, and other times I think maybe she just really loved having him as her son-in-law.

"Andre was so clever," she says now. "What he wouldn't have done with that house."

Shit, I think. If Andre hadn't crashed, there wouldn't have been money for the house. And since he did crash, it's me that's working my ass off on it.

"Can we maybe change the topic?" I says, "cause you're upsetting Jess." I've got some other things in mind to say, too, but Jess squeezes my hand and I shut up.

"I know it's the time of year," she says in a shaky voice, "but I'm trying to move on." Jess stands up and pushes her chair back and starts picking up her plates and mine.

"That's my girl," says her dad. "You've done all right." He reaches over and pats her arm. Sal Senior is just the opposite of his wife. He's awkward and kind, while Mrs. P is little and clever with some agenda of her own going. "Why don't you leave Leon with us for the afternoon and have a little time to yourself?" Sal Senior asks.

Jess looks uncertain about this.

"Cathy's kids are coming by," her mom says. "Be good for Leon to have some company."

Jess nods and says okay, and I thank them for lunch and help her carry stuff to the kitchen. Jess stands by the sink for a minute like she's going to start on the dirty dishes and then she puts down the sponge and says, "I've got to get out of here." She strides into the living room to talk to Leon for a minute and then she's out the door and down the walk and wrenching open the door of the truck. I see she's half crying.

"Why the hell do they do that?" she asks.

"Maybe I shouldn't of come for lunch," I says. "Maybe that looks too permanent." Maybe this whole idea is crazy. Maybe I'm really pushing my luck. Maybe I'm not up for Sunday lunches from here to eternity with Mrs. P and Michelle's parents.

"I loved Andre but it's not as if he was perfect or anything," Jess says. "And it's not as if I don't have a life now. But Ma just goes on and on about him like nothing will ever be quite right again. What does that say about me? About us?"

"Hey," I says, "it's all right. You're making out just fine." And I put my arm around her. "You know how she is. It's the way she worries about you."

Jess wipes her eyes and blows her nose. "Yeah. Just sometimes it gets to me. Andre died at 21; I didn't."

I start the truck and drive until we get to the main street. It's beginning to rain now, and everything feels dull and heavy. "So, where we going? You want to go the movies or what? It's kinda wet to go to the park."

"There's nothing good on. I'm sick of gun fights and car chases."

"I still gotta turn one way or the other," I says.

"Go right. Go up to River Street," she says, "I'll take you to my favorite place."

I look at her. "I've known you all this time, and I haven't seen your favorite place?"

"I've been saving it," she says, "til we really needed it."

"We didn't need it the day I went through the porch roof?" I says. "Or how about the day we had to pull the upstairs lath?"

"It was too hot then," she says, but she's beginning to look more cheerful.

"Yeah, so what is this?"

"You'll see," she says and steers me through the little streets near the high school to an asphalt shingled colonial with a mess of greenhouses, sheds, and plastic covered hoops sprawled behind it. There's a funny looking black, yellow, and white cat with a bunny tail sitting on the porch and bundles of dried weeds hanging in the front window.

"This is it?"

"You've never been in here?"

"I've been by, sure. It's a nursery."

"You wait and see," she says as she climbs out of the truck into the chilly drizzle. "I love to come here. I used to bring Leon when he was still in his stroller. It's like another planet."

The dark office smells like dust and dried plants. Jess talks to the old guy at the desk for a minute and then takes my arm and we go down a couple steps into the light and warmth of a big glass house. There's plants everywhere, all different shapes and sizes. Little ones no bigger than a thumbnail are set out in flats on each side, and big ones with ears like elephants and queer furry skins roost on the big center tables. Complicated vines trail down to the floor, and pots of bright flowers hang under the beaded and dripping glass of the roof. It's like being in a jungle right in the middle of November: humid air, damp earth; water bubbling in a little fish pond and strange, soft blossoms opening everywhere.

"Don't you love the colors?" Jess says. We're looking at acres of begonias and enough orchids for a Mafia wedding. There's jasmine like a strong, expensive perfume and hibiscus unfolding pink and white. Lemon, orange, and grapefruit trees with real fruit shoot up toward the glass. Rows of camellias with waxy green leaves and big round buds are coming into ruffled red and white blossoms, and mysterious shrubs with dry, grayish leaves and lavender flowers lean over the narrow aisles. We wander around this weird indoor garden, past a couple women dickering over scented geraniums and a fellow measuring the topiaries to get just the right one. We squeeze by thick plants and thorny plants and duck under overhanging branches. Outside, it's serious rain now and cold; inside, it's permanent spring with the cool smell of fertilizer and the thick, sweet scent of pollen—another place entirely, where you get new and strange thoughts.

The last door leads into the biggest of the glass houses: flowers everywhere and perfume; mysterious fleshy shapes and twisted branches; gleaming, leathery leaves. We start down a narrow gravel path lined with big impressive shrubs and tables loaded with gardenias in bloom. We're all alone. Sunday lunch is history; Michelle's folks and everything else are a thousand miles away. Jess stops for a minute and touches a plant with sapphire flowers, and I stop, too, my throat aching with mysterious and complicated emotions. I put my hand on her thick hair and pull her into my arms and start to kiss her.

"It's nice here, isn't it?" she says between kisses. She sounds short of breath, and I says "yes" which is all I can say. I run my hands up and down her slim body and she says, "I love you, I love you", and I'm halfway lost in the jungle—the jungle of plants and emotions and strangeness, the jungle where only Jess knows the paths—before I hear the greenhouse door opening at the back. Damn scented geraniums and topiary are coming back through. Jess steps away and takes my hand. I bite my lip, and we don't say another word until we get back home and into our bed. And then I says, "Will you marry me?"

And she says, "Not right away. Not right away, I can't. But maybe later."

CHAPTER 13

Funny that we're ever surprised, seeing how often we get screwed by life. We fall in love with normal, that's what it is, and refuse to see normal's the exception, the stroke of luck, the winning Lotto ticket. I'll give you an example. I come home this one afternoon just as the sun drops behind the barn like a big red cinder. There's some early snow in the air, and I'm thinking maybe a sled for Leon and wondering whether Jess's tires can handle the winter. I got purely ordinary things in mind, so I'm surprised when I brake for the drive and see a big dark cruiser with state insignia.

First thing I think of is Jess and the damn van, an accident, a break-down, some sort of catastrophe. Then I'm thinking Leon and the cars that come screaming down the road and the neighbor's iced over pond and foam-mouthed raccoons psychotic with rabies. I go racing into the house, shouting for Jess. She answers me from the living room, where I find Lt. Stankus and Benny exercising their professional hard guy expressions and ever ready notepads. Stankus is tilting south on one end of the couch, Benny's perched on the wicker chair, and Jess is in the recliner with Leon. They all turn towards me, and there's silence for a beat before Leon starts to wiggle around in Jess's lap.

"Well," says Stankus, "this is a surprise. Isn't it, Benny?"

Benny nods, his face as yellow and cadaverous as ever. "Hadn't expected to see you here."

I think their surprise is phony, but you never know. Perhaps they had forgotten about me; perhaps they're amazed at this show of innocence; perhaps they've just realized I live dangerously.

"Christ, I thought there'd been an accident," I says to Jess. "Is everything all right?"

She nods her head. "They were hoping Leon would be talking," she says.

"We're counting on Leon to help us," Stankus says in this smooth voice that wouldn't fool a day old infant. It certainly doesn't fool Leon, who rears back and starts to shriek. I recognize the sound that used to greet me, the sound of a child scared out of his mind.

When Jess lets him down, he bolts up the stairs to his room. "You can see this isn't going to work," she says. "All you're doing is frightening him. He hasn't behaved like this in months."

Stankus gives with this sour face.

"Don't you see, he remembers you. He remembers all the tension and fuss," Jess says.

"He remembers us," Stankus says softly. "If he remembers us, he must remember the park, the perpetrator." He looks at me with his slow cold eyes.

Jess shrugs. "His doctor says he may not remember. The shock of it."

"Or may not say," says Stankus. He keeps looking at me like he's finding inspiration in my features. "Or maybe afraid to say."

"He doesn't say anything yet," I says. My voice sounds funny, like a voice out of some dream, where you'll do and say any damn thing and wake up surprised for sure by the consequences.

"He's how old? Past three?" asks Benny, sounding doubtful.

"He'll be four in March. He hums now and he understands everything," Jess says, defending Leon. "He just doesn't talk."

"I can see he's a bright little boy," says Stankus. "Don't you think so?" he asks Benny.

Benny sucks on his pen and nods his head. "A bright little boy. Maybe a little nervous." And his eyes, too, shift in my direction.

"It's no wonder he's nervous," Jess says. She's not as calm as she looks at first. Her eyes have gone very dark and she's twisting her fingers the way she does when she wants a cigarette. "With what happened and then all the questions and strangers since."

"He's our only witness in your cousin's death, Mrs. Simeone."

"He's a child, a baby. I don't want you questioning him again," she says quickly.

"Of course, not right away, but whenever he starts to speak..."

Jess shakes her head vigorously. "You're not going to mess with my kid again. It's not going to happen."

"I don't want to upset anybody," Stankus says, "but short of a confession, Leon's our only resource. That right, Mr. Woodbine?" And he shows a lot of his perfectly capped teeth.

"You always have a choice about hurting kids," Jess says. Lucky for me, she's totally focused on Leon and tuning out all the other implications.

I put my hand on her arm cause I can see her losing her temper.

"Perhaps a policewoman," Stankus says smoothly, although I can see he's not pleased. "He might be more willing to talk to a policewoman." And he gives me a look like he sees my whole life laid out.

"Perhaps," I says, and Jess says, "We'll see about that."

Out on the porch with me, the Lieutenant stops being subtle. "Settled in quite comfortably, aren't you?" His breath forms whitish puffs in the air and the boards of the porch creak under foot as he shifts his weight. Lt. Stankus has a way of getting in your personal space.

I don't answer.

"Nice old house. New roof, I see. Interior work. A serious interest?"

"What do you want?" I says.

"What I've always wanted: to nail your ass," he says, perfectly calm, impersonal almost, like this is just a job and not how he really gets off on life. "How much does Mrs. Simeone know any way? Not much, I'd guess. For some reason I never filled her in fully on our investigation. Perhaps I should. It might change her attitude. It might make her more willing to cooperate."

"Why don't you get the fuck out of my life," I says, fighting the urge to knock him off the porch. "You don't have a thing on me."

"We've got Leon," he says. "Leon had worried me. We'd been concerned about his abilities. But he'll talk eventually. Perhaps to a child psychologist, a trained pediatrician, someone who can gain his trust." He smiles slightly, his jaws all smooth and shiny like some fishy carnivore. "We'll see how you like that," he says and follows Benny over to the cruiser.

I watch them go out the drive and turn down the state road, taking normal life with them. I was afraid of this before Florida. Now it's a thousand times worse cause there's Jess and Leon and her folks as well as mine and complications everywhere. I feel a very strong need to jump in my truck and get a beer. Instead, I go on inside. I can hear Jess talking to Leon upstairs, and I want to put my arms around them both and tell them it'll be okay. But I know I can't, because something we'd carefully glued together is in danger of coming apart at the joints. I know that right away, and Leon does, too, though Jess does not.

Maybe if he'd been older, we'd have worked it out just to protect her. Maybe. But he's too young, so he shrieks and cries and wets his bed and acts up at the table. I try to avoid him. I start stopping for a brew with the guys after work. I resume Saturday dinners with my folks and bowling with Frenchie. Jess isn't too pleased, but things settle down, then, wham, the cops are back, accompanied by a gal with oversized glasses, a bright, artificial expression, and a big time vocabulary. She impresses the shit out of us with "trauma" and "repressed memory" and "therapeutic strategies" before producing a box of dolls for Leon, who's chiefly interested in how the hinges work and the top fastens. She doesn't see that right away, just bores on about "avoidance behavior" and "home vs therapeutic environments" and "stress", while Leon leans against Jess's knee and watches indifferently.

The fallout comes later, after Jess talks to the pediatrician at the clinic. She's got an absolute veto on any questions, the doc tells her, and from then on the door's shut to the troopers with or without their pet psychologist. Since Leon's out of reach of the law, I should be sitting pretty, but now the hangup's Michelle's folks. They want everything done whatever the cost, and they start putting the heat on Jess and turning family pressure up into the danger zone. The worst is the day her uncle comes over. It's a cold, dank Saturday and we've just come in from the bowling lanes, when Uncle Louie pulls into the yard. We'd gone out to avoid his wife, who calls every weekend and keeps Jess on the phone until she's nearly in tears. This particular Saturday, Jess finally runs out of patience, hangs up on her aunt, and says, "Let's get out of here."

So we hit the lanes and it's not a bad afternoon, cause Leon loves the automatic pin setters and the ball returns, and we're all in a pretty good mood, until, bingo, there's Louie getting out of his car.

"I'll handle him," I says, though the thought of talking to him about makes me sick.

"No," Jess says, "I got to talk to him about Aunt Vi. He'll be mad I hung up on her, but I got to explain what's going on."

She goes out on the porch, cause she doesn't want him in the house and I feel like a coward cause I'm glad I don't have to face him.

"You hung up on your aunt," Louie starts. I can hear him even with the door closed. "Your Aunt Vi's known you since you were in diapers and you hang up on her."

He's had a few and his voice's got this indignant whine that sends my better instincts south.

Jess's voice is a murmur beyond the door; she's trying to explain, to pacify. As if that's possible. Michelle's whole family are tapped into grievance as a permanent thing.

"What the hell're we asking from you anyway? A few questions...." I can see him though the window, short and stocky, a fireplug in a parka, his face red with the cold. He'd be ridiculous except for the tears in his eyes.

"You don't understand..."

"I sure as hell do understand, Missy. I understand that you don't give a goddamn about your cousin."

"What about Leon?" Jess says, her voice rising to match his. "You don't know what it does to Leon." She brushes back her loose hair and runs her hand nervously around her throat.

He starts shouting, now, really shouting, and I open the door and step out on the porch, just as he says, "Leon's always been odd. There's been something wrong with Leon from Day One and not a damn thing you can do about it. A few questions...."

Jess goes white and then red. "Michelle was an interfering bitch," she shouts. "Leon would be fine if she'd done what she said she was going to do and she's be alive, too. Don't you say anything about my son."

Louie runs through his whole vocabulary. He's so gross and yet so pathetic, that I focus on Jess and on calming her down, because I really don't want to deal with him. "Just get off our porch," I say to him. "This isn't going to do anyone any good." He swears for a moment, then turns and takes a step and slips on an icy patch. I grab his arm to keep him from falling, and he hits me in the side of the head, thinking I'm trying to push him off the steps.

I put up my hand and release him, and he almost fucking slips again—he's too mad to see straight. Now he starts screaming he'll sue us. "I hope you have insurance, cause I'll sue you both. I tell you it would break Andre's heart if he saw you living with this jerk. A good Catholic girl."

"Hypocrite," Jess shouts back. "You don't give a damn about Leon, do you? You don't have to live with the consequences."

"Consequences!" he says. "Consequences! Your aunt loses her baby and you don't think there are consequences? What the hell's the matter with you since you start living with this dickhead?"

I start edging him to the car, not saying much, cause I don't entirely trust myself. At the same time, I'm sorrier than ever about Michelle, which makes me feel guilty about this certified asshole.

"Go see about Leon," I says to Jess, and she swears and says it's Louie's fault for upsetting him and that's what she tried to tell Aunt Vi who won't listen to anything. "I've been on the phone for hours with her and I can't stand any more. Tell her that," she shouts to Louie. "Tell her that. Nothing's going to change my mind. I'm sorry, sorry, sorry, but Leon comes first, no matter what you think!" She runs into the house and the door slams and Louie turns to me and holds up both hands like I might start beating up on him.

"I got nothing to say to you," he says.

"Great," I says.

"A young guy like you living off Andre's benefits," he says and spits on the ground.

I get him by the coat collar and turn him around and one, two, three, four steps to his car. He's hollering the whole time, but I open the car door and in he goes. I start to close the door, but he snatches at the handle and almost smashes my fingers.

"Don't come back," I says. "Leave Jess alone."

"With you," he says, and he gives this skeptical little grunt like he knows more than he's saying.

"What's it to you?" I says like I don't know better. "What the hell is it to you?"

"They'll get you yet, you little prick," Louie says like he hasn't forgotten anything and like Stankus has bent his ear. He starts up the car and backs up with a rush, then jerks the wheel and swings around so fast I gotta jump outa the way as he goes barreling by, his heavy face peeking over the steering wheel, his features all distorted with hate and frustration. When he gets to the street, he doesn't even brake; he just swivels out and accelerates away, leaving me cold in the January chill and full of weird emotions, including surprise. Surprise at Michelle's dad, who may be dangerous, and surprise again at Jess's passionate energy.

She has some other surprises for me, which I'll get to later, but watching her with her relatives and the troopers gives me a hint. Even Stankus gets battle weary, cause all of a sudden he and Benny start leaning on me at work: stopping by to see if I'm around, calling at odd hours so management knows there's something going on, turning up in the parking lot about the time I'm going home. All this attention doesn't do me any good, especially since the work load is down with the cold weather, and, right before the holidays, I get cut back to part time, though they let me keep on benefits. The cutback is only temporary, they say, but the way the winter's going, I'll be twenty-five hours a week through March, and if Stankus and Benny keep on my case, I'll be lucky to have a job at all.

By Christmas, every little expense becomes a crisis. We'd be totally broke if it weren't for the military survivors check. Jess gets obsessive about coupons and grocery specials, and I go dump picking instead of shopping the home centers. Leon gets an ear infection which just about wrecks us, and every time the van makes a funny noise, Jess panics. The only good thing about being on half time is that I can spend the other half lying under the van persuading the clapped out old junker to run. Financially, I'm right back where I was before I started at the Bargain Barn, and I'm remembering pretty clearly just how come things happened the way they did. I get down about that sometimes and stay out too late and drink too much and nearly screw up the best deal of my life.

That's how December is, anyway, with a break for Christmas which isn't too bad. Stankus and Benny must of been doing Toys for Tots or working some good cause, since they're absent the whole holiday. My dad makes Leon a little tool box and I buy him some small tools and package up some scrap lumber and that's okay. We find a tree out back, Jess makes cookies for all our friends, and we catch our breath and think things will get better. We're still hooked on normal.

New Year's Day, we wake up early, way too early: the heat's come on and the old furnace smells like the back end of a bus. I celebrate the new year down in the basement, but no amount of cleaning and tinkering can diminish the heavy, soiled odor of inadequate combustion. That night, Jess runs the figures. I check them over, cause she's not much at math, but the result's the same: there's no way we can replace the old burner, pay our taxes, and come up with the house insurance. We've got a choice between freezing and suffocating, and since Jess knows all about carbon monoxide poisoning, there's no doubt which we're going to choose. I tell her carbon monoxide never smelt that bad, but the furnace goes off and stays off. We shut up every room we don't need, pile sweaters on Leon, and rely on the wood stove to keep the downstairs liveable.

Right then our view of the world changes. Everything gets classed as burnable or not burnable. Dead branches, unpainted lumber, and downed trees stop being eyesores and start being cordwood. After we've scavenged the neighborhood, I get myself a permit to hit the woodlots in the state forest, and on the weekends Jess goes with me to load the truck. We bundle Leon into his snow suit and get out as soon as the sun's right up. Saturday and Sunday mornings are plenty busy in the forest with chain saws whining up and down the sections marked for thinning. Families fill station wagons and trailers and the back ends of old sedans, while, along the logging road, guys stand by their pickups, taking cigarette breaks and lying about the deer season.

Wood cutting's hard, sweaty work in the cold, but on those noisy mornings in the forest, Leon is almost back to normal. With me, too; I'm once again the master of tools and his pal. He hums along with the saw, rhumm, rhummm, rhummmm, and watches it cut through the logs with a greedy and concentrated expression.

When I've cut enough to fill the truck, I lock up the saw and show him how to put on the goggles and the ear protectors. Leon grins the way he does when he's got something really interesting going and stamps his feet and jumps around like a demented elf in his red ski hat and mittens. Then, real quick, he's all business. He sets up a small log and braces his feet just the way I do and picks up a stick and starts growling rhummm, rhummm, like he's working the chain saw.

"That's right," I says. "Feet well out of the way." And I show him how to hold his arms. When I turn around, I see Jess watching us both. Her face is red from the cold and her hair is blowing in her eyes. She's so pretty and so worried that my heart turns over with wanting things to be right for her. When she catches my eye, she shakes her head. "If they'll only leave him alone," she says softly. "He's fine, if they'll only leave him alone." They meaning the troopers and their assistants, but also certain Portinari relatives who've tried to talk to Leon.

"Yeah," I says. I know it's true. All the tension and anxiety reminds Leon of what he's trying to forget—or of what he really doesn't remember except as an unfocused and lingering fear. Every time he's questioned, every time the family zooms in on him, he makes trouble for days afterwards, especially for me, and I'm starting to wonder whether it would make any difference if I left, moved out, put some more space between us. Maybe he'd be okay. Or maybe they'd still keep after him, and maybe he'd remember and then where would I be?

That's the kinda stuff that creeps into my mind whenever things get too much, when Jess and I get to quarreling or when Leon throws his food or bangs his head on the floor or starts shrieking the way he does. There are moments when I'm tempted to leave her, to head out, to sell the truck and buy that Harley and get my butt south of the snow line. I'm tempted but I don't do it, because soon as I start making the actual plans and calculations, I'll see the way she looks at Leon, so full of hope, fear, and love, or I'll hear her laugh in spite of all the accumulated shit or feel her breath against my cheek in the night. Then I can't imagine leaving, or rather, I can, I can feel the great empty space of not having her, of absence, of loss. Although I can see the hopeless stupidity of it, I'm realize I'm in love with her, and there are times like the visit to the greenhouses, when I understand the doors she's opened for me and what she's added to my life and how she brings out the best in me. And then there's Leon, who I really have come to understand, no kidding. Leon's jealous of me and anxious about me and admires me and relies on me. Without doing anything special or deliberate, except walloping Michelle one, I've become responsible for Leon.

CHAPTER 14

We survive the winter with the usual minimum wage improvisations: late bills, cheap dinners, second hand clothes. Jess worries about the bills and power washes recycled sweaters, but cheap dinners are a challenge. She gets all enthusiastic about the food coop, which is full of veggie types fussing over fiber intake and pesticide residues. Like they're going to live long and prosper and die with pure intestines. I go along to lug sacks of dry beans so that she can convert those farts in a bag into the legume du jour, which is the Frenchie way of saying beans for dinner. We get beans a la French and beans Chinese and beans Thai and beans Tex-Mex and beans real Mex. Sure, she's a genius cook, but there are days when I sneak out at lunch and blow money at the diner just to get something that used to run on hooves.

Still, I gotta say that beans, delays, and discounts keep us going. The weird thing is that the real grief begins in the spring, when I'm back on installations, Jess is selling food at the community college, and our money worries have lightened up. This time the trouble is Leon.

On the surface, we're cool. He tags along when I'm working and keeps out of sight when I'm not. He's pretty good about meals and bedtime, so I rarely have to yell at him, and when Jess is gone with the van, he stays with her mom. That's how we work it out, if you can say a grown man and a speechless kid can work anything out. Underneath, of course, there's other stuff going on: the screaming fits, the occasional tantrum, the moments of deep, bitter rebellion.

"Just his age," my mom says. I'm not so sure, especially when he fixes his recording eyes on me. He still does that. The little person behind them vanishes and you can almost hear the wheels and gears turning and everything going down on some invisible spool of tape. He does that when he's studying a new tool or a new machine and he does it sometimes with me. I suppose I was just unlucky. An ordinary kid would of remembered straight out or forgotten entirely and that's the end of it. Leon's different. He's gotta study everything; he's gotta know; he's going for the meaning of life. Even that weird child psychologist couldn't get over how he'd examine the hinges on the toy box or fiddle with the joints of the dolls. What I've done is given Leon the biggest problem of his life, and he's gonna keep onto it until he knows. That's one thing.

The other thing is talking. He's got himself in a bind, and he's sure sick of it now. But with Stankus and Benny and Michelle's folks and nosey relatives, he has to keep quiet. He's committed himself, and it's getting him down. Instead of asking for things like a normal kid, he's gotta do some kind of war dance, and when things are too much for him, he falls back on screaming and crying, which he knows is baby stuff. You might not think his mind works like that, but you don't know Leon's silences and his rages and his powers of concentration.

I don't, either, not right away, and when I first realize what's coming down, my main thought is to cover my ass. It's a Saturday morning, I remember that, warm for March, one of those sudden spring days before winter's really over. They got some special open day over at the college, and Jess is doing the coffee and refreshments and all excited since it's her first real catering deal except for friend and neighbors. I'm out back, tidying up the woodpile and splitting logs. The sun's starting to warm up and the smell of saw dust and wood chips and damp earth is real nice.

Leon helps me pile kindling for a while. He likes to see the logs split and crows with satisfaction when the wedges do their work. Then he gets tired and goes to mess with his own tools in the barn. Toward lunch time, I put away the saw and the ax, check the mailbox, and get washed up. I'm putting on a clean sweatshirt when I realize something's different. I don't know what. But there's a kind of detector you develop around kids.

"Leon?" I calls. No answer. I go out to the barn. Nothing. I call again. Not that Leon ever answers, but there's no sound of running feet, either.

I check the loft and, coming back down, I take a look out the cob-webbed side window. Leon's crouched by the big pile of sawdust and chips, playing with one of his little metal trucks. He's loading the dump-er with damp sawdust and running it over to a new pile he's got going. He has this little car out too, and after a trip with the sawdust, he brings the car around a sharp turn on his imaginary highway and smashes it into the truck. "Boom!" he yells. "Boom! Got ya!"

My chest constricts the way it does when I almost hit a dog on the road and sends my heart rebounding at double speed.

Leon sets his truck back upright and sends it toward the little car. "Get out of my way. Over you go! Boom!" He laughs. I guess now it was an ordinary kid's laugh, but at the time, it's got all these sinister implications. "Outa my way!" Leon yells at the car. I can hear Michelle in his voice, and when the car bounces over, I see stroller wheels revolving and the kid tipping out on the walk and everything that happens afterwards.

With all this, it takes me a minute before I'm mentally back in the barn. I'm standing there, thinking he's got to know, he's got to remember, and, all at once, I understand he really can talk and my stomach seizes up like a bad gear. For a few minutes I don't know what to do. I'm trying to figure all the implications, but since I don't want to face any of them, I hustle out the door and round back where I says to Leon, "Didn't you hear me calling?"

He looks at me, real innocent.

"We gotta get lunch ready for Mommy," I says. The funny thing is I'm waiting for him to answer and dreading it and yet one part of me is kinda hoping at the same time.

Leon runs the car in a circle around the truck and makes with automotive noises. Then he picks them both up and smiles and looks at me and kinda glances over at the barn and the window. You know how a cat or dog can tell you stuff without saying a word? That's what Leon does. He tells me he knows I was watching him; he tells me he knows I heard him talking to himself.

I should of called him on it; I should have of said, "Won't Mommy be pleased." Instead, I'm thinking Seattle or Denver and what my chances are and wondering how long he can keep quiet—and why he has kept quiet, until the possibilities just start multiplying like rats.

Leon hops up without a care in the world and starts humming to himself and doing little dance steps. At lunch I don't eat much, what with watching Leon and listening for the van. I'm figuring that's it; soon as she comes home, he'll start rattling away, and the first thing he'll say is "Jeff hit Michelle" or maybe "Jeff hit the woman", and some major league shit'll hit the fan. That's what I'm thinking, but when Jess comes home, Leon runs out just like usual. He hauls her over to see the sawdust pile he's made and demonstrates his truck route with sound effects. Otherwise, not a peep. Maybe it's just my guilty conscience that I keep thinking he's watching me and that every now and again he looks over toward the barn window and smiles.

So Leon and me, we've got secrets from Jess. I got a serious desire to be outa the house and outa the atmosphere which is closing in like fog but twice as heavy; at the same time, I want to keep an eye on Leon. I find myself creeping around the yard when he's playing and listening outside the living room door when he's watching tv or building with his blocks. I want to catch him talking again; I want to have it out with him. At the same time, I don't want to bring it up; I don't want to give him any ideas.

Meanwhile Jess's got spring fever and making plans. She wants to rent a rototiller and cut out a big garden. She wants to make cold frames, too, and a pen for some chickens. Plus, she's saving every penny for the down payment on a new van, and, come weekends, she's after me to go with her to look at the second hand wheels advertised in the shopper and the auto sections.

Sometimes when we're out—with Leon, too, cause a trip to a car lot is as good as the circus for him—I'll catch a glimpse of us reflected in a showroom window. We look like a nice, normal absolutely unreal family, and I'll start thinking how easy things would be if Leon was different or if Leon was some how not there.

That's how easy evil sneaks up on you. The business with Michelle, I feel bad about it, but it's not eating my gut. I'm sorry it happened cause it's just so much shit for everybody, but I don't take it personal. Leon's another matter. One minute he's sitting up beside me listening to an engine, and I can see he's cute, a great kid with this fantastic ear for motors; the next, I'm thinking things would be a whole lot easier without him. I'm thinking about the kid who got run over by a truck last week, or the one in Thompson who took meningitis and died; I'm thinking fluky, no fault stuff like that.

Sure, I raise hell if I see Leon playing too near the road or messing about with the saws, but you can see what's in my mind, and once an idea's in your mind you don't know how far it will go or how much territory it'll take over. Look at the things people do, like the guy who's trying to ski to the South Pole. They run flights to the South Pole now, they run charter tours, for Christ's sake, but here's this fellow off on skis hauling a sled behind him. That's what I mean. There's no point and yet the idea's overrun his mind so that he can't do something sensible like taking up bowling or farming avocados or raising pigs. I'm just at stage one with Leon. The idea's in my mind, all right, but it isn't the only idea, and I'm still uncertain whether it's going to take over or not.

I don't know what would of happened if things had gone on. Maybe I'd of split in half and never gotten the parts together or left Jess and run away to points west or done something I don't even want to imagine. As it turns out, when the storm comes, events go to warp speed, and I don't have time for ideas at all. I'd really like to blow right by the storm and a whole lot of later stuff, too, but I got so many daily reminders, there's no way. So we got to skip ahead to early April, when the long, cold spring suddenly turns hot, too hot for the cold front that comes screaming in with torrential rains and thunderstorms and the first documented tornado we've had in twenty years. The weather guys and gals go on about it for days afterwards, but at the time, all we know is that a sultry day turns black about two o'clock. Me and Tom don't start another side of clapboards, and I pick Leon up at his Gran's before three.

Mrs. Portinari notices and wonders have my hours been cut back again? She says she's all worried, even though I know she's not, cause it's a chance for her to remember Andre and to mention what a good provider he was and how reliable. I just point to the sky so I don't say something I'll regret and put Leon in the truck. He's a little hyper going home, bouncing around and humming. I don't usually pick him up and never early; this is something out of the ordinary and Leon's not sure he likes it.

By the time we get home, the rain's started, so I figure I'll do some work on the stair rails we've been repairing. I get the little pry bar and a mallet and pliers and start knocking out damaged spindles and yanking old nails. Leon gets his tool kit, too, and sets up higher on the stair, and everything's just fine until the lashing rain turns into a real storm. We lose one of our shutters, and across the road a tree explodes, freezing the world with this fucking big crash and a blue-white bolt as bright as the sun. The wind winds up to a screech, and Leon puts down his toys and turns on the recording device. He goes into the living room and sits watching the storm with the kinda blank look he gets. I'm a bit nervous, myself, because Jess isn't home, and the street's a river.

Five-thirty comes, then six, and Leon's jumping up every couple minutes to see if the van's back. Finally, the phone rings. Over the static, Jess says she's made it as far as her mom's. The state road is closed with a downed tree and she doesn't know when she'll be home.

"We'll manage," I says.

She tells me about a casserole in the fridge, and then I tempt fate and put Leon on, but he just listens up real alert and doesn't open his mouth. When I start dinner, he hangs around the kitchen and gets underfoot like a hungry cat.

"Mommy'll be home," I says. "You heard her; she's only down the road at Gran's."

He looks sick; he's actually pale with worry.

"It's the storm," I says. "Mom's okay, but she can't get home; there're trees down across the main road."

Leon's leaning on one of the chairs, rocking it back and forth.

"She'll be home later," I says. "She wants us to go ahead and have dinner."

Leon gives me a sulky look and begins kicking at the wobbly table.

"Don't do that," I says, "you'll knock stuff off."

He gives the table another shove and tips over one of the glasses I've just set out.

"Hey," I says. Leon retreats into the living room. The tv's out, of course, and he howls about that. Then he gets one of my hammers and starts pounding on the stair. Pretty soon we've got a storm atmosphere inside, too, and I'm just getting Leon straightened out when the power goes. I know he's frightened cause he starts hooting like a psychotic owl, but I'm fed up with him. Instead of kidding him along, I tell him to shut up. When I can see the greenish gray rectangles of the windows, I feel my way into the kitchen for our kerosine lamp and some matches. Leon sidles in behind. He's mad at me but drawn by the light.

"That better?" I says. There's no way I can touch him. He cuddles Jess but he's wary of everyone else. Leon gives me a cold, noncommittal stare, climbs up onto his chair, and concentrates on the long wavering shadows.

I cut up some bread and a banana for him and take out the casserole—macaroni with ham and cheese. "Mommy left this for us," I says, in case he's scared of my cooking.

He takes a few bites, then without warning, his face distorts and he begins crying, not just little kid sniffles, but violent, heart rending sobs.

"Hey," I says, "it's all right. You wouldn't want Mommy driving in this storm, would you?"

He gives a shriek which means that's just what he does want. And maybe that's all, just a little kid's lack of proportion, or maybe it's the darkness and the shadows and us being alone together, or maybe he's doubtful and anxious and wants to know one way or the other about me—who knows? Even at his age there's more going on than I can calculate.

"Just stop it right now," I says, but of course he doesn't. Leon's got stamina in the crying department. Pretty soon I've got that half angry, half helpless feeling you get with difficult kids, a feeling that's only satisfied if the brat turns belly up.

"What would Mommy think?" I says.

He's crying so hard, he's gone bluish-red in the face, and when I reach across the table toward him, he knocks his glass to one side and a big splosh of juice hits the table.

"Damn it all, Leon," I says. I grab a wad of paper towels and start mopping up. I've been slaving away for this kid, putting up with crap of all sorts and really sticking my neck out, and what do I get? Tears and juice over everything, friction between me and Jess, and the chief witness for the prosecution shrieking like a Sawzall hitting nails.

"When're you going to grow up?" I asks him. "You're not fooling me with all this." I've caught his attention now and he stops wailing and glares at me. "I know," I says, "I know you talk just fine. It's time you stopped all this baby howling and carrying on and acted like a big boy."

Leon's face changes and he shakes his head.

"'Boom,'" I says, "'Over goes the truck.' Right? 'Outa the way. Over goes the car'. You talked just fine the other day behind the barn. I'm sick of playing games with you."

He scrambles down out of his chair.

"Where you going now? You stay and eat your dinner."

He's awkward getting up and down, but once his feet hit the floor, Leon's damn quick. I make a grab for him, but he somehow reaches back and tips hot macaroni in my lap. While I'm letting him know what I think about that, and he bolts from the table, snatching the kerosine lamp from the counter as he runs by.

"Leon!" I says as my heartbeat revs up. "Leon, you be careful with that. Come back here and put it down."

Instead, I hear him peeling off down the hall and banging into the living room. Shit!

I scrape the macaroni off my jeans and stamp down the hall toward the yellow circle of lamplight. Leon hears me coming and makes for the stairs. Whenever he's in trouble, Leon heads straight for his room. I know where he'll go, too, right under his bed, light and all. "Leon." I says, trying for calm, "You tip that light, we'll have a fire for sure. Put it down."

Instead, he's up the stairs. Yellow splotches of light bounce across the stairwell and down the steps. He's carrying the lamp with both hands and he's looking back at me and I can see disaster coming without being able to do a flying fuck about it. I can see him falling and kerosine every-where, and I try the last thing, I yell, "I never meant to hurt anyone! That day on the river-it was all an accident!"

Maybe it was me yelling or maybe Leon just ran out of luck, because right at the next to the last step, he stumbles, and the lamp slips out of his hands to break with a tinkle of glass and the smell of kerosine. Leon scrambles up, too scared to cry, and glances around in horror at the little blue and yellow flames jumping across the darkness.

I'm frozen, too—scared by the situation and by confession. I smell evil possibilities, and I recognize the moment when I can be off the hook, safe forever, outa the mix; the moment when the idea that's noticed every child disaster in six states can make a power grab. All of a sudden I hear myself yelling, "Leon, quick, come down! Come down!"

Instead, he tears off to his room. I hear him running along the hall in the dark, banging into something, screaming and crying, then the door of his room slamming.

Meanwhile, fire's dripping down the steps, and I feel a big time aver-sion to going anywhere near it. I grab the throw rug in the hall and start beating at the flames, which simmers them down without quite putting the fire away. There's a fair bit of smoke, too, and the wall's getting dark and I think about the phone and the fire department and professional help. Then I think of Jess. I think of explaining to Jess about leaving Leon alone with fire, even for a moment. I know the house and everything in it is nothing in comparison to Leon, and, on a shock wave of adrenalin, I go crashing up stairs into the fire and dark after him.

"Leon," I'm yelling, "We've got to get out of here."

It's fucking dark except for the nasty flickering light in the stairwell. "Leon," I says, "Leon, please! Leon, it was an accident!" I'm feeling for the doors. I bang into the spare room, only I don't know that until I fall over some cartons. I get myself up. There's a very definite fire in the stairwell now, but I can see better, and I get to Leon's door and open it and grope over to the bed, shouting all the time for him. I pat the top of the bed, then lift the cover, reach underneath and get my hand kicked. On the second try, I grab a leg and haul him out.

"We've got to get out outa here," I'm saying over and over. Leon's shaking so much I can hardly hold him. We manage the door, but when he sees the fire he starts to shriek and struggle. "We gotta go down," I says, "We gotta get out." I sling him over my shoulder and go like hell. I can feel the heat on my jeans—the damn rug's caught, too, and there's plenty smoke and the heat's leaping around my ankles. I'm doing two steps at a time, jumping down, and I'm more than half way when I hit a toy or one of the spindles or my hammer or something, cause I slip. I grab for the wall, for the rail; Leon's clinging on and we're falling into the fire, and, just as I hit the step, I kinda throw him forward into the hallway. I hit the step with my right leg folded underneath me, and there's this sharp crack before I land in pure, hair tearing agony.

For a minute I'm too stunned to do anything but notice the flames headed down the stair and along the floor in my direction. I try to get up but the pain's a bulldozer. I raise my head and see my jeans smoking. Then I see Leon. He's on his feet, looking shit scared but not moving at all; he's standing perfectly still watching the fire, watching me.

"Run," I yell, cause I know all about panic. "Run now. The Holbeins. Tell them 911, Leon."

He takes a step or two down the hall, still silent, his eyes blank. "Quick," I scream, "Quick! You gotta get out! Get to the door!"

He's like hypnotized by the fire. I wrestle off my thick work shirt and smack at the flames around my legs. When they disappear under the shirt, Leon takes off. I hear him rattling with the catch on the front door, but his hands are too small or he's too nervous, cause he can't get it unlocked.

"The kitchen door, Leon! Go out the back!"

I hear his feet clattering on the bare boards, then only the sound of the fire, magnified by pain.

My shirt's smoking; I dump it and start thrashing my way towards the door. Something serious has happened: my hands feel all bones and all my bones are on fire. I'm out of the flames, but they're still in my leg and the dizzy expansion of pain wipes my mind clear. I see dancing cinders glowing on the edges of my clothing; I see the darkness going gray with smoke. I see an endless, but rapidly contracting, tunnel where the air's turning solid, too solid to breath, too heavy for my lungs. But though the flames are after me, my legs have stopped working, and my hands aren't making contact with the door. I shout, "Call 911, call 911!", until even the fire becomes remote, until I feel a rush of cool air, until I'm falling again.

Some rubbery item's clamped over my face and I'm trying to tear it off when a strange voice says, "Take it easy, and breath normally."

"Fire," I says, cause apparently they haven't noticed. "On fire." I mean me; my arms are white hot; my leg is burning with a sharp, steady pain.

"It's okay," the voice says. "The firemen are here." And I guess that's right because I can hear sirens.

"Leon," I says. I try to sit up; all I remember is that Leon's somehow involved.

"The little boy's safe," the voice says. I remember that later, when I struggle through mind warping pain, and a face with a white mask appears. I ask, anyway. "Leon? Where's Leon?"

"Leon's all right," says the voice.

Nothing else makes much sense. I remember a white room with lights and a flat silver reflector, and another, dimly lit, with glowing dials and remote electronic beeps. Otherwise no landmarks. I'm lost in thick, tangled dreams of scalding pain so all encompassing and inescapable that even when I come out of shock and anesthesia and narcotics, I'm different somehow, a different person. Trauma's left a residue like a ring in a bathtub, and I've had experiences the old Jeff doesn't know and wouldn't understand.

Course the hospital brings some other situations that are dead easy to grasp. There's no rest from burns, that's the first lesson; they're the nearest thing to the eternal fire. Burns hurt like hell from Day One and only get worse as they heal and the nerves start coming back to life. My arms and legs have second and third degree burns, mostly second, fortunately, but more than bad enough. Basically, I've been half skinned alive and my bodily fluids are leaking out through the bandages. To prevent infection, the dressings gotta be changed regular and the burns cleaned and dressed and the dead tissue scraped away—a real horror show sensation.

Every day I wake up around five a.m. when the morphine tapers off and lie awake dreading morning when the R.N. will come in with her tray and her scissors and her bandages and medicines to start work on me. No matter how long I'm awake and prepared, when I hear the rattle of her little cart, my heart shrinks and I could cry with fear. That's the major daily misery. Special days are the skin graft days, when I get hide stripped off my sides and my butt to patch the worst of my hands and legs. I haven't even mentioned my leg, my right leg, which is broken as well as burned. The shin is all raw and oozing, so they can't cast it. Instead, they pin the break and put the leg in traction. The basic situation is I lie immobile with my right leg in the air, counting the hours to my next shot and distracting myself with ESPN and X-rated fantasies about Jess—and sometimes, I admit, the Red Gal, too, cause my mind's all adrift. I'm awash in so much pain and dope that a queer hospital stink of disinfectant, antibiotics, fear, and narcotics rolls off my skin like I'm inhabited by alien life. Though there're guys a lot worse, and I don't even want to think about the kids upstairs in the pediatric burn ward, I've still got nights when I don't want to wake up, and days when death looks like the best of my options.

There are other changes, too, for me and for others. Take Stankus and Benny. They come to see me early on, almost my very first visitors, wanting to know about the accident, of course, but also wanting to fish my psyche to see what's floating helpless on the surface. Fortunately, they're a little premature; I'm too dazed to say much. Then my folks arrive and are helpful. They tell the story of the fire, at least as they know it from Jess and from Dad's pals at the fire house, until the nurse comes in and packs everyone off home. A week later, Benny returns, alone. I'm nervous and crabby, cause I feel like hamburger on the grill. If he hopes for any revelations, he's lost the moment.

"Where's the Lieutenant?" I says.

Benny's expression turns doleful. He looks around the room at the flowers and cards and studies the big silver balloon with "Get Well" in pink letters that's gently descending towards the floor. "How're you doing?" he asks.

"I feel like shit."

He nods and waits and sucks on a tooth. Maybe that's his trouble, lousy teeth. "We've been talking to the kid," he says at last.

Even though I've been expecting this, a rush of adrenalin zaps my damaged nerves.

"Yeah," says Benny, "he's talking good. I suppose you know that."

"His mom's real pleased."

"Oh, yes," says Benny. "He talks like a grown up. I gotta kid three years older who doesn't talk as good as Leon talks right now."

I nod my head. I got two ideas in mind, both sharp and vivid, which is something I get now, courtesy of the medicine or immobility or my recent experiences. I see my ass in a sling and indictments and disaster, and I see Jess the way she sat beside my bed, stroking an unburned patch on my right arm. I've just had my afternoon shot. I'm starting to drift out from land and her face seems particularly beautiful, with the large, heavy lidded eyes, the neat, wide mouth, the long nose with the slight curve just at the bridge. She's got her thick hair pulled back, but it's getting away as usual and makes a kind of halo against the afternoon light. I've got such an intense sense of her beauty and her body that it's hard to concentrate on what she's saying. I know she's concerned and upset but I feel she's happy, too, like sun under a cloud. And when I says, "How's Leon? Is Leon all right?" her face lights up. I understand now what they mean when they say someone looks radiant. The damage to the house, my injuries, money worries—they can't reduce the joy of Leon's sudden speech.

"Oh, Jeff, you won't believe how he's talking. Whole sentences, just like an adult. We'll call you. He wants so much to see you. It's just wonderful to hear him."

So I says, "yes", to Benny. And then I wait.

"He's got a lot to say," Benny says, looking at me slyly. I wait, feeling not just faintly sick, the way I normally do now from too much pain and too much dope, but like instant puke. I don't dare open my mouth, and after a long pause, Benny sighs cause he's played his best card and come up short. "He's told us all about the fire," he says. "About the storm, stuff left on the stairs, calling 911. It's a remarkably complete account."

"Good," I says now. "I'm afraid I wasn't much help on the fire."

"Detailed," Benny says sourly. "Precise. Kid would make a helluva witness. Trouble is, all he remembers is the fire."

"Ahh," I says. That I understand. The fire transformed me, and I'm still not entirely familiar with the result. That's how powerful the fire was, so I'm not surprised if it wiped the park and Michelle—and the mysterious stranger who might or might not be his friend Jeff—for Leon. I close my eyes and lean back on the pillow and regret hesitation and bad thoughts. When I open my eyes again, Benny is gone, and I realize with a jumble of emotions that the new Jeff, having in some mysterious and painful way paid for Michelle, is finally off the hook.

CHAPTER 15

I have plenty time to digest my new status, cause I'm in the hospital for nearly nine weeks. I come out shaky and tender skinned, seriously underweight and deep in debt. I have lizard arms and a bum left hand, and a leg gone bionic with a set of stainless pins that ache in wet weather. My right leg winds up an inch shorter anyway, so I got the hardware plus an old guy cane. On the hot July day when my folks arrive to take me home, about all I'm fit for is worrying about the collateral bills and damages.

We go to their house, cause Jess is working long hours with the van, and Dad'll be home to keep an eye on me. I'm relieved in a way. I don't want to see Jess's damaged house, although she says it isn't too bad. Frenchie's come and boarded the front door and shored up the porch. He's torn out the flooring in the hall, too, and replaced the damaged joists underneath. The hall's patched, she says, just plywood, but solid for now. The insurance is paying and the porch and the front clapboards are going to get done. The stair needed work, anyway, and she's cleaned up the smoke damage and started repainting. Not bad; just a heartbreaking illustration of how you can never really start over fresh.

I don't even try. I get myself installed in a hospital bed in Grampa's old room, and Mom force feeds me morning and night. Dad keeps me company by talking town politics, which keeps my mind off other things, sure, but probably does him more good than it does me.

I'm awake a lot at night, feeling sorry for myself and sorting unfocused thoughts. I haven't a clue what I'm going to do next or even what I can do next. After the hospital, I'm better acquainted with my bodily components than I ever expected to be, but, at the same time, I'm no longer at home in the whole machine. It's an odd feeling which spills over into everything else—even Jess and me. I get bad moments in the wee hours, when everything seems uncertain and useless, when my life's in the dumpster and I'm content to leave it there. At the same time, I freak out over little things, and in particularly suckless moods, I find myself crying about nothing at all.

This goes on until one Saturday Jess and Leon arrive in my truck.

She's been after me to come home, but though one part of me wants to go, another part's afraid of the whole scene and keeps making excuses. I want her and I'm afraid at the same time. My body's betrayed me so stupendously I'm not sure about anything, not even about going to bed with Jess, although the idea was mighty sustaining back in the hospital. But this afternoon, she only comes in for a moment. She kisses me and then says she's got a recipe for my mom and goes dashing out. Leon, surprisingly, doesn't follow her. He hangs back, looking at Grampa's pictures and trophies and at the polished and varnished hoof of a favorite thoroughbred.

"Grampa was a jockey," I says.

Leon just nods like he still doesn't speak. He's not much interested in animals, it's the starting gate he's examining. I explain how it works and how you have to train horses to charge out soon as the doors open. Leon listens and studies the picture and then comes and stands beside my bed. I'm all dressed and everything, but I've been lying there not wanting to get up.

"When are you coming home?" he asks, just like that.

"I don't know. When I feel better maybe."

"It was my fault," he says now. "Running with the lamp."

"A bad move," I agree. "But you're never going to do that again, are you?"

He shakes his head, like he's taking this really to heart.

"We all do stupid things," I says. "Grown-ups, too. And things we don't mean to do and things that turn out bad."He looks very serious, and I wonder for a moment what was in his mind, whether he'd been afraid of me as well as the storm, whether he knew me better than I thought, maybe even better than I knew myself. Leon and me connect below the surface, you might say. We've both experienced certain intense and confusing moments.

"Listen, you saved my life," I says. And come to think of it, I saved his. Which I knew, of course, but which didn't have the same meaning lying in the hospital as it does when Leon's standing in front of me all bright and solemn. I feel better, like I owed him for the stroller tipping over and the fear and the hassles with the Lieutenant and the relatives. Now I've squared accounts. "You know that? You saved my life."

He looks away and rubs one foot along the floor. "911," he says with shy pride. Jess has told me, and the Holbeins have, too, how Leon ran next door through the wet and rang their bell, shouting, "Call 911, call 911!" Which they did, before they rushed over with their fire extinguishers and garden hose to turn a total disaster into a salvageable mess.

"Hey," I says, "you came through when it was important." And I tap him on the shoulder, very lightly, cause my hands still hurt and Leon's shy of being touched. But instead of flinching the way he usually does, he gives a half smile, an innocent smile, a smile with no hidden meaning but happiness. "You got out and you saved my life and that's what matters," I says.

Leon reaches out his hand and lets me take it for just a moment before he says, "We want you to come home."

"You, too?"

"Yes," says Leon, very serious. He seems to have gone from being a baby to being a miniature adult in one dizzy jump, and now he waits silently for my answer. I wait, too, and into my mind comes a Sunday when I'm still on the burn ward. There's a chapel in the hospital, and Jess knows the time for Sunday mass. She wants me to go, too, since they've finally been able to put a cast on my leg. She prayed for me while I was really sick. And for Leon, always, so she says she owes Our Lady double. Though protestant Grampa turns over in his grave, I say okay and let her push me down in the wheelchair.

The chapel's small—cozy, I guess is the word—with a tile floor and brick walls. It's got plain benches with spaces in between for wheelchairs and stretchers, and there's a table with flowers and a pair of candles for a kinda all purpose altar. As we arrive, one of the staff's hanging up the crucifix in preparation for the Catholic service.

The priest comes in a few minutes later. We're not a big group—Jess and me, a couple of elderly women wearing hats with their bright bathrobes, a thin young guy in a wheelchair accompanied by a woman who might be his mother, and an old fellow with tubes and bags lying flat on a gurney. The priest looks us over and nods to the regulars. He has a smooth, hospital pale face with wide cheekbones and the careful eyes that come from seeing a whole lot of sickness and misery. He gets right to work with his cups and wafers, reminding me of Michelle's funeral, so that I tune out the whole deal until he comes to the little speech that Jess tells me is the homily. He's going along about God's will and the usual, and then he says, "We are creatures of the moment, but we are destined to be creatures of eternity." That strikes me, I guess, because of my recent experience and my sense of being a new and pretty much different person. I listen up until his conclusion that "we must live, not in the moment, like creatures of the moment, but as if we are creatures of eternity, and as if each of our actions has eternal life."

I don't particularly believe in eternal life, which I'm not at all sure would be endurable. A whole lot of things would sure have to change. But to a point, he's right about our actions—they've got a life of their own that's too damn long sometimes, and if we'd think about that first, we'd be better off. Yes, indeed, though we can't predict. I couldn't. I never would of thought the park would bring me to this point with Leon.

"Go tell your mom," I says. "Go tell your mom I'm getting packed."

Going home is kinda like having my first swimming lesson. I'd been waiting and wanting to do it, but when the moment comes and I'm standing on the edge of the Y pool, big as the ocean and deep, too, with blue and green shadows slanting away to shark depth, I'd just as soon wait a little longer. That's how I feel. Maybe Jess does, too, cause she's gabbing away about the house and the van and the garden, while Leon is even quieter than usual. I can feel his eyes fixed on the back of my head, and I know his recording device is going like crazy.

When we pull up to the house, I'm not just apprehensive but scared. The porch and the door and the hallway and the stair all have bad vibes. My scars get hot like my skin remembers, and my chest tightens up, expecting smoke. Then Leon rattles off to get something to show me, and Jess and me look at the plywood subfloor and start figuring how many bundles of oak and whether or not we could salvage something cheaper—forgetting, momentarily, that my hands are too messed up now to handle hammers and squarecut nails.

Still, the cost of red oak bundles gets us through those first awkward moments, and, later on, home renovations keep us off more sensitive ground. Even when we're in bed at night—lying on our backs staring up at the ceiling—we're talking about my health insurance coming through and how the stairs got fixed. Neutral stuff which sure as hell beats some other topics, like my horror show arms and leprous looking hands and the dead chill that's dampened even my longing for Jess.

That's how homecoming goes, a thin ice business, but we avoid all talk about the chill, and it's a good decision, really, cause I'm on disconnect. When Jess isn't around—when she's out digging her garden or working with the van—I can't get her out of my mind. When she's right in the house, right in bed next to me, it's like I'd been fed a paralyzing drug.

Pretty soon we settle into a routine that's safe without being satisfactory. Jess gets up early and gets the van ready for the breakfast trade at the community college. Leon and me get up an hour or so later. We have breakfast together, and round about ten I take him over to his Granny's for a few hours. I'm supposed to get over to the hospital around noon to work off some of my monster bill. Sometimes I do. I put on this dumb slate colored smock and march around the wards with magazines and newspapers. It's slow work. The old ladies wanta have a look through the magazines before they buy and the old guys wanta talk about the ball scores or else they got political ideas they just gotta vent. I don't need any more politics than I get from Dad, who keeps me up to speed on all the fat cats and grafters from Slatertown to D.C. There's a couple guys my age in traction, who're a big time delay, too. They want me to let them read the comics gratis and peek at the baseball scores, and they're all the time after me to make a special trip to the corner newsstand and buy them some girlie mags or their favorite biker books. If I'd landed up in traction off of a motorcycle, I'd never want to see another one, not even in newsprint.

Other days, I've got the flower detail and have to drop off ceramic planters filled with greenery or bunches of flowers wrapped up in plastic or mylar balloons with pink script messages. I get to know all the florists: who's cutting corners with week old plants and who does nice work and what the container of the moment is. Sometimes when I'm bored, I'll sneak a couple carnations outa the big bunches and take them home to Jess or give then to patients who need a little cheering up: "spreading the wealth" as Grampa used to say. I do a lot of walking, which is good for my leg, and it's an okay job. The only thing is, I figure that at minimum wage I've got fifty years of being the Sunshine Guy ahead of me.

Days I start thinking that way, I go AWOL. I maybe go to The Kitchen and have a couple brewskis. Not a good idea. My system's gotten sensitive to alcohol or something, cause I get wasted quick. I find myself one afternoon in a motel off the interstate with a woman I met on the trauma floor and another day I put the truck in a ditch up on a farm road and damn near get stuck there. Although depressing, it's safer to hang around the hardware store, getting in the way of the trades guys and seeing my old pals, who're half embarrassed and half sorry and basically just want to say "Hi, Jeff" and clear the area.

So the best plan, when the weather's good, is to go down along the river or up to the lake, with or without my pole. If Dad's feeling okay, I take him, too, cause he's another drop out and kinda knows the disability score. We watch the water like a couple of geezers and talk about fish and keep other thoughts to ourselves.

Whatever else's on the docket, when three o'clock comes, I pick Leon up. If I still have Dad with me, we stop at the Dairy Queen to get Leon a cone. Dad and Leon get on real well, and if Jess is going to be late, we sometimes go over to the house so the two of them can play with Dad's jigsaw and cut out little wooden cars and trucks. Wet days, I sometimes don't take Leon to his Granny's at all. Instead, we go out to the barn, and I teach him how to use the small hand saw I found for him and let him hit nails with the tack hammer and generally do stuff that makes Jess nervous when she's home to keep an eye on things. One way or the other, I put in a full day without doing squat. Killing time without going crazy is an art, and, by the end of the summer, Leon and Dad and me, we've got it down pretty good.

That's how we go along, living off Jess's military benefit and the food van. Jess won't say too much cause she knows I'm still in pieces, and I don't say much because I don't feel worth a damn. Then one day I'm crabby and out of sorts. We're getting a storm coming, and, god-damnit, I'm getting like Grampa: I can feel it coming through the pins in my leg. Some of my scars are itching, too, the skin on my arms feels like sausage casing, and I'm generally in a shit mood. Jess is late back with the van, and Leon and me've been playing in the barn and haven't started dinner. Just the normal day to day aggravation, but, anyway, she says something, and I says something and before you know it, I'm saying mean things and she says it's about time I stopped feeling sorry for myself and got off my butt.

"Sure," I says, "I'm ready for siding."

"You'd think there wasn't another job in the world," she says.

"It's what I do," I says, "and it used to be good enough for you."

"Grow up," she says. "Listen, I see people at the college every day much older than you. You're a smart guy. Go back and get trained for something where you won't have to use your hands."

"Shit," I says.

"You always have an excuse," she says. "You'd rather just sit around drinking beer with the guys at The Kitchen."

I don't know how she heard about that and I hope she hasn't heard anything else. I sure as hell don't want her to know about some of the dumber things I've gotten up to recently. At the same time, I strongly feel I need a drink some days, and I guess she would, too, if she hurt as much as I do. Anyway, things pretty much deteriorate from there, and, before you know it, I'm swearing and carrying on cause I don't really want to talk about my lousy present and my scary future. Jess is starting to cry, though she tries to hide it, and I suddenly stop being angry and start feeling like crap.

"I'm not worth it," I says to her. She turns away and I get up and start patting her back. "I'm not worth it."

Now she really starts to cry.

"I don't know why you stick with me," I says. "You could get any guy you want, not someone with messed up arms and a bum leg and a bad temper." There's some satisfaction in saying that. It's what I've been afraid of and now it's out and on the table.

She shakes her head.

"You know I'll leave if you want me to. You know I will."

She stops crying, bang, just like that, and she gets this wild, furious look I've only seen when something's threatened Leon. "No," she says.

"It's not going to work, Jess," I says.

She wipes her eyes and straightens up and goes over to the sink and starts shuffling dishes around. When she's real upset, Jess likes to be doing something with her hands. "No, we'll stick it out," she says. "I'm not going to fail with another man."

"Jess, it's not your fault," I says. Christ, she doesn't know the half of it. She doesn't know about Michelle or Leon talking or the night of the fire. She's outa the loop. "It's nobody's fault," I says real quick, cause though I really feel squared away with the past, I don't necessarily want to dig it up. "I'll bet it was nobody's fault with Andre, either."

"You don't know anything about it," she says in this cold, determined voice. For a sweet person, Jess has sure got a hard, stubborn streak.

"Listen, Jess," I says.

"You listen. Andre volunteered to get away. He didn't have to go. He didn't even wait to be called up. He was on the phone the moment they first began to talk about mobilization. If things had been going well, he'd of waited and he'd probably be alive today. But things weren't going well at all."

"So was it all your fault? Christ, Jess, you couldn't know how things would turn out. You couldn't know."

"I know now," she says.

"I'm not Andre," I says. "I'm not about to get in any fucking helicopter. I'm scared of heights above two stories. I'm not going to get in anything that flies, for Christ sake." I want to cheer her up, cause I'm scared of the deep water, but Jess isn't.

"What will happen to you?" she says.

And there's the bonus question, plopped on the table like a dead fish.

"I don't need any help," I says, and I'm getting angry cause this is so obviously untrue I'd rather not face it, and, anyway, I'm overwhelmed by Jess and deeper in debt to her than even to the hospital.

"Well, I do," says Jess. She puts down the dish towel and turns away from the sink and says in a rush, "I've always wanted a home of my own and someone I love to share it with and Leon and a father for Leon and I need you for all those things."

This is the moment and I know it. I've been putting off and putting off this discussion, and I'm scared to death. I wait and I hesitate, and her face starts closing down like a shop grating sliding shut at the end of the day, and I can't disappoint her. I just can't. Sometimes you've got to do stuff whether you're ready for it or not. What I know that Jess is my best ever shot at happiness, so I stretch out my hand and I says, "Jess, I love you for keeps."

She steps across the room, across miles and miles, across caution, uneasiness, and fear. Then she's in my arms and I feel like the old Jeff, horney as hell, but different, too, cause I can feel tears on my face. I'm kissing her and telling her I'm sorry and that I've never loved anyone like I love her, and pretty soon we're really getting into it. At this moment, Jess says, "Leon's in the living room."

"Leon's watching tv," I says. "He won't come upstairs."

She's not sure about that and cautious, and we tease back and forth until I convince her. We go upstairs with our arms around each other, tramping out the bad memories that rise like yellow and blue flames. In our room, we put the hook on the door and make love. Everything works like normal even if my leg starts itching and then aching and my one arm still looks like a prop for a horror movie. I lie back and look at the ceiling and stroke Jess's lovely thick hair. "I've been worried about this," I says to her.

"I know," she says. "Darling, I know."

"The shock," I says. "The shock and being sick for so long and not knowing what was going to happen."

"You're getting better," she says. "You're going to be lucky and get all better."

"I thought I was pretty good already," I says, and she laughs the way I like so much and pokes me in the ribs. I start kissing her again, and I know right then that we'll make it somehow.

A week later Jess brings home a catalogue and a stack of application forms from the community college. She sets them in the living room and doesn't say anything, and for a few days I just let them sit there. School's involuntary confinement, and I'm not real enthusiastic about getting more. At the same time, I want to do my share and encourage Jess and get my butt out of the house and feel like I'm working again. Besides Leon's ready for pre-school, Mom and Dad are talking about trying Florida, and even I can't kill time all by myself. Eventually I spend an evening going though the catalogue, and the next day I sign up for a couple computer courses.

Off I go, prepared for nerd city, for guys with pocket protectors and gals with computer pallor. What I find is ordinary dropouts, and gals raising kids alone, and beat-up looking fellows who've gotten too old to work the loading docks and warehouses. We're all in the same boat—even the old guy with the accent who reminds me of Grampa—and, after our first computer final, the whole bunch of us go out and order pizza and beer at the Kitchen and sit around talking about the questions and the professor and the relief of the whole thing. I know what they mean, although the courses are basically no sweat for me. It's gearing up for something new; it's seeing yourself in a new way. Like now I'm starting to feel at home with these guys, more so than with my buddies in the trades who feel awkward cause they remember me from before I got hurt; that's what I mean.

Besides, I kinda get into the work: computers are precise, and I like the fact that there's no margin for error and no surprises. I especially appreciate the no surprise angle, so the next semester I sign up for a full load, get myself some state money, and start putting "student" on nosey forms. Pretty soon I'm doing data entry for the hospital and helping their programmer and working off the books for Frenchie and his dad and some of the other businesses around.

I begin to think I'll make an honest living some day, and when I get my computer certificate, I'm pretty satisfied. But Jess isn't, though she's as excited as me when I get my certificate in computing. More so, really: Jess associates math skill with genius. She thinks I'm the smartest guy in the whole town if not on the whole eastern seaboard, and I have moments when I promote the idea. Course I have no intention of acting on it, but Jess has. "Accounting," she says to me one day. "You need more of a business background."

"Oh, yeah?" I says. "Who says?"

"You say your hands aren't good enough for repair work."

"Naw. I'm sticking with programming."

"You know I can barely add," Jess says. "I am totally stupid with figures."

"Keeping the van expenses straight is no bother," I says.

"The van is easy," Jess says. "But a business is different. For a catering business or a restaurant, you need accounting and bookkeeping."

"Who said anything about catering or a restaurant?"

"I'm not going to be selling lunch from a van all my life," Jess says.

Right there I see a vision of the future. I realize that Jess, who I love, is sort of an unknown territory. She's like some other women I know, the Red Gal included, the women who'd been wild, agreeable high school girls, willing to go to ball games and drinking parties and drag racing on the back roads, women who expected us—I mean me and Frenchie and the other guys—to shape their future. No more. Children changed all that. The easy going girls went into a sort of cocoon and when they came out, the polarity of the sexes got reversed. Now it's the women who're driving toward unexpected goals and expecting us to pitch in to help get them there.

I don't mind, though I'm not sure I want to run a restaurant. Days and nights of watching people eat strikes me as feedlot duty, but Jess would be a terrific chef and pretty soon I'll know how to balance the books for her and all that. For myself, I got other ideas. I see possibilities in the computer line for a sharp guy who knows how to get along, so college is an okay prospect. Besides, after the fire and south Florida and the park, I'm ready for precision, for networks and flow charts; I'm ready for the utility and stupidity of machines.

CHAPTER 16

Get a bright hot day with enough stars and stripes against a blue sky and even a beat up burg like Willi feels festive. Along the main street, families are setting up with lawn chairs and baby carriages. They've brought dogs and eats and radios; they're wearing red-white-'n-blue and funny hats and t-shirts with slogans. Some have tuned in already, and as we walk toward the start of the parade, we hear a stereophonic mix of marches and songs and WILI station promotion. Leon is clutching his small portable, and, once we reach the route, he switches onto an excited guy telling us we've just got minutes before the Boom Box Parade begins.

Leon gives a small, satisfied smile. I can see he loves the idea of it, not the parade, which he can't visualize yet, but the synchronized machines, the coordination of many radios.

"What a nice crowd," Jess says, waving to some guys across the street. The whole town's turned out, the down-and-outers at the residential hotel, dealers in their gang colors, local merchants, yuppies from the Windhams, moms from the projects, farmers and villagers from farther out. Kids are running last minute errands across the empty street or hot-dogging on their bikes and rollerblades to impress the crowd. The Main Street apartments have their windows open, and the tenants are leaning out on their elbows to watch the fun and wave to their friends. Jess knows people all along the way—construction guys from the road crews, students from the community college, workers from the industrial park. "Where's the van?" they yell, and she laughs and says "Next year." And I call back, "I finally got her to take a day off."

In fact, she'd wanted to work the parade, but I said 'no, we gotta take Leon'. So she's walking along beside me, wearing a straw hat with red, white 'n blue streamers, a white shirt and little pale shorts. She's tanned from working in our new garden, and she's easily the best looking woman in the county. I put my arm around her shoulder and whisper that I wish we were home in bed, so that she blushes and looks more beautiful than ever.

"You were right," she says, "this is fun."

"Three minutes," says Leon importantly. "Three minutes to the start." He's never been to a parade before and he's taking everything in. The dogs, the kids, the flags.

"We should have gotten him a flag," says Jess.

"There may be some on sale," I says, but the station's already starting to crank up John Philip Sousa. From down the hill, we hear the first of the trucks with the heavy duty speakers, and a police car flashes its lights and leads off the parade. Leon checks his dial to be sure he's still on the station, then turns up the volume with all the pride of participation.

Leon's past five now, first grade in the fall. He's been in kindergarten, but he's looking forward to being in "real" school—like me. When I'm doing homework at night, he sometimes comes and sits beside me. He can read all the titles of my books and some of the programming symbols, too. Jess was right; he's a smart kid.

Applause ripples up the street as a dozen or so elderly and stiff-legged vets swing around the corner onto Main. They're carrying black MIA flags between the red-white-'n-blue, and they look tired and sorta sad, like they're eaten up with the kind of memories "The Stars and Stripes Forever" can't dispel. Our honored survivors: the only down note in the festive Fourth parade. I wonder what seems more real to them, the crowd, the sun, the applause—or bad times in rice paddies or frozen fields. Probably sometimes one and sometimes the other, that's my guess, speaking as a survivor of personal, local disasters. Though I've had my time under fire, so to speak, the time of raw burns and oozing dressings and endless nights, right now, I'm sun, flags, and parade.

That kinda surprises me, but not entirely. I'm starting to understand my grandmother, the one who went crazy in bits and pieces but kept trying to immitate normal life. Gran was an extreme case. I guess the vets are another—and I've had my moments, too. The thing I've realized is that life's all thin ice—it's got these spaces, moments, danger points that you can disappear into and not come out of. Or come out of like you don't want to. So you gotta live on the alert, "watch your step" as Grampa used to say, and you gotta get across the bad places the way me and Jess have or like me and Leon did the night of the fire. You gotta keep trying. I see that and so I see grandmother different now. She was making stuff up to fill in the gaps; she was doing crazy things, because she was still struggling to make sense even with half her deck missing. Which we gotta do. The world's beyond us, that's true, but a lot's in our own heads, and we gotta decide how we want things to be and try to make them come out right.

Take me; I thought I wanted to go West on a Harley, but it turns out I don't. The river's still there, running, running, and the fire and bad thoughts, but for now I'm on top of them all. I'm standing with Jess and Leon, listening to the boom boxes swing into another march: an introduction for folks pushing baby carriages and pulling wagons; for a guy carrying a young goat; for smiling women leading fat, nervous dogs with ribbons and bandannas around their necks.

"How's he doing that?" Leon asks, hopping up and down all excited. What we've got's an eight foot Uncle Sam in red pinstripes and a high hat, striding along on stilts. I explain about stilts, about how you balance, about how I've used them. Leon looks skeptical. Stilts are magic; friend Jeff is strictly down to earth.

"Before my leg," I says. "Used them on drywall. You ask Frenchie sometime to show you his stilts."

But we're distracted by the floats: the local boxing club, one of the nurseries, someone who's brought his chickens and guinea fowl in cages on the back of a flatbed. Don't ask me what that means. See, that's where people are different and surprising, especially Windham people. You get a radio promotion, right, strictly cornball and self serving, an excuse for patriotic folks to listen to the local on the big holiday. And what happens? It takes on a life of its own. Frenchie, now. He's passing with his truck. A little bunting, a few flags, his sister's kids in the back with balloons, Carla throwing candies to the crowd. Free advertising. A pretty good idea, actually, and Jess is saying "Next year, we'll do that," and Leon's hopping up and down and asking to get picked up.

"Take it easy," I says, "hold my cane." I put him up on my shoulders and then I take back the cane and lean on it a bit, cause Leon's getting heavier and my right leg still aches with extra weight. He starts ooing and aawing, cause now he can see everything: fine old cars and decorated junkers, rollerbladers with banners, day camp kids marching in their red shirts. Here comes a radio guy in a clown suit with boxes on his feet. That's about what you'd expect: wannabe celebrities making fools of themselves. But then outa the pack a pretty gal swoops by wearing stars and stripes angel wings. She's on roller skates, and she's weaving in and out, around the cars and Uncle Sam and the kids carrying boomboxes. She's on a roll with her hair flying, and her wings are moving as gently as a butterfly's in the hot air. Well, what about that? Or the Traveling Fish Head Society, who come dressed in painted sheets shaped into bony-looking green-brown fish heads and followed by jellyfish made of umbrellas decorated with swaying tentacles of crepe paper and mylar. That's unexpected, isn't it? I started out assuming all the surprises were bad ones, and it's true that life tricks us in lousy ways and reality breaks apart when we least expect it. But that's not all. There are girls with angel wings occasionally and not all jelly fish sting.

"Oh, look," Leon cries. Leon's not concerned with poetry and pretty women yet. What he sees is a little neon orange car driven by a kid not much older than he is. "Oh, we could make one, couldn't we? How does it run, Jeff? Do you know how it runs?"

"Probably a lawn mower engine would do," I says. Now he wants down, he wants to see it closer, and I give Jess my cane and lift him off.

"You stay down now," says Jess. Leon doesn't care, he's leaning into the street, his intent face full of yearning and joy.

"Can we make one?" he asks me when the little car has passed. "For next year's parade? For Mom's ad? It could say 'Jess's Catering'."

His mom laughs, and I says, "We'll see. That one had a pretty fancy body."

"We don't need anything fancy," Leon says. "Please, Jeff."

"You'd have to do a lot of the work," I says. "My hands aren't so good for details any more."

"I want to," he says ultra serious. "I want to do it all. You just have to show me how, Jeff."

"If I can find a mower engine cheap," I says. "That's a big 'if', now."

"Yes," Leon says, and he takes my hand the way he does when we're great pals.

So we stand there, watching the Fourth of July Boom Box Parade, where everything orderly and official and organized keeps getting interrupted by whatever people dream up as fun to do. Next year, I'll probably be wearing a 'Jess's Catering' t-shirt and trying to keep Leon's little car going. Probably. I look at him and wink and feel water going over the dam as Grampa used to say. Sometime, maybe, we'll have to have it out. I mean the park and Michelle and the night of the storm. Maybe when he hits adolescence and the monster years. Maybe when he's as old as I am now and getting reflective. Maybe when I'm real old like Grampa and there's not much else to lose. Maybe.

But maybe not. Maybe there'll be no need. We've both been in dangerous places and done good and bad things without really meaning to, and, as a result, Leon and me connect on some very deep level. That's the most surprising thing of all. I love Jess, who's changed my life and given me happiness—and is going to marry me whenever I can get the medical debt down so it won't swamp us. But Jess will always be partly mysterious, separate, a dark continent, and I will always try to keep part of myself unknown to her, so as to present the best side I can. But Leon and I have had terrible moments without deception, moments half forgotten but always present, and, in the end, he's the person I understand best in the whole world.